Shadow or Flesh?

Hanse rounded a corner to face a slavering red wolf with red eyes like smoldering coals. They glowed like torches to surround the creature with an eerie dark-pink illumination. The creature walked on hind legs and wielded a sword and buckler. It wore a nice gold ring in its left ear. Hanse froze, staring at new impossibility.

"Go away, wolf. I know illusion when I see it." The wolf advanced a half-pace. Fiery red eyes stared into Hanse's black ones. Hanse decided to be certain.

With the speed of summer lightning he slammed a throwing star at its left eye—and watched in astonishment as the animal interposed its green-and-red shield. The shield caught the deadly star of steel with a heavy thud of impact. It was no illusion. Hanse turned. He saw three more wolves. All walking erect. All bearing shields painted red and green. And all of them coming for him . . .

Ace Books by Andrew J. Offutt

KING DRAGON

War of the Gods on Earth Series

THE IRON LORDS
SHADOWS OUT OF HELL
THE LADY OF THE SNOWMIST

The Cormac mac Art Series

THE MISTS OF DOOM
THE TOWER OF DEATH
WHEN DEATH BIRDS FLY
THE SWORD OF THE GAEL
THE UNDYING WIZARD
THE SIGN OF THE MOONBOW

SHADOWSPAWN
THE SHADOW OF SORCERY

THE SHADOW OF SORCERY

ANDREW J. OFFUTT

ACE BOOKS, NEW YORK

This book is an Ace original edition,
and has never been previously published.

THE SHADOW OF SORCERY

An Ace Book / published by arrangement with
the author

PRINTING HISTORY
Ace edition / February 1993

ISBN: 0-441-76026-0

Ace Books are published by The Berkley Publishing Group,
200 Madison Avenue, New York, New York 10016.
The name "ACE" and the "A" logo
are trademarks belonging to Charter Communications, Inc.

PRINTED IN THE UNITED STATES OF AMERICA

10   9   8   7   6   5   4   3   2   1

Prologue

THE CARAVAN WAS a great snake, curling its way southward on the desert. A multicolored snake, shimmering in the sun.

The sun; the demon. It hated men, and Hanse hated it right back. It was hot, unbelievably hot. The air was hot; the ground—ugly, glassy sand that supported nothing and got into everything—was hot. The dry heat drew the moisture right out of the bodies of humans and beasts. The desert was even hot underfoot, right through the soles of boots or buskins. And woe to him whose soles were worn thin! Only those improbable uglinesses called camels, with their ugly noises and ugly habits, were equipped to travel in this earthly preview of the Hot Hell.

One day the gods quarreled, the story went, and soon they were all angry, and that day they created this thing called desert. In their anger they populated it with poisonous scorpions and maddening sand fleas, strewed it with stones and bad imitations of plants, and as an afterthought arranged for winds that would darken the sky with sand driven with the force of hailstones.

So the story went.

Hanse of Sanctuary plodded along astride the horse he had with good cause but no imagination named Ironmouth. Ironmouth was his favorite among the several horses he owned; several, now, in this time of the most prosperity he had ever known. He had not stolen them, not really; he liberated them from the stockade of the desert people who

had stolen from him and left him to die in the desert.
Ironmouth sweated under the sun, and except under his dark
gray mane, the sweat was gone as it appeared, greedily
drunk by the dry heat. The desert saddle with its high back,
leather over wood, was hot against his rider's lower back
and under his buttocks, which were damp despite the fact
that on the desert humidity was only a word.

Horses were no better equipped than humans for this
garbage, this taste of hell on earth. Only the white ones were
at least reasonably clothed to survive on the desert. Ironmouth's coat was not white. Like his far more economically
built rider, the big horse also suffered under the blazing
white glare that eventually turned orange and then blood-red
late in the day when it came to ground and disappeared—for
all too brief a time.

The sun. Among the desert people up here far north of
Sanctuary, the sun was called Vaspa. It was also their word
for demon. Hanse had learned why on his way from
Sanctuary up to Firaqa. Now, on his way back north to
Firaqa from Suma, he felt no better and no different about
this seemingly never-ending sand, pallid yellow and heat-
shimmering so that things, animals, people, the world
seemed to waver. He still despised the desert he had planned
never to be on again. All was as he remembered: today
Vaspa was a demon straight from the Hot Hell, just as it had
been yesterday and the day before, and would be tomorrow.

On his very first day in this sere ugliness he had soon
been thinking almost wistfully of the Cold Hell. To some of
his people that was the preferable place to go, later. Others
were stupid enough to hope for warmth after death; the Hot
Hell. Not Hanse! After a few hours on the desert, however,
he learned that which was still true on this dull trek: the
desert gave a taste of the Hot Hell by day and the Cold Hell
every night to those so fearless or stupid to travel it. How
was it possible that such heat could become positively cold
such a short time after sundown?

He missed Notable. He missed Mignureal.

Damn! I thought of Notable first!

Mignureal was Hanse's woman. Notable was his cat, insofar as most cats and most especially Notable could belong to anyone other than his unusually large self and the rules of catdom. Hanse did not have trouble with Notable.

Just now his scalp and his thick mop of curling black hair sweated and itched within the flowing white headdress he had to wear. Its long tail was hot on the back of his neck and sometimes it acted as a blinker, interfering with his vision. The alternative was worse; the sun baked his head until his hair was hot to the touch and his scalp grew just as itchy and he had a headache besides. Too, when the wind blew sand that stung like so many hard-flung darts, it was more than pleasant to be able to pull across his face the tail—the camail—of his standard desert headgear.

He had decided that letting Arcala talk him into "being a good citizen" as the master mage put it, and accepting this dull job of escorting an overly wealthy caravan down to Suma was the dumbest thing he had ever done . . . just as creating desert was the dumbest thing the gods had ever done.

Hanse was sure that the primary god of his people had had nothing to do with it. Ils just could not be so cruel to his chosen people, the Ilsigi.

Hanse was restless, Arcala had mentioned quietly.

"Oh, does it show?"

The youngish, pleasant-faced mage had only smiled at that and pointed out that the biggest bank in Firaqa was transferring gold down to a smaller bank in Suma. On its return, the transferring caravan would import silver from Suma in exchange. Such a caravan, Arcala had pointed out unnecessarily, made the finest of targets for raiders. Or for one of the several bank employees and mercenary guards hired to ride with the shipment. Someone just might decide to meander off in a different direction with a saddlebag or two full of the Firaqi coins called hearthers. Or now, on the way back, with some of the flat oval plates of fine almost-pure silver.

I at least wish I'd argued and got them to let me just take it alone, Hanse mused as his mount plodded past a high dune like a wall or a mountain range done in pale yellow, stretching for over a mile. *At least that way I could have galloped and stirred up enough air to pretend it was a breeze!*

Sure. A banker was about as likely to trust one man—and a youthful foreigner, at that—to carry so much wealth as he was to cut interest rates just because he was tired of making so much money and having to buy so much real estate to bring in more money.

And of course if the fellow happened to have any inkling that the chosen occupation of the dark, youthful foreigner was thief—cat burglar—Hanse wouldn't have been taken on as caravan guard at all!

I wish I'd told 'em, he thought morosely, and muttered it aloud to hear the words: "As you know my name is Hanse, but see I'm also known as Shadowspawn, the best wall-climbing, night-seeing thief you ever heard of or even imagined, your honored worshipful bankership sir, but see I never snatch a purse even when it would be easy and wouldn't think of snatching any of your money 'cause there's no challenge in it."

He laughed aloud at sound of his ridiculous words—ridiculous and true—then sobered quickly and glanced around to see whether anyone had heard.

No. The caravan was still back there, following in his wake at a distance of about an eighth of a mile. At least he had insisted on that, and been able to make it stick: he would not be one of those poor bloggy wights who had to follow the caravan, eating all that dust and sniffing horse- and camel-droppings all the way!

And at least the edge of the desert was just about in sight, and Firaqa would not be much farther along. Firaqa, and Mignureal.

He missed Notable. He missed Mignureal.

I mean I miss Mignue and then that damned cat!

The whole unpleasant, dull trek down to Suma and now back to the City of the Flame was so thoroughly unpleasant that he had engaged in all sorts of thoughts darker than storm clouds—which would have been a welcome sight! It had even occurred to him and then begun to gnaw at him that Mignureal liked Arcala and his children, and the good-looking widower wasn't *that* old, and besides he was the most powerful man in mage-ruled Firaqa . . . and he was most responsible for Hanse's taking this job—a job!—that made Mignureal so happy because she had come to despise his chosen occupation especially now that they didn't need the money or whatever else he stole, and suppose the charming Arcala—hmm!—both literally and figuratively—had merely wanted to get Hanse out of town so he could weave a tighter pattern of *friendship* with Mignue . . .

Or suppose the two of them had planned it together!

No, he kept telling himself. Mignue wouldn't do that.

Mignue loves me. She's always loved me, even back when she was just peeping at me from behind her mother's skirts. She wouldn't do that.

He blinked his eyes dully and realized he was slouching in the saddle, half hypnotized by this uninterrupted plodding across the desert. One day the gods became angry, and that day they created this thing called desert for the punishment of humans and animals alike.

And they were really *angry,* Hanse mused. *I sure wish a band of baddies would attack!*

But not too *many of them!*

Or even that they'd start yelling back there, and I'd see somebody galloping away at a tangent to the caravan heading almost due north: galloping to the east or west who cares with some of that raw silver we're lugging back to Firaqa!

That led to more fantasizing, whether it was really wishful thinking or not: *Even that big swordslinger who swears he really is from a place called Barbaria! I could take him. Besides, how fast could a horse gallop, carrying a man the size of a tree?*

He sawed his mount's iron mouth a bit to get him to stop, and took a good long squinting look all around.

No one and nothing. Sand. That and a few garbagey plants here and there. He put back a hand onto his saddle's high cantle and twisted half around to look back again. He sighed. No attack. No robbery. Just yellowish-white sand flashing here and there in the sun like gemstones and sparsely dotted with imitation plants, and the multicolored snake of the caravan, shimmering in the heat of the sun.

He muttered the sour thought: "Where else but on a damned desert would heat be something you can *see*!"

He shook his head and clucked to Ironmouth.

The oversized Tejana horse affected not to notice.

Hanse twitched his heels against the horse's flanks. "Go," he said quietly, and Ironmouth began plodding again. Hanse had taught him that; the Tejana word "haiya" was to be used only in emergencies.

The high point of the whole trek had been the fight that night in Suma, in the inn of the sign of the Happy Lizard. And even that was flawed. The first attacker had muffed it; in a drunken lurch he stumbled into the table so that it rammed into rising Hanse and sent him backward onto the floor, chair and all. In an instant that huge damned Brimm had grabbed the off-balanced fellow and hoisted him right up into the air to beat the other two with him until one fell down and the other ran—as well as could be expected of a man who had been drinking for hours and was so far gone he picked a fight with a lean dark mean-looking youth and a man with a chest like a wall and hands the size of cats.

And then Brimm had thrown the one he had been using as a club several feet across the room and right through a window.

All the while Hanse, his two legs tangled in the three of his chair, stared up from the floor.

"That could have been an interesting fight," he told Brimm a few minutes later, "if you weren't so damned greedy!"

"Greedy!"

"And strong," Hanse had muttered, "and in too much of a hurry," and he bought a round, and later that evening he ascended a wall and a roof and made himself happy by stealing, which to him was life itself. He took from that small third-floor apartment not anything valuable, but only a pair of old green tights, while their owner lay snoring a couple of feet away. And he had walked back to the inn, giggling all the way and wishing Notable were along.

Notable. Hanse sighed. What a cat that beer-guzzling red rascal was!

Hanse slid his hand into the slippery wet heat under his mount's mane and tugged it up to let in a little air. "You're a hell of a horse, Ironmouth, you know that? As horses go, you're the best, iron mouth and all. But I have to tell you, you're pretty rotten company. All in all I prefer Notable. And Mignureal," he added hastily, and frowned, for once again he had thought of the cat first.

And Hanse of Sanctuary plodded along astride the big gray horse he called Ironmouth. And nothing happened, except that he wallowed in unhappiness and the desert roasted and shimmered. And he missed Notable. And Mignureal.

He was slump-slouching in the saddle again when the yells erupted from behind him.

Without interrupting Ironmouth's plod Hanse twirled about to look back. Instantly his skin tingled and his body heat began leaping upward. Men were yelling and shouting, one waving a sword and another loosing a crossbow quarrel . . . while another, bent low in his saddle to make himself a smaller target for arrow or quarrel, was galloping away at a tangent to the caravan's direction. It had happened! One of the bank's own men had snatched a saddlebag or two of silver and was running for it, hoping for a life of luxury . . . someplace.

And already Brimm had kicked his horse into a gallop and was racing in pursuit. The huge man from Barbaria looked as if he should be carrying the mostly-tan horse he rode, but surprisingly the animal was making good speed despite its rider's weight.

The fleeing one was laden with nearly as many pounds of silver, Hanse's racing brain reminded him, as he hauled Ironmouth around. This could not, surely, be much of a race. He calculated direction and intercept point, clamped Ironmouth tightly with both lean thighs, took a good grip on the reins with his left hand and on the saddle's high pommel with his right, and shouted one word:

"Haiya!"

He was just able to stay on Ironmouth as the beast instantly launched himself into a gallop as if he had been hurled from a catapult. The gallop became a dead run almost immediately. Hanse stayed on.

The wind he created was hot against his face. He knew it was against his quarry's, too, and he was glad. He glanced over to see that Brimm's horse was still making good time, and that the two pursuers and the fleeing silver-thief formed a triangle.

"Let's get there first, Ironmouth! Haiya-a-ahh!"

Ironmouth stretched long with every stride, and surely all four hooves at once were off the sand about every other second. Hanse hung on with thighs and knees and hands. Both hands. He would worry about drawing steel later, when he overhauled the quarry. Now he saw that he surely would. Few horses were so fast as Ironmouth, and besides his rider was far from a heavyweight while the horse they chased bore both a bigger man and at least one leather bag stuffed with heavy silver plates.

He glanced to his left again; Brimm was well behind in the race. Assuming that all went well for everyone but the thief, the giant would arrive several seconds after Hanse did. Good. Hanse had learned that being a hero felt really good.

He was close enough now to see the reddish boots and know that his quarry was Fejjlas, the bank employee with the reddish-brown hair and ratty moustache. The poor fellow had had to wait all this time to find his opportunity, and now it was about to be all over.

Then Ironmouth was racing alongside the other man's sweaty roan and for a moment the gazes of Fejjlas and Hanse met. Fejjlas's were an odd pale brown, and right now they were huge.

"No good being a thief unless you're good at it," a more-than-competent thief yelled across to his incompetent quarry, and then Ironmouth's left flank was passing the other horse's neck, and with the extreme pressure on the reins that Ironmouth needed Hanse dragged him leftward, to force the other beast leftward and make him slow down.

It did not work quite that way. The roan shrilled the scary, high-pitched sound of a horse in distress as he banged into the gray and his neck twisted, and in mid-gallop he lost his footing. Two horses and two riders went down. Fortunately, one of the latter hurtled free. That way Hanse covered seven or nine feet through the air and came down with a bang to push up a yard or so of sand with his gloved hands and his nose, which was admittedly large, instead of having a leg crushed under his horse as Fejjlas did.

Both horses were up and trotting with heads jerking and tails high before either rider was quite certain who and where he was. Hanse was up on one knee, gasping and hurting, when he glanced over to see that Fejjlas, too, was on one knee—the only one that was functioning—and here came that great big Brimm on his great big brown horse and one of his great big—bigger than Hanse's waist—thighs gripped his mount hard so that he could lean far out to the side, and his long, broad-bladed sword swept through the steamy air with a tenor *whoosh* sound that terminated in a heavy chunking thunk, and there went Fejjlas's head flying to roll on the sand in a dark red wake.

Fejjlas died in gore and silence; Brimm's yell of triumph was loud. When he reined around and came trotting back toward Hanse, he was wearing a smile as big as the whole face of the man he had just beheaded. The Barbarian was obviously superlatively pleased with himself and that one massive stroke. Despite stories men liked to tell, few men indeed could take a head off with one stroke, even aided by the momentum of a galloping horse.

Brimm was holding his dripping sword well out from himself and his horse. "You're not hurt, are you, Hanse?"

"No," Hanse said, because this was Brimm, who might possibly admit to being a bit discommoded if someone lopped off both his legs and wrapped them around his neck. The hard part for Hanse was going to be keeping up his macho pretext when he had to remount.

Brimm made his horse sidle up beside a smallish mound hardly worthy of the name dune. He slid his sword into it, turned it, drew it out, and cursed. "Thought the sand would clean the blood off—instead it's stickin' to it! Going to have to wipe it off on ole Fejjlas's clothes." He reined in close, and suddenly Hanse was completely in shade. "Leg all right?"

Ah, opportunity to excuse difficulty in remounting! "Not quite. Twisted it the wrong way," Hanse said.

"Ah, I'll help you get back on Ironmouth," the big man said, looming over the much smaller dark one like a wall. He nodded past him at the caravan. "No one else is coming. Want to just take that silver and see what's on the other side of whatever's over there?" Brimm gestured.

"Can't do it, Brimm. I've got people in Firaqa. But go ahead; I did stop him and it's easy for me to pretend to be hurt more than I am."

"Naaaah. So far, whenever I take a man's money I work for him until the job's done or he fires me—or I find out I can't trust him. That's what happened to the last one, and that's how I got this good horse. My ignoble employer was in no condition to pay me my wages." He wrenched his giant's body around to gaze northward. "Well, not too long till we get to Firaqa. Maybe we'll get a bonus for this. We should. Let me handle the asking, Hanse, and we'll have enough for a good roaring drunk the night we get back!"

What Hanse was thinking of most was bed, not beer, but he nodded. "Sure, Brimm. What'll you do if Anoraise says no to a bonus?"

"Chop the son of a bitch's head off and take it myself!"

Hanse nodded. The reply was about what he had expected. Brimm did not intend to hint, or even merely request a bonus for the two who had saved the bag of silver. When a man was as big as Brimm he didn't have to hint, or request, or even think much. He could just depend on the size of his body and the fighting skills it had learned. And Brimm did love violence.

I'm going to have to drink with him once we're back in Firaqa, Hanse thought, *and if we don't wind up in a fight I'm a Rankan's grandmother!*

Then: *Oh damn. Now I have to get back on that horse, and my whole body feels like it ought to be on a funeral pyre, not a horse!*

THE
SHADOW
OF
SORCERY

1

THE AIR OF the main room of the Bored Gryphon was filled with the odor of cooking food—which added a certain murkiness, as if a grease-bearing haze had invaded the place—of the oil of cheap pressed flowers, of greasy hair and sweat mostly old. The dive was also filled with noise. It was nearly full tonight, with a wide-varied crew of eaters and drinkers. Some few were quiet. Perhaps the only truly silent patron was the great big red cat. It lay on a shelf well above the floor as if it owned it, disinterestedly surveying the inn and its denizens with sleepy-droopy eyes greener than polished emeralds.

Two patrons were recognizable as men of the City Watch in their dull khaki tunic-and-leggings. They had put by their leather cuirasses now, off-duty policemen guzzling too much wine from pottery mugs and all the kisses they could get from painted lips. That fat man with a lot of hair and the revoltingly oiled beard over there was a moderately successful trader from somewhere or other; if he had been more than moderately successful he'd have been someplace more respectable than the Bored Gryphon on the Street of Merchants in that section of Firaqa called the West End. He sat well apart from the men of the Watch, who had gone deep enough into their cups to be of little value if trouble arose. With him was a large man who was not fat, evidently a bodyguard. He wore a hand-ax, a dagger, another knife, a mean look and very little hair.

15

Some noticed that he had a companion or fellow body-guard, although the hungry-looking one sat well away, alone and watchful. His hands were restless spiders and he bore a scar that would have made his mother wince, if he'd ever had one. He was eyeing—or pretending to eye, some noticed—a couple of fat wives and three painted chippies with vast areas of breast and leg on display, one far past her heyday, if she'd ever had one.

In the murky room's center, beneath the swinging lamp charmingly fashioned from an old torture device or a copy in dull brass and black iron, four loud Meditonese warriors lolled in bright tunics and billowing blouses that were definitely not Firaqi. They had fled here from their harridan queen to offer their services as mercenaries in a city with no need of their kind, and looked surly enough to chew building nails. And there were others, native Firaqi, less boisterous and colorful although over half of them wore yellow tunics. They sat sipping at watery wine or slightly better beer and pretending to pay no heed to the less timid carousers.

Already one of the Meditonese had offered them trouble and one of the four quiet locals had indicated that he possessed some small sorcerous ability. The would-be merc from Medito had been suspicious. With his fingers tickling the black stone pommel of his sword, he asked, "How come you ain't runnin' this sorcerer-run city, then?"

"You have your betters with blades and I have mine with the *art*," the Firaqi told him in an equable voice. He wore an expression to match. "I'm no major mage; just a few small talents. You know, trembly hands, warts on your feet, inability to get it up, that sort of thing."

The Med had decided to leave the man alone.

Now voices fell and heads came up as, one by one, they regarded the two new arrivals in the doorway.

This unmatched pair did not belong, particularly the gaudy one. In addition to the attention-getting clothing he

wore a superior, even supercilious look that seemed quite at
home on his face. The other, more plainly but hardly poorly
attired, had skin like old pewter. A lot of hair in back
counterpointed a lot of shiny forehead and scalp in front as
if, cheated by nature and his genes, he flaunted what hair he
could where he could. The gaudy fellow's gold-trimmed
tunic was the same mulberry tint as his silk-lined cloak.
Below the tunic's three-quarter sleeves his arms were
sheened with tight-fitted, silvery cloth. Soft boots in red
leather rose just to his calves. His face ended in a short
black-and-silver beard, but his upper lip beneath a great
hawkish nose was hairless. His eyebrows were curly and his
hat matched his boots. Its great big feather was yellow. The
sword at his hip he wore with the careless air of a man who
had never had to consider it as other than ornament. The
eyes above his beak of a nose were oblivious to the many
gazes he attracted, or affected to be.

He had a lot of presence, this large fellow of slightly
above average height. He stepped forward past his retainer
and moved carefully among the tables to the trio by the back
wall. Many eyes watched.

As he approached, the female member of the trio looked
up. She was faceless beneath a Sissæn veil the color of old
wine. That covered her from hair to bosom, save for a
smooth forehead and her eyes. They were the color of night
after a rain. Despite the prevailing style of display among
the women of Firaqa, her bosom was fully covered.

She touched the arm of the lean, youthful-looking male
with her and the other man.

The wiry young one, with a nose that was a rival for the
approacher's falcate beak, turned to look. Two sheathed
knives clung to his right arm, high and low. The upper one
was strapped on upside down. He wore black, black, and
black. His hair and even his eyes were the same color.
Above those discomfiting midnight eyes his brows were

trying hard to meet, yearning toward each other like parted lovers.

The third member of their party was a veritable giant with an uncombed shock of black hair and several scars on the hairy backs of his outsized hands. He wore the leggings and cross-strapped buskins of some sort of barbarian. The gesture with which he cleared his sword's hilt of his cloak looked like pure reflex.

The newcomer stopped beside their table and peered at them around his nose, which angled a bit leftward. It was not a pleasant protuberance. *Looks like his mother spent a steamy night with a potato,* the dark young man thought.

"I do not ask names before giving my own," the newcomer said, bordering on the sententious. "I am Cathamarca, of Suma. I seek another foreigner, a southerner who I know has seen the inside of the keep of a certain *late* sorcerer of this city."

The trio looked at him. The woman glanced at each of her companions. Sand trickled away second after second of silence.

The giant spoke one word, in a flat voice rising from deep in his massive chest. "Interesting."

Cathamarca directed his gaze at him, obviously detecting the obvious test and passing it by showing no emotion and saying nothing.

After a time the big man said one more word: "Why?"

"A fair question. This southerner obviously brought to Firaqa a great talent for certain night-time activities. I seek such a man."

The big man's face did not change. The gaze of his blue eyes, cold as the winds of winter, remained fixed on Cathamarca's beard. His lips hardly moved as he repeated himself. This time he used both words:

"Interesting. Why?"

Cathamarca's servant started forward angrily and several hands moved weaponward. Glaring eyes met and crossed gazes like the swords not yet drawn; not quite. His master's hand, which was gloved in slate blue, stayed the servant, although Cathamarca did not take his gaze from the seated giant.

"No, Yole." Cathamarca gazed at the giant without changing expression. "Is it my clothing or my manners or your nature that makes you so rude, friend?"

The big man stared at him and his scar-crossed knuckles turned almost white with the clenching of his fist. He rose, unlimbering an immense, solid body that towered over the table and the retainer. His face rose shadowy above the light of the single lamp.

"You speak bluntly, friend. Maybe it's because I'm from Barbaria."

At that, his younger, leaner companion looked up frowning.

"Aye," the very big man went on, "it's your garb makes me less than eager to invite you to sit. I don't like to be turned down and this is not your sort of place, or company. And you've been less than honest in the giving of your name."

The buzz of other conversations in the Bored Gryphon had ceased as suddenly as a summer rain. Many eyes stared at the five people in the rear, and those that didn't stare were only pretending. They were looking, just the same.

The silver-sheathed arm moved in a carefully modulated gesture. "I am Cathamarca, Count of Rockwall, outside Suma. I came to this . . . *place,* rather than send servants, for the same reason you gave. I dislike being refused."

"Well said. I am Hansis, of Never Mind, far to the south." The huge man's smile showed no teeth; barbarians, like other animals, bared their teeth only in anger or warning.

Cathamarca peered into their mugs. "If you and your friends would care to accompany me to the Broken Wing, Hansis of Never Mind, I assure you my wine will be neither sour nor watered."

"We're drinking beer."

Cathamarca shrugged and made a gesture. "Surely you would appreciate a better quality brew."

The giant inclined his head. Taking that for agreement, Count Cathamarca turned and walked from the now silent inn. His mulberry cloak flapped at his heels just beautifully. The very slender Yole followed him closely, gliding ahead to open the door. The giant turned back to his companions.

"Come."

The girl or young woman rose, but paused to look down at the other, youthful-looking man.

He lifted black eyebrows that came close to being one. "He wants you, *Hansis*."

The big man from Barbaria shrugged. "You're with me same's she is, Brimm," he said, also emphasizing the name he used. "Come along."

He took from an old drawstring wallet a coin that had little company there, and left it regretfully on the table. Brimm and the woman rose and followed him from the inn. She was about four inches shorter than he; he was about a foot shorter than the one called Hansis. The shorter man picked up a huge-brimmed hat with a big trailing green feather and settled it on his night-black hair, and they headed for the door. He noticed that his far bigger companion lurched a bit as he passed through the doorway.

The four Meditonese warriors had gone . . .

But not far.

Just over a block away they were engaged in attacking the Sumese nobleman and his retainer. It was hardly well-lighted down that side street of pink-stucco houses that was also a cul-de-sac, but the moon was high and bright, done all in sculpted silver. All six men were visible, along with flashes of steel. Hansis chuckled and swept back his cloak with his huge left hand while his right slapped across his middle to drag out his sword, a full yard and more of copper-hilted steel. His huge hand enwrapped it totally, and more.

"Uh . . . old friend," his smaller companion said, "you've been drinking quite a bit . . ."

"Arrrgmmm," the giant said, or something like. "A few cups put meanness in a man's sword-arm!"

"Wait a moment, you walking temper tantrum—there's four of—" the lean and youthful other began, but the giant was still moving, and clearly overjoyed to be doing so.

He had roared out a cry and was running down the street of laid stone. His shorter companions were left in open-mouthed shock.

The soldiers turned at the Barbarian's shout. One pointed. "Stop him Ortil, Blenk! We'll take care of these two!"

Two Meds swung to meet the giant's manic attack, doubtless wishing they were the two who got to deal with Cathamarca and Yole. Cathamarca was proving he knew his way about with a sword, at that. The slender Yole was hard to attack; he wielded sword and dagger simultaneously and moved like a snake.

Hansis had not lessened his speed even at sight of two professional sworders coming to meet him with naked blades in their fists and death in their eyes. At the last moment Ortil wavered before the seemingly uncaring, even insane charge of the very big man. The giant's gaze was on Blenk, but he saw Ortil falter and in that instant Hansis's sword leaped sidewise. Its first two inches glided across and through the fellow's throat.

Ortil looked very surprised. He gurgled and blood bubbled from his neck and from his mouth. He dropped his sword to clutch his throat with both hands, trying to stop the flow. Already he was sagging, sinking to the brick pavement.

The long sword that had given him his death swung back in time to clang loudly off Blenk's leaping blade. Sparks flew and danced like sexually excited fireflies. The shrill scraping skirl of steel on steel was far from musical. Not a man among them carried a buckler, which was close to idiotic in such an encounter. Blenk stumbled a half-step but held, watching his blade shriek down the bigger man's with a noise to rip eardrums, bang off the guard, and slide easily

into the giant's abdomen. Inch after inch went in and into
the man called Hansis, and Blenk thought it wise to
relinquish his sword temporarily. He wore a couple of good
long daggers, after all, and the damned barbarian was dying.
Cling to that sword and Blenk might well join the damned
nosy barbar in one hell or another.

The huge man actually cursed as he banged down onto
his knees, wavered, and fell heavily forward. The pommel
topping Blenk's hilt struck the pavement first and a second
or so later his point emerged from Hansis's back. More and
more swordblade appeared as the giant went prostrate. His
legs twitched. One foot kicked.

Blenk glanced past him at the young couple who had
accompanied the dead man and immediately forgot the
problem of retrieving his sword. The wiry youth was
moving, throwing . . .

Blenk's eyes went huge as he knew instantly what was
happening. He tried to duck. With a *chuk* sound the hilt of
a guardless knife appeared in the hollow of his throat. For
just a moment he stood, eyes open, mouth working, unaware
that he was just as dead as the giant at his feet. Then Blenk
fell across that body.

"*Hah!*" Cathamarca grunted, as he took a wound across
his arm, right through the fine expensive cloak he had
whipped about it as makeshift shield.

Abruptly his assailant stiffened and he too made a
guttural noise, less loud. He assumed a look of surprise. The
count slashed his sword across the fellow's face without
opposition. He thought it wise to chop the Med's sword-arm
on the backstroke, just in case. Cathamarca stepped aside to
let the man fall. That was when he saw that the fellow wore
two throwing stars in his back, six-pointers. Four points of
each showed; the other two were imbedded.

Yole's attacker had heard the noise. His peripheral vision
showed him badness. He glanced over, half-shouted a name
that sounded like "Toop," and received Yole's sword right

across the face. He staggered back, blinded in redness, and Yole gave him another cut: his backstroke went low, into the man's thigh. He fell down.

The sinuous Yole gave the fallen merc a good chop into the back of the head, wiggled his blade free, and regarded the Meditonese cautiously, ready to chop some more if the fellow should happen to prove that necessary.

The lean and wiry youth in black seemed almost to appear out of the shadows, almost as though he had not trotted up, not at all winded. Cathamarca stared in considerable surprise and some alarm at the dark, hawk-nosed face of the sinister night-worker called Shadowspawn. With the merest glance into Cathamarca's eyes, he hurried back to drop to one knee beside the fallen giant.

"Aww, damn it, man . . . damn it . . . we spent all that time on stinking desert and down in Suma and I got to *liking* you! Now you've gone and . . . aw, damn it!" And he stroked the dead man's thigh-sized upper arm as if mourning a dead pet.

He rose with a sigh, took a few steps toward the thoughtfully watching Count Cathamarca, and slid sinuously into a squat to wiggle his throwing stars out of the dead attacker's back.

In a conversational tone Cathamarca said, "I did *not* hear that he was a giant, that southerner who has seen the inside of the keep of a certain late sorcerer of this city. I *did* hear that he was good with knives."

"That's true," the squatting young man said. "Damn! This thing's really stuck! You had a real opponent here, Cathamarca—this jackal's back is all muscle." He drew a dagger to aid him in working the star out of the corpse.

Cathamarca blinked hard and looked away.

"Damn," his savior muttered again, perhaps to himself. "This killing has gotten all too easy. I remember telling a certain royal prince not too many years ago that killing was the business of princes and the like, not of thiev—not my

sort of person. I remember the first time! Wasn't all that
long ago. Also at night, in an alley. Attackers, like these:
cowards who waylaid an unsuspecting *victim,* just the way
these four came after you. That time I was helping out a
friend. A sort of friend. Well, we were acting friendly then.
I threw up and went around thinking about those dead men
for days. It really bothered me. Damn! All I've been through
since then . . . and all the corpses I've seen!''

The squatting southerner shook his jet-haired head. ''This
time I guess I was avenging a friend . . . a man I hardly
knew. But I liked that walking tree of a man, damn it. Ils
knows why I kept on coming, and took this one for you.''

Cathamarca said, ''Because you're a born hero. Ils I've
heard of. Who is the giant, then?'' he asked, and looking up
the street at obvious corpses, he corrected his verb: *''was.''*

''His name was Mitra,'' Yole said, ''of Barbaria.''

''Damn,'' the dark youth said. ''I've just spent two weeks
with him, off and on, and he told me he was Brimm, a
Simmerian.'' He was meticulously wiping his throwing
stars on the tunic hem of the dead man, where there was no
blood. ''Why *will* people lie!''

Cathamarca chuckled. ''And just for my benefit you two
decided to change identities tonight,'' he said, reminding
the dark youth that he too had lied, at least in omitting to
correct the nobleman's misassumption.

''Uh,'' the dark youth said, and that was that. He took off
his big hat, ran his hand through extremely black hair, and
restored the hat hurriedly lest the count think he was being
respectful.

That was not paramount in Cathamarca's thoughts. He
was noting eyes black as the bottom of a well at midnight,
sinister and arresting eyes that could meet and hold another's gaze, and yet were set deep into a face that held its
expression almost to one of blandness. And the count knew
that expression masked neither blandness nor stupidity, but
confidence and competence. This youthful man all in snug
black knew what he was doing, and was good at it.

And he was speaking, low and quiet: "I decided to come to this wrong section of town tonight because I thought it would be fun. Met Brimm-I-mean-Mitra and I-forget-her-name in that dive. He really was a barbarian—from Barbaria, eh!—and has a lot of fun in him. Had. We were having a pretty good time swapping tales—probably mostly lies—when you came along and spoiled everything."

He straightened, having somehow caused the deadly stars to vanish, and met the gaze of Cathamarca from eyes blacker than any the count had ever seen. Darkness and shadows had surely spawned this so-lithe thrower of knives, so that he was sinister as well as sinistral.

"My name's Hanse and I'm from 'way down south and a week or so ago I was in Corstic's keep."

"Well met, Hanse from away down south!"

"We'll see."

Yole didn't like that: "A night for vicious attackers and arrogant allies, my lord."

"Hush, Yole," Cathamarca said, noting how this Hanse person had turned to stare from those black, black eyes when Yole spoke. "It's likely that this man saved our lives." *And is extremely competent with weapons, you idiot, and pretty swift to take offense too!* "Hanse: I suspect that I can talk us through an encounter with the Watch, but I fail to see why we should waste the time. Let us hurry along."

Hanse noted with approval that the Count of Rockwall was as cool now as he had been in the inn. He tested that cool a bit more. "I have lots of friends with the Firaqa police."

Cathamarca gave him a look that was beyond skeptical. Yet Hanse did not smile. Indeed his eyes had gone large and preposterously innocent and ingenuous—chillingly so, in view of his obvious skill and his recent actions.

"I mean, five bodies is a bit much just to leave lying about," he said. "Besides, I sent that woman back to the inn when I uh went to uh work."

"Woman?" Cathamarca said. "Oh, you mean the girl in the scarf."

"Woman in a veil," Hanse said. "She's sensitive. Ah!" He jerked violently and looked down. "Damn! Startled me, you damned cat!"

The unduly large and emphatically red cat from the Bored Gryphon had just appeared, seemingly materializing behind the young man in black. Immediately the cat paced past his leg from behind, swerving to bang his flank against Hanse's calf in passing. Hanse stared down at him.

"Missed the fight, you dummy. Shouldn't've lapped up that second mug of beer, should you! Count Cathamarca, this is my dog, Notable. Notable, Count Cathamarca of Suma. He seems all right. This is his, uh, man, Vole."

The cat's reply was a low-voiced r-sound.

"Yole," Yole corrected, and his lips were tight.

"Notable," Cathamarca said, repeating that most unusual name with exaggerated enunciation. The impossible cat, he noted, responded to the sound of his name:

"mmaowr?"

"I didn't name him," Hanse said, but he wasn't defensive about it.

"Your . . . dog."

The youthful-looking man named Hanse shrugged. "I've never liked cats and Notable and I are definitely friends, so he can't be a cat. Also, he follows me everywhere I go. Anybody knows dogs do that but cats don't." He shrugged again.

Cathamarca nodded. "I . . . see," he said, wondering if this youth was crazy or in shock and had no idea that he was tending to babble.

"Excuse me, Cathamarca, Notable. I think I'll just step over here and throw up."

Ah, Cathamarca thought. *Good, then. He was in shock. Killing is not all that casual a thing for him. I do prefer that to the prospect of trying to deal with a man who kills with ease, much less that enormous Barbarian.*

2

HANSE FROM 'WAY down south, Cathamarca learned with some surprise, did indeed know people in the Reds, Firaqa's City Watch. Although they had not worn red for many years, the Firaqi police were still called Reds. To Hanse, all police were still grabbers.

A sergeant Hanse hailed as Rimizin turned up, with four men in shiny helmets at his back. They wore the same yellowish-tan tunics as the recent patrons of the Bored Gryphon—now nowhere in sight—but topped with front-and-back body armor of leather. Those cuirasses, along with crotch-armor, weapon belts and boots, gleamed with small-ish square plates of dull metal that appeared to be iron rather than steel. All were well armed with sword and dagger, and three bore lances. Helmets and body armor were marked with the stylized flame emblem of Firaqa. The sergeant wore a darkish blue cloak and his helmet was uncrested.

Sergeant Rimizin's squad was accompanied by a driver and a wagon, presumably for the transport of prisoners, corpses, or both.

By that time Cathamarca, Yole, Hanse and the cat had returned to the Bored Gryphon, a lot of its patrons had disappeared and the woman/girl picked up by Mitra/Brimm had bustled out to strip the corpses of valuables. She returned with angry eyes; someone had beaten her to them, that fast.

Hanse met that news with a tiny imitation of the ghost of

a smile; more a look of longing. "Ah, that does remind me of home," he muttered in a tone of happiness.

"We have waited for you men of the Watch only because my old friend Hanse insisted," Count Cathamarca said, wearing that imperious look well and going back to his sententious way of making declamations. "It was a matter of cowardly attack, four against two, and of simple self-defense with friendly assistance."

The word is Rescue, Hanse thought, but said nothing.

Rimizin nodded. "Uh. And never a one of us around when you need us, hmm? Landlord! What happened?"

"You could ask two of your men who was here," the innkeeper said, in a voice he must have bought used. "They seen it."

"Uniformed?"

"Tunics only, Rim," Hanse put in. "They were off duty. I don't know them."

"Drunk?"

"Uh . . . working on it."

"That's why you wouldn't say so if you had recognized them," Rimizin said.

Hanse shrugged and managed to look as if he was considering a smile. It didn't quite happen. The sergeant turned back to the innkeeper, who wore a string of the square copper coins the Firaqi called sparks on a bit of twisted wire about his fat neck.

His story was brief: "Them four Meds was a noisy lot, and I picked up that they come here—to Firaqa, I mean—looken for weaponish employment and didn't find none. I was polite with them, and quiet; it's the only way to act with weaponish men who're angry and surly. They tried to give trouble to them honest men over there—oh, they've left. Well, you know how it is when somethen happens and you fellows come along! Even honest citizens get nervous. Anyhow, one of 'em said somethen that backed off the Med—the soldier from Medito—and I c'n hardly wait for 'im to show up 'morrow night an' tell me what he said!"

"Who's that?" Rimizin asked.

"My customer," the innkeeper said, all large-innocent and sweet of eye. "I forget his name."

"Uh-huh."

"Well, like I was sayen, this young fellow come in and pretty soon he joined the big barbar and this girl here, and they was nice and quiet right over there by the wall. Best behaved cat I ever seen, and the big barbar paid when they left, too. Then this gentleman and his man here come in and went straight to them. They talked a little. I thought the barber was angry there for a while, but he settled down and obviously they got along all right. About that time I noticed that the four Meds had their heads close and was talking low for the first time since they come in. They left fast then, and quietly too. Left me just enough to cover what they drank. Nothen for the house, you understand."

"Why didn't all of you leave together, Hanse?"

Hanse stared into the eyes of the homely policeman. "Maybe you want to separate us and see if we all tell you the same story, Sar-junnnt."

Rimizin looked pained. "Oh dammit Hanse, don't be that way. I have to ask questions. We keep records."

"Count Cathamarca invited us to join him at the Broken Wing. As soon as Brimm-I-mean-Mitra agreed—that's the barbarian, Brimm of Simmeria he told me his name was but Mole here says his name was Mitra, from Barbaria—Cathamarca just turned and left. We got ourselves together, paid, and ambled out. We didn't take a dozen steps before we heard the noise and saw that the four Meds had these two citizens of Suma backed up in that dead-end alley."

"That's *Yole*," Yole said, through very tight lips.

"That's a street!" the innkeeper said.

Hanse made a boyish gesture. "Sorry."

"My Lord Cathamarca," Rimizin said, "did you know those four Meditonese? Why did they attack you?"

"I did not know them. You can guess why they attacked

me as well as I can. They came to your city looking for work
and found none and were disgruntled. They sat here and got
drunk—mean drunk. I appear to be a man of some worth,
and they went outside to lie in wait to strip me and my man
Yole, here, of our valuables.''

"Not to mention clothes," Hanse muttered.

"They didn't even demand purse or anything else,"
Cathamarca went right on. "They just attacked. Their
swords were already out, which is why we were able to
prepare ourselves. In a way, that is; Yole saw the glint of
steel in the moonlight. I don't care to fight four men,
especially drunk men, who can't be reasoned with and are
harder to hurt besides! Therefore we chose flight. Unfortunately we chose that cul-de-sac. We had drawn sword as we
ran and whirled my cloak around my arm.''

"I see it served you well," one of Rimizin's men said.

Cathamarca deigned not to glance at either him or the rent
cloak. "Once we saw we were trapped, we turned to defend
ourselves. Almost immediately there was a wild yell, and
here came that huge Barbarian at the run.''

"Sword out?"

"Absolutely. Two of them turned to meet him while the
other two kept at Yole and me. I don't really know what
happened after that—to those two and, uh, Mitra, I mean. I
was busy."

"Brimm uh Mitra attacked at the run and killed one in the
charge," Hanse said, before Rimizin could ask. He snapped
his fingers. "That fast. The other one stuck him right
through the middle—stuck Mitra, I mean—and he fell
forward, onto the blade. There I was, still thirty or so feet
away and staring at this damned murderer across Mitra's
corpse. Mitra's legs were twitching and I knew he was dead.
I don't remember throwing—I threw, didn't I, uh . . . .''

The girl nodded. "The knife went straight into that
murderer's neck," she told Rimizin. "I never saw anyone
throw so true, so far, and not even in daylight! I mean, I
could barely make out pale spots I knew were faces.''

She paused to glance at Hanse. Several people were looking at Hanse, who suddenly took on a more youthful, ingenuous appearance.

"I, uh, I've always had real good vision at night."

"We know," Rimizin said. He returned his attention to the veiled girl-woman. "What else?"

She shrugged eloquently. "Then he shoved me, told me to get back here, and that's all I know."

"I know," Cathamarca said. "Naturally I was looking into the face of the man I was fighting off. Suddenly he went all stiff and shuddery and his face took on a shocked look. Surprised. That's when I slashed him, but when he fell I saw that Hanse had already put two death-stars in his back. The fourth Med saw, and that distracted him for a moment."

"So you killed him?"

"No, I did," Yole said. He touched the scratch on his cheek. In this light it looked like saffron faded by being left too long in the sun. "About a second before he had almost cut my face open!"

"Sergeant," a youthful grabber called, tramping in with that noisiness a small man used when he had found a moment of importance. "Not a one of those five has a purse and only one's wearing a ring—a cheap one."

Rimizin looked questioningly from Hanse to Cathamarca.

"Don't be looking at us, Rim! Would you call this a neighborhood of well-off people? Is this the kind of neighborhood where people who come across corpses with purses leave 'em that way, or not?"

The Watch sergeant managed a pallid smile. "Not. Milord Cathamarca doesn't appear to need money or be the sort to search dead men anyhow, and we all know you don't need money, Hanse."

Immediately an arm slid around the back of Hanse's waist and a small but long-fingered hand attached itself to his side.

"Shhh," Hanse told Rim, glancing around. He looked down to see that the hand at his waist was a small one. It belonged to Mitra's pickup. Somehow he remembered her name at that instant: Jemise.

"I ain't been outta this place all night," a voice said, and they glanced over to one of the Bored Gryphon's few remaining patrons. He sat slouched at a table, hovering over a mug of beer like a cow protecting her newborn cafe. The grizzled fellow looked as if the reason he hadn't been out of the place all night was because he was incapable of getting up. His voice sounded as if it were coming up out of a well. Or a tankard, perhaps.

"Them as needs to pipe up an' protest innocence has a habit of bein' guilty of things," a burly Red told him.

"Hush, Gid," Rimizin said, and addressed Cathamarca, Hanse and company. "All right. I'm convinced that everything is just as all you have said. Damn! This is what happens to some poor barbarian who comes to town and trusts his brawn . . . just charges trained men of weapons without pausing to use his brain! Count Cathamarca, are you staying at the Broken Wing?"

"Yes."

"I won't ask your business in Firaqa, but my superiors may want to."

Cathamarca looked at him imperiously, over and around his nose. "I shall be there tomorrow."

"Thank you, sir. Eternal Flame! Five foreigners, all dead in a few minutes! Oh—I'll need your name."

Pressing close to Hanse, she said, "I'm Jemise."

"From Sissæa?" He was looking at her deep red veil.

"From Mrsevada, really. But that was . . . a while ago."

"Recently from Sissæa?"

She shrugged, against Hanse. "I like to wear the veil, at night."

"Should I ask to see your face?"

Still pressed close, she shrugged again. "It doesn't matter, Sergeant. I never saw any of you—including you and your men—before tonight. I wasn't with Mitra; we were

just talking when Hanse came in. I noticed *him* right away.''
Her emphasis indicated that Hanse was just the most
attractive thing she had seen in years.

''Uh-huh. I think I won't bother asking what you do,
Jemise.''

''Actually I'm a wealthy noble.''

''Uh-huh.''

''We were on our way to the Broken Wing, Rim,'' Hanse
said, ''and none of this was our fault. Can we be on our way
now?''

''Oh, Sergeant,'' Jemise said. ''I live right around the
corner from the Broken Wing, by the way.''

Rimizin glanced at her, said ''Uh-huh,'' in that same
persimmony way, and answered Hanse: ''I think we're
through here, Hanse, yes. You're entirely too good with
throwing weapons, you know? Are you maybe planning on
leaving Firaqa soon?''

Hanse met his eyes with a bland look. ''As a matter of
fact, yes. I have to go back to S—south. Home.''

The sergeant looked uncomfortable. ''Oh, damn. Now
I'm sorry I said that. I didn't mean it really. Just a joke.
Ashes and embers, Count Cathamarca . . . this man is a
hero in this city.''

''He is to me, after tonight!''

Rimizin nodded. ''Uh-huh. You should have known
Corstic.''

The ears of the big red cat went back.

''No,'' Hanse said darkly. ''No one should have known
Corstic. I don't like to think of him as human. Otherwise I'd
have to be ashamed to be a member of the same race.''

''Well, thanks for ridding us of him, Hanse. And, believe
it or not, I'm sorry you're leaving. Anyhow . . . Singlas,
are the bodies loaded?''

That brought a nod from the older, overweight Red he
addressed. ''All on the wagon, Sergeant. Gid's ready to
drive.''

"Let's all be on our way, then."

"Uh, Hanse," Singlas said. "We've never I mean we've never met or anything but uh, Hanse—I live in Firaqa. Always have. Thanks. For Corstic, I mean. Getten rid of him, I mean."

Wooden of face, Hanse looked at the Watchman and nodded. "Sure," he said. "With him gone, Firaqa is a nice safe place to live now, right?"

Singlas nodded with enthusiasm and his jowls bobbled. Hanse felt Jemise jiggle against him, and knew she was silently giggling behind her veil.

"Right," he said. "Well, thanks, Singlas. It's nice to be appreciated. I know you have to go now—got to get those five nice safe *corpses* someplace else in this nice safe town, right? Good night. G'night, Rim."

They left, with Hanse thinking that far too many people knew about that night at Corstic's, despite Arcala's efforts to keep it quiet. If he had really made such efforts.

Hanse looked down at Jemise. "This tunic is a pretty new one, Jemise, and I'd appreciate it if you wouldn't dig holes in it with your nails. I can feel them biting into my side."

She trembled, and kept her hand right where it was. Its nails matched her veil. "I'm af-fraid to let go of you, Hanse. This started out to be a nice night and now I'm just scared half to death."

"It seems to me you've had about your limit for one night, Darry," the innkeeper was saying to the grizzled patron who had felt it necessary to avow that he had not left the place all night. He still sat at table, drooped over his mug like a dying flower.

"Seems t'me one of them Meds said they had work," Darry said, low-voiced and slurring.

Hanse glanced that way, but Cathamarca's words were a lot more interesting just now: "Let's be out of this place," he said.

Yole showed that he was more than ready. Hanse nodded,

and moved. Seeming somehow to have become glued, Jemise moved with him. So did the big red cat.

"Needn't be in no hurry," the innkeeper said, in manner jovial.

He received four cold stares, followed by the sight of four backs. The nobleman's mulberry cloak flapped at his heels just beautifully.

3

In a nice room on the second floor of the inn at the sign of the Broken Wing, Hanse took off the big blue hat and set it down carefully so as not to crimp the feather. Meanwhile Notable prowled in quest of cat-eating monsters, found none, and pounced atop a tall red-brown armoire to nap. Count Cathamarca showed surprise when Hanse turned down ale, beer, and wine. He merely gazed expectantly at the Sumese from those dark, dark eyes.

"I propose not to ask too many questions," Cathamarca said. "But will you tell me something of how you learned about Corstic, and gained access to his keep?"

"Probably not," Hanse said. His eyes were dark and chilly, yet they burned, burned.

"Just a little, perhaps. A summation."

That was when Notable rose and stretched briefly. He pounced to the floor, a bit too close to Yole, who jerked and gave the cat a look entirely without love. Notable bestowed a green, dull-eyed stare upon the very slender man. He paced some more, re-checking these new premises in the yellowish light of the lamp, before slumping on the round, four-colored rug beside Hanse's chair.

"mew," he said sweetly in his practiced but never perfect imitation of a kitten, and lay there as if he had just been struck dead.

Hanse regarded a wall that appeared to be solid oak and

surely was not, and addressed it as he responded to Cathamarca's request.

"This city is ruled by a sort of guild of sorcerers. Oddly enough, that seems to work. The mages have rules and laws about how they can and cannot use their talents. Corstic and another really advanced mage, Arcala, were the most talented among them. The most competent, anyhow. That wasn't enough for Corstic. He wanted one-man rule, and worked at it. He'd gotten so powerful that he broke their rules and laws and nobody could do anything about it. Understand now, this isn't my city and I'm not political anyhow. I had another reason for wanting in Corstic's keep, and I'm not going to tell you about it."

Cathamarca nodded to let him know that was fine with him.

I said it again, Hanse was thinking with some distress. *It's been a habit so long I can't stop! Damn, I wish I could quit saying I'm not political—it isn't so.* He resumed a narrative he knew would be very, very brief:

"The second time I tried, he had killed several friends of mine in a way too horrible to talk about. Awful, sorcerous ways. Gods, how I hate sorcery! I saw one man die with a tree limb big as your leg all the way through him. And yet Corstic made him alive and was keeping him alive, that way, to suffer. The other three . . . ah gods, he had turned those poor wights into human pyres, shooting flames up more than three times my height. In short, Corstic nearly got me, but thanks to this cat I got him instead."

"Your dog, Notable."

Hanse looked at the count and almost smiled. He nodded, and slid fingers through the lurid fur of the cat snoozing beside his interestingly wrought, crook-leg chair. Notable's tail twitched in response. His eyes slitted partway open. Since the pupils were not in sight, that vision was less than appealing.

Cathamarca nodded. "I suppose no one's ever going to hear the whole story of that night. Corstic can't tell it and you and Arcala aren't going to."

"I suppose you're right."

"Might I ask what you brought away with you, from Corstic's estate?"

"That's pushing, Count."

"For that I would apologize, Hansis," the count said, with a loose gesture. "Just natural interest. You did a great deal for Firaqa that night and I wondered whether you had benefited yourself."

"I'll tell you anyhow," Hanse said. "This time. By the time all the horror and excitement was over, that place was full of people; Arcala was there, and another Watch sergeant I know, Gaise, and a herd of his men. I didn't come out of there with a damned thing and I am not going back."

He turned his head to stare at Jemise, still wondering how he had been so weak as not to thrust her into a doorway, any doorway, on their way here. Appeal to the ego, maybe; a shapely and attractive young woman who displayed such high interest in Hanse was very good for his ego.

Hanse shook away that memory, and frowned. *Attractive! I don't know whether Jemise's attractive or not, behind that damned curtain!*

"Would you please take off that silly scarf, girl? No one here is going to attack your—whatever you might have that you value."

"I have a name!"

Her eyes flashed and sparkled like dark jade dipped in oil. She jerked aside her veil and the first thing Hanse noticed was that full-lipped mouth, stained the same burgundy hue as the veil. Almost a point at the bottom of a piquant face, her chin was dimpled and her nose was . . . her mouth was . . .

Hanse blinked and sighed. Damn. "Eminently kissable," was the phrase he wanted. This Jemise of the streets was beautiful or nearly! *And Mignureal's probably waiting up for me, too!*

"You are wise, my dear," Cathamarca said. "I can understand that you would wish to cover such beauty in that neighborhood!"

Interestingly, Jemise didn't bother to preen.

"You came into that Gryphon place looking for me, without knowing what I looked like," Hanse said. "You mentioned my talent for getting around at night and said you were looking for such a man. You've heard my recent business, Count. What's yours?"

"Yole is with me, always," Cathamarca said. "You want her to hear what I have to say to you?"

"I didn't exactly bring her! She *attached* herself to me. What d'you propose now, tossing her out the window?"

Jemise made a small high-voiced sound that made Notable's tail twitch.

Count Cathamarca glanced past her at the window, a veiled arch with shutters open. He smiled. "That shouldn't be necessary." He gestured loosely. "Yole, give her a few coins. Jemise, just pop down to the common room while we discuss a bit of business."

"Hmp!" She stared. "Hmp!" she said again, unable to find words at being summarily dismissed when she thought she had done a very good job of insinuating herself into this fascinating collection: the hero of Firaqa and a wealthy noble. Her hand had already begun drawing up her scarf when it occurred to her to say, "And just suppose I'm not there when you *pop* down, hmmm?"

Three men stared at her. No one spoke.

"Hmp!" Jemise departed, flouncily.

Yole went over and locked the door.

"No, Yole," his master said. "Just open that door and stay near it, hmm? An open door cannot conceal an eavesdropper."

"Very good," Hanse commented. "An old Sumese saying?"

Cathamarca laughed. "Not yet. Oh, Hansis, she called you just Hanse?"

"I noticed that too," Hanse said, face and tone bland as tepid water. "Shortened my name 'cause she likes me, I guess."

"Oh. Well, at any rate, Hansis . . . have you heard of the Rings of Senek?"

Hanse shook his head. A certain tension formed inside him and writhed, just a little. A monkey rode his back; an addict dwelt within him. Hanse of the Ilsigi people of Sanctuary, as the handsome master mage Arcala had recently pointed out, was addicted to danger, to adventure. The addiction had another name: it was Shadowspawn. It was Shadowspawn who pricked up his ears.

"'Rings' is always an interesting word," Hanse said. "Rings that have a name are even more interesting. '*The* Rings of Someplace or Someone' sounds important, and even more interesting."

Yet he had not hunched forward in a display of interest. Instead he sat back, legs apart and asprawl. Cathamarca wondered idly just how fast the youngster could come up from that indolent position. Probably very rapidly, if need be; the southerner moved with the grace of a dancer, or a cat.

The count was nodding. "You read me aright. The jewels of Senek are very old, so old that many think them mere legend. That is not so. They exist, or at least three fine finger-rings do, and I know where they are."

"Hmm," Hanse said casually. "Valuable, are they?"

"Oh, I'd say we could rule Firaqa with them, if we so desired."

Within Hanse, Shadowspawn picked up his ears in full cat-burglar alertness. Hanse snorted. "Firaqa! I can think of better things to do with rings, Count! I am no citizen of this town and as a matter of fact am not staying here long. Meanwhile you know a thing or two about me that you shouldn't, too. Cathamarca: are you a mage?"

"No."

"No kind of sorcerer?"

"No kind of sorcerer."

Hanse nodded, considerably happier. "You know where some old rings are and want them. You also want me. Presumably to fetch them for you."

"True twice. Fetching them will require an individual of your talent and skill, Hansis. Abilities Yole and I freely admit we do not possess."

'Cause you're so lordly and superior and honest and trustworthy, Hanse thought, but said nothing. He made sure that his eyes said nothing, too.

Count Cathamarca was gazing at him around his beak. "Shall we make an agreement before I say further?"

"What makes these rings hard to get, Count? What protects them?"

"Hansis . . . I haven't the faintest idea. Good men have tried, in past."

Hanse chuckled without smiling. "And bad men too, I'll bet!"

"Without doubt. But what I meant is men good at entering places meant not to be entered, at detecting and getting past barriers and traps or guardians, and coming away with . . . this and that."

"Uh. Men not as good as I am," Hanse said matter-of-factly. "But . . ."

"I accept that," Cathamarca said. His silver-shining arm was stretched out to his cup, his hand turning it slowly, over and over without his awareness. "As a matter of fact I assumed that you must have come to Firaqa because you'd heard of the Rings."

"Didn't," the younger man said. He looked quite comfortable and relaxed, slouched asprawl in the chair, black-clad legs stretched out, one arm dangling. His fingers lightly touched violently red fur. "I just . . . came here. You mentioned barriers and traps and guardians? What kind of traps and guards?"

"Hansis, I repeat and assure you: I haven't the faintest idea."

The two men looked at each other in thoughtful silence pregnant with surmises about guards and traps set around three Rings. Three very, very valuable Rings. It was the Sumese noble who spoke:

"I remind you that I asked whether we might make some agreement before I say further."

Hanse shrugged and Cathamarca went on:

"I will tell you the whereabouts of the trinkets, and we will go to the area together. We will fetch them together. We make a seven-and-three split and go our ways in safety and friendship. And wealth."

Trinkets, Shadowspawn thought with a mental snort. Nevertheless he nodded. Then he saw that the count awaited a formal reply. *Am I to believe he trusts me, then?* The answer came swiftly and easily: *Of course not. And he knows I know he doesn't. Doubtless also knows I don't trust him.*

"All right," he said. "The split sounds fair, too. Without me you'd never have a chance at the Rings. Obviously I deserve seven portions to your three."

Cathamarca smiled. "You mistake my meaning. Without me you'd never have known about the Rings, and without me you will never find them. The seven parts are mine."

Hanse sat back and gazed steadily at the other man. "Let's be sure I understand what you want and what you are *offering,* Count. You want me to go into some extra-dangerous place and fetch out some extra-valuable little objects that have been there a long, long time. They are in some place hard to get at and guarded by who knows what or how many who-knows-whats. You want them for some reason you have not stated, and I have this naggy notion that it isn't just because you like jewelry or need more wealth. One of them would be roughly thirty per cent, but you are not about to give me one of them. Do you intend to sell them?"

Cathamarca was able to meet that level gaze with his own. "Hansis, more is there than the Rings. It is just that they are all I want. Anything else you find is yours to carry away and do with what you will, with good wishes and in good health. No, I do not intend to sell the Rings of Senek."

Hanse was impressed with the nobleman's refusal to be

intimidated. "And the idea is to hope that I don't get too attached to them once I find 'em and bring 'em out, hmmm?"

Hanse blew a breath out through his nose in what could have been construed as an audible smile. He rose, all in one fluid motion that had Yole's hand moving weaponward and brought Notable's eyes alertly open. With a beautiful and astonishing suppleness and soundlessness, the dark youth in black took a couple of paces away in what they recognized now was his normal gait, a smooth gliding pace that jarred no part of his body.

With no seeming attempt at drama he turned again to face the others. "Count Rockwall, it seems to me that we can't do business. I don't know enough. You won't tell me why you covet those Rings or what you mean to do with them, except that you aren't going to sell them but offered me a third. A third of what?—whatever else I *might* find in . . . wherever it is I'd be going if I were going. That is a very one-way arrangement. I have other things to do. True, I won't have the Rings of Senek, but I'll get by. I always have."

Cathamarca sighed, and did not hesitate. "What I was trying for was a business partnership rather than an employer relationship, Hansis. However: I shall hand you twenty Firaqi gold hearthers tonight and twenty more when you hand me the three Rings. And you still keep whatever else you bring out of there."

Hanse sat right down and clonked an elbow onto the table. The sleeping cat's tail snapped and curled while Yole's hand pretended that it had merely wished to scratch his hip, all along.

"I seldom refuse a man's second offer, Count Rockwall," the black-clad youth said in a voice bland as his expression. Let's make it twenty-five and twenty-five," he went on, gazing into Cathamarca's eyes, "but forty *silver* hearthers tonight and the balance in *silver* when I hand you the loot." He corrected that hurriedly: "I mean the rings, the Rings."

Cathamarca looked surprised, but nodded. Rather than forty gold coins marked with the flame and hearth of Firaqa's religion, this black-clad strangeling demanded fifty—but wanted payment not in gold but in silver.

"I will agree to that, Hansis . . ."

"Good. Where are the Rings?"

". . . except that I have only twenty with me tonight. But I admit to being curious. You turn down gold and want silver? Please pardon me, but why?"

For the first time the two men saw Hanse smile. "Gold is a magic word. Gold attracts attention and usually demands change," he said quietly, even slowly. "Hand people gold and they get all excited and others notice and they talk about it after you leave. Silver, now . . . well, any man might have spent all his coppers and have only a bit of silver amid the cobwebs in his purse. I certainly don't like attracting attention, Cathamarca, not that way."

Cathamarca gave Yole a significant look, and smiled, nodding. "I understand you, and I am appreciative of your answering an idle question, Hansis. However if you wish I can always go to a changer and hand you the payment in innocent, common coppers."

Yole snorted.

"In a wheelbarrow," Hanse burst out, smiling, and then he was laughing aloud. Notable's tail twitched and his ears waggled a bit. His eyes, however, remained closed.

Cathamarca laughed with the man he needed, and made a show of unstrapping his purse. He started to toss it onto the table, but thought better of that and passed it over to Hanse.

"You asked a question about the Rings of Senek. You were very close to them, Hansis." Cathamarca's chuckle was a dry sound like the falling of dying leaves. "They are in the keep of the late Corstic."

Hanse stopped laughing.

4

NOT A MAN to be trusted, ever, Hanse thought as he walked home—the apartment on Cochineal Street he shared with Mignureal. *His first* instinct *was to cheat me. He took that seven-and-three split out of the air—we're not talking about any seven or three or even nine and one parts of anything. Three rings, that's what it's about. And Cathamarca's instinct is to mislead, to cheat. Someone who hasn't had as much experience with that as I have might well have been taken in!*

Under the big plumed hat popular among Firaqi men, he was enveloped by his still-favorite cloak, which was a dull black, lined with black. One reason he liked it was its color; another was that it made him look a lot taller. Under it he wore five visible knives and the sword with the fancy hilt and guard. Although his pace was rapid, he seemed to glide, never coming down on his heels. He stared straight ahead, wearing the forbidding look he affected. It tended to frighten away footpads and cutpurses, as well as honest citizens who feared that the sinister fellow in the long night-colored cloak might be a foodpad and cutpurse.

On the other hand the fact that he was accompanied by the outsized red cat strolling along at his side, tail high, did attract glances and more. Hanse's eyes and the presence of so many sharp blades worn openly here and there about his person persuaded people to keep their comments to themselves or low-voiced.

47

Notable accompanied him, walking or trotting on this side or that, occasionally running ahead with tail high or turning off this way and that to inspect something interesting. Once a dog barked and Notable looked hopeful. But nothing came of it. The dog was tied in his yard and would never know how lucky that was for him!

As he walked Hanse was wary of the occasional passing or overtaking horse rider, although in this city riders held their mounts to a sedate pace, and kept scrupulously to the center of the street, and as ever he was grateful for Firaqa's law prohibiting chariots within the city. He did deign to step aside to give easy passage to the pole-mounted conveyance, all draped in fluttery green silk, that swayed by on the shoulders of four knotty-calfed slaves or servants in matched tunics. He knew they bore someone of wealth or importance—*possibly* even both, and was not interested in offending anyone. Not tonight.

He was also not interested in who this might be, or in the bare-breasted whore—well, she was bare of breast so long as one discounted the way her "wrap" contrived to hide her areolae. He was thinking about rings, and about the one wrapped and snuggled in the bottom of his belt-purse. That reminded him of That Night at Corstic's, and the words of the rival mage Arcala:

"Hanse," Arcala said, "what did they promise you?"

For once Hanse told the truth: "Whatever I could carry out of there in addition to the figurine."

Arcala chuckled. "Please pardon me. I do not intend to laugh at you. It's just that you and that cat saved this city, and you came away from there with nothing at all for yourself!"

Shadowspawn had shrugged, feeling an unaccustomed sensation: embarrassment. And he had thought briefly on the ornate ring worn by the dead Corstic. He had transferred it to his possession . . .

It and its slate-colored stone reposed snugly in his

concealed belt-purse as he walked along well after sunset, thinking about it, and the Rings of Senek, and Cathamarca, and what other things might be among the late Corstic's treasure. After a while he was almost smiling, thinking that he would talk this over with Mignureal.

His Mignureal. And now he frowned a little; still his Mignureal, the girl he had taken away from Sanctuary after the murder of her mother and Hanse's slaying of the killer. Still his woman as he was her man, but oh how she had changed, just since they had been here in this far northward city!

He had changed too, of course, and much without realizing it: in taking her out of Sanctuary with him and heading up here to Firaqa, he had accepted responsibility for someone other than Hanse, perhaps for the first time ever. Along the way he had fought for her, easily succumbed to her desire to rid herself of her maidenhead, accepted responsibility too for the red cat and then the calico—both of which turned out to be products of sorcery, of Corstic's consummate and incessant evil. Next he had become a man of property, with the sale of the horses he had taken from those robbing dogs of the desert, the Tejana; and then of that robbing dog of the forest not far south of here, Sinajhal the predator. He had even learned about interest, about how money could earn money while being left alone, and he had bought things: not just for himself but for Mignureal and the apartment they shared.

But Mignureal! What had happened to her was womanhood, responsibility, a man, and then considerably more. She was eighteen as of two Ganedays ago, the product of a sheltered life amid a large family with a wonderful mother back in Sanctuary. And she had the Gift; the Seeing ability of some of her S'danzo people.

Now she had something Hanse had never had save on a temporary basis: employment. His S'danzo woman was better than talented in the Seeing ability of the women of her

people, and now that Corstic was dead the S'danzo would
fare better in Firaqa. She had gained confidence. Now she
practiced her gift as a trade, in the bazaar along Caravan
Way. Now she was able to look directly at him and express
disapproval, this very young woman who had so admired
him for so long when she was only an impressionable girl
under the protection of her mother and father.

She loved Hanse, and while she was several years
younger she often felt older for she had not so many of his
inner needs, not so many things to prove, and prove again.
She no longer found his comings and goings by night so
romantic. Now she could not seem to help disapproving;
trying to change the very things about Hanse that had
attracted her to him for years as a dashing, romantic
figure—an Older Man (older boy)—to begin with.

She had been happy that he had taken the temporary
employment of caravan guard, despite the danger.

They had money and she had work and he had an
employable skill; why must he steal?

He could only sigh and try to answer—or more charac-
teristically, refuse to answer and take shelter in acting
offended.

He was not sure of his age; maybe twenty-two, maybe
more or less. He had never had a father and hardly knew his
mother, who had barely known his father. He had grown up
on the streets, raised by a thief. In matters of the street he
was more mature than somewhat; in other ways he was a
boy, and in some way he was aware of that, whether he
admitted it or not. The cockiness of this bastard orphan was
an act to cover his being filled with inner needs and pain and
unsureness. And he was the best roach there was. That was
what it was called down home in Sanctuary; roaching,
because a roach was a creature that came out only at night.
Why did he continue to do it? Because he must, he tried to
tell her. It was what he did. He did it better than anyone, as
far as he was concerned, and he was probably right. His

abilities at climbing, at moving silently, at disappearing into any pool of shadow, were unparalleled.

Beyond that, it was a need in him. By scaling the unscalable wall or building, by stealing the unstealable, he proved himself. At the same time, he achieved that happy fusion of work and play enjoyed by so few people.

And there was that other thing, that which Arcala had recognized in him at once That Night in Corstic's keep; Corstic's last night alive: Hanse was Shadowspawn, who was addicted to adventure but more than that, to danger. He did not admit, ever, how much he loved the rush of adrenaline that made him tingle all over. Yes, he was addicted to that.

Mignureal heard Arcala say that, and she did like and respect Arcala, but still she could not quite understand, could not approve. There was in Hanse something else that Arcala did not mention. Perhaps Mignureal knew it now, whether she quite admitted it or not. Despite his charm and his often giving ways, Hanse was a self-devoted loner.

Trying to be one half of a couple was difficult. He was good at dealing with difficult physical matters and indeed he loved doing so. He was not at all good at dealing with emotional ones, he who admitted little to himself and even lied to himself, who had so much to prove, and so he avoided such difficult matters. The trouble was that was the very worst way to behave when one was trying to be part of a couple.

He had not ceased to succumb to the occasional sexual adventure with others, either. That Mignureal probably did realize and probably did understand. She had an incredibly mature attitude about such things: bodies, she quoted her mother, were not for the owning, much less one part of a body.

The effect on him of a thought she'd had, one night after he took refuge in being offended and then became aggressive and then stormed out, would not have been salutary:

Sometimes I know what an immature girl I am, she
thought, one night after he had stalked angrily out rather
than try to talk reason. *It hurts, to realize that he is such a
knowing man of the world, so experienced, while I'm such
an ignorant girl. I rile him because I don't know how it is
that I should behave, and so I behave as some mixture of my
mother and me and—a silly girl. And yet in other ways he
is such a boy! Sometimes he makes me feel old, more like his
mother than his . . . than his . . . his woman.*

*Oh Hanse, Hanse, why must you be cursed with such
deep needs!*

Why can't I be more a woman and you more a man?!

But the bastard orphan did not know of those thoughts,
and as he walked home he decided to lie to her about
the kind of job he had accepted. She had employment and
he did not, which was uncomfortable. Now he had. Yes,
he decided, he would not be wholly truthful about its nature.
He was feeling good about that when he reached the
two-story building fronting on Cochineal and backing on an
alley—which he had found convenient, more than once. He
even nodded politely and as if respectfully to a hooded
oldster. He knew the fellow was aged because he covered
wrinkled legs and knobby knees under a robe as no younger
Firaqi did. The darkish blue garment was multiply striped in
a medium green at hem and sleeve-ends.

Hanse had gotten used to the strangeness that in the City
of the Flame, whose temple rose tall, no one wore red.

The hood nodded in polite response or acknowledgment,
and the robe went its way.

Naturally Notable decided to hold matters up while he
relieved himself. Hanse heaved an exaggerated sigh and
waited without patience while the cat took time to make
certain he was satisfied with his ritual sniffing of his urine.
Hanse was through with that before Notable was, and
started in. After a final sniff to prove his independence, the

cat snapped his tail to attention and hurried after him, showing dependence by making a complaining noise.

"Be quiet, Notable," Hanse muttered. "Mignue may be asleep."

His improbable cat replied with a small burbling noise from the throat.

They ascended to the second-floor apartment to find her waiting, seemingly doing nothing but waiting. Of course, Hanse realized with a pang of guilt; it was pretty late, well past dinner time. Notable went straight to his bowl, which was larger than anyone would have expected a cat's bowl to be. Finding it empty, he turned to sit and stare accusingly as if he had had nothing for days.

Mignureal was not asleep. Mignureal was sitting up, waiting. Of course she was miffed and a little stiff about her man's lateness and about the fact that he had eaten, for she did like to cook for him. She was irresistible, beautiful with her mass of dark hair and her lovely body draped in the long, colorfully embroidered robe he liked even though it had been a gift not from him but from a grateful client. Yet when he embraced her it was more as if she allowed herself to be hugged, and his attitude, too, stiffened.

"I'm sorry I'm late, Mignue. My new employer paid for dinner, and I couldn't turn the man down!"

Her face changed for the better; sunshine breaking out of clouds. "Oh, I understand, Hanse," she said in her soft, girlish voice. "I realize you couldn't let me know—now tell me about this new employer."

He showed her Cathamarca's money; down payment, balance to be paid on completion of the *mission*. "He's a mighty well got-up and well-off fellow from Suma who is fearful about traveling back down there without protection. I'm going to act as guard. Me!" He smiled as charmingly as he could, since he was lying. "So—we've agreed I *have* to go back to Sanctuary, and this way I'll be busy and paid all the way!"

She looked fearful. "But . . . a guard! A weapon-man's employment with a caravan. Suppose he has reason to worry, darling. His danger would be yours! You might have to fight."

He gave her a sideward look and a teasing smile. "Uh, Mignue . . . remember our trip up here? Suppose we'd been with a caravan then . . . we wouldn't have been robbed by those damned Tejana, would we? Or been waylaid in the woods by good ole Sinajhal, either."

After the nomadic Tejana robbed them of horses and provisions out on the desert, Shadowspawn waited until night and stalked them into their very camp. He took back more than they had taken, including lives and limbs. As for Sinajhal: well, he was the sort of charming lying cowardly thief who had charmingly given them directions into the woods, where he had lain in wait for them and would have killed Hanse. That led to a fight with swords, and to Hanse and Mignureal's having two more horses, as well as the blessings of those people who were more than glad that Sinajhal's career had been brought to an end with his rotten life.

Now Hanse hoped that Mignue would not think about the fact that had they not traveled alone—foolishly—but had been with a caravan, they would not have come into all those horses they had turned into money. She didn't:

"But . . . oh Hanse, I had hoped . . ."

Already feeling defensive because he had decided to lie about his *job,* he pushed: his voice, tone, and face hardened. "Damn it, Mignue, you're always worried about me being in danger! You *don't* want me to climb walls, *don't* want me to steal, *don't* want me to take a harmless little ride down south pretending to be the noble count's guard. What do you think I'm going to do, become a tailor or let you teach me how to pretend to do what you do?"

And then, gazing into her suddenly dolorous face, he added to his lie: "At least this is a *job,* not stealing!"

She was immediately apologetic, feeling guilty when he had so obviously come in excited with good news, and so he immediately felt guilt, too. He always did when he hurt her, or lied to her. He was sure that lying was not what a man should do with his woman. In Hanse as in most others that led to defensiveness, which as in too many others led to offensive behavior.

He had not consciously looked for it, but he had found his excuse not to deal with it; to storm out of her presence once again. He did, this time leaving the broad-brimmed Firaqi hat with its flamboyant plume. She did not call after him, but he knew he left her weeping, and took absolutely no pleasure in that.

I can't be as different as she seems to want me to be, he thought unhappily, *but damn it I wish I could be* some *different!*

Notable caught up to him down on the street, making that weird uncharacteristically cute burbly noise he did when he tried to speak while trotting. Hanse knew Mignureal had to have let the cat out, and pretended to ignore him. The gods knew that Notable had done that to him often enough!

"Mmmaw?"

"Hush, Notable, I'm mad right now and need to think."

Notable paused to sniff at a blade or three of scraggly grass in a cat's pretense of being unconcerned with the big bully he had attached himself to. The clop-clop of hooves and the jingle of bells—another city ordinance—on a passing food-wagon had no visible effect that most people would have noticed; Hanse saw that the cat took notice of the wagon and huge steeds with a swift twitchy wagging of his tail.

"Need any melons, young fella?" the wagoner called.

"Nah; my woman has two big ones," Hanse called back, and went on his way while the fellow giggled and went on his.

Needing to Prove Something even more than usual,

Hanse made his way into a well-to-do neighborhood and
scouted for a likely house. Notable had busied himself
lurking and sniffing, and had to be summoned and advised
to stay. He got the drift of Hanse's meaning, but did not
pretend to like it. Shadowspawn parked his cloak and
companion while he went up a wall as easily as another man
might have climbed a ladder. He flitted like a silent shadow
up the roof and down to pounce onto another building of the
pink stone that was so prevalent in Firaqa.

One with the shadows and just as soundless in his
soft-soled working buskins, he edged along to peer through
the open window of a third-floor bedchamber.

The eyes of the human shadow pierced the dimness of the
bedroom. Ah, now here was a nice challenge: a large man,
asleep on his side in his dark bedroom and not even snoring!
It was not Hanse who slipped into that room, moving as
quiet as time and seeing far better than nearly any human
could have seen in that darkness. It was Shadowspawn the
professional, and his buskinned feet made no sound as he
entered. Staring at the sleeping man, he moved slowly
toward him.

He froze at sound of a little change in the sleeper's
breathing. Stepping back into one of the room's deep
shadows—and vanishing—he waited until he heard the
man's breathing return to what he had decided was normal.
He smiled when he picked up the jeweled cloak-clasp from
the chair beside the bed, then slithered back into the
masking dark when its sleeping owner made a chuffing
noise and turned over onto his back.

Minute after minute dragged by while Shadowspawn
stood in silence, flat against a wall, gazing at the man on the
bed. He was a thief, a roach proud of his abilities at
roaching, not an attacker. Not a man who admitted incom-
petence by having to harm those he robbed. After a time the
fellow commenced to snore, and the extra shadow in his
bedroom left it.

Out the window and onto the ledge like a ghost done in black and freeze at a sound below; then onto the roof and across to the other one and down, without waking the former owner of the handsome clasp, and without anyone's seeing. Notable was waiting beside his cloak. He was none too happy at being left, and voiced that feeling in a long, querulous r-sound. But not even the cat had the climbing ability of his human and this time Shadowspawn had elected not to take him along.

Notable stared accusingly at his human, who was showing his teeth in that odd non-menacing way humans did.

"Easy as slicing pie," Shadowspawn muttered, and Notable made a belly-deep r-sound.

Buoyed, the successful thief decided to celebrate by going uptown to that nice inn called the Green Goose. As he walked, ghosting through the nighted city dark as darkness itself in every shadow, he fetched out Corstic's ring from the leathern purse at his belt. He slipped it onto the middle finger it fitted, because it was ornate and he fancied that it made him look rich. As if he, the bastard brat-thief from Downwind in Sanctuary, *belonged* where he was going.

And once again it was his own liking for the game of skulking, of seeing while not being seen, that led him into trouble.

In a dark-shadowed side street that was not quite an alley he heard a familiar sound and went to one knee while a sword's blade swept over his head. He did not have time to think on the fact that no one had demanded that he stop, or hand over this or that; someone had merely tried to kill him. Apparently someone who had lain in wait for him! Insofar as he was capable of thinking when pure automatic reflex took over, Shadowspawn might have given a sixty-fourth of a second's thought to those Meditonese mercenaries who might have a vengeful friend or two.

But he was moving, staying alive, and when he rolled over against the wall and stared out from black shadow with

steel in each hand, sight of his assailant dispelled any
thoughts about Meditonese.

His attacker was an impossible creature, a man with the
head of a bird of prey, including the bright yellow beak that
curved and clacked as no mask could. Even as he swept out
his sword at that outré apparition, Shadowspawn's peripheral vision showed him the other one, also swinging a
long-bladed chop. Desperately wrenching himself aside,
Hanse dropped into a squat and aborted his attack on the
first vulture-headed attacker long enough to chop the leg out
from under the second. He fell without a cry and Shadowspawn had no time to gloat; he must hurl himself away
again from vulture-head number 1. He, without a sound or
seemingly any feeling for his companion downed in agony,
coldly tried a second sweeping blow at what was supposed
to have been an easy mark, in the dark of an alley that only
pretended to be a street.

Meanwhile Notable was squirting about as if in confusion, tail down and ears back, and yet making no effort to
attack the attackers. That was as uncharacteristic of the
attack-trained watch-cat as if he had suddenly taken a liking
for milk in preference to beer.

Blade clanged and skirled on blade with a sound made
more frightful and ear-assaulting by the walls of buildings
on both sides of the narrow street. Even as they noisily and
jarringly crossed blades in what Hanse considered desper-
ation since they were both without shields, the vulture-head
jerked a knee up into the crotch of his intended victim.
Hanse went backward in agony, fighting not to drop his
sword and bend forward to grab himself in agony, as he very
much wanted to.

When he did drop the sword it was a decision, not a
reaction. The echo of its clang to pavement was still in the
air when Shadowspawn's hand flashed forward and put the
long slim lozenge of hiltless steel into the assailant's throat.

At that Notable took off straight along the center of the streetlet, at tail-out speed.

Mortally struck, the impossible attacker wavered—and disappeared.

Not that he danced away, or ran, or faded into shadows the way his chosen opponent did; the vulture-headed creature simply disappeared. Even in the shock of that Shadowspawn wasted only about a second before turning to face a new challenge from the one he had downed.

Furthermore Hanse could find no blood. What he did find was his throwing knife, which would be of little value until he had sharpened its tip. It was blunted from having struck the wall of pink stone behind the vanished attacker.

Sorcery, he realized, sweaty and angry rather than fearful. *Some son of a bitch has attacked me with sorcery. Illusion! O gods, O father Ils, how I hate sorcery!*

Hardly panting in that place of darkness that was as home to him, he was assailed by the memory of the shadow of sorcery that had so long hovered over him and Mignureal. It was a list of names and a handful of sorcerous coins that had had so challenged his and Mignureal's mental stability, and indeed their very relationship.

And maybe destroyed it, Hanse thought morosely. *One more thing to lay at the door of that monster Corstic!*

Now and again a name would vanish from the list, at the same time as one of the coins also disappeared. All Hanse's efforts to get rid of the pieces of Firaqi silver had failed. Sorcery. Corstic's sorcery, it eventually turned out. Hanse trusted Hanse and his abilities, and despised sorcery, the introduction of a factor that robbed a man of his skill and competence. And yet always it reappeared in his path.

Much of his life, far too much of his life, had been taken up by his attempts to grapple with the shadowy things of horror that menaced life and limb and sanity.

And now what the devil had come over Notable? Hanse whistled, and waited. Warily.

Ah, he realized. Sorcery. Illusion. Notable had seen no attackers, for there had been none. Only Hanse had seen them. *So would I be any the less dead or maimed if I hadn't fought them off?*

He had no answer for that, and here came Notable, acting skittish in his nervousness. But his human's insanity had been only temporary; he scooped the huge, bristly cat up and stroked him while making nice sounds. In spite of himself Notable's throaty growls became a purr, and man and cat went on uptown. The latter was happy to get to ride.

5

AFTER THE SOBERING experience in the side street, Hanse changed his mind and headed elsewhere. He returned Notable to the pavement while he surreptitiously removed the ring and concealed it in the flap of fabric Mignureal had sewn inside his tunic.

Maybe his feet took him to Jemise; maybe his subconscious guided his feet. At any rate he found her, or was found by her. He succumbed with alacrity. She was wearing little and soon wore less, and then less than that. At her smallish place, she showed him her bemazingly obvious feminine assets and an interesting ability or three. He succumbed. While she watched him undress, he tried to conceal from her the singular plenitude of sharp steel things he carried here and there on his person. He was only partially successful.

"You certainly carry a lot of weapons."

He glanced over at her, naked on the couch but not quite sprawled; she had arranged herself to be fetching. She had done a good job of it, too.

"You have about the most beautiful name I ever heard," he said.

Jemise's talents were more physical than mental, but she took that compliment as a strong clue that this walking arsenal did not wish to discuss his armaments.

They did not quite wreck her bed, but they certainly made a tangled, sweat-damp mess of it.

"Stay," she said, when they were able to breathe and talk again.

He shook his head. "I can't," he told her, and was kind enough to give her the night's spoils.

"You don't have to give me anything, Hanse," she said, giving him a cute and thoroughly fetching look from under the tousled hair pasted to her forehead by the sweat of their lovemaking. Her hand didn't seem to hear; it was making the handsome cloak-clasp disappear in the flimsy little lavender shirt-thing she almost wore.

"Good," he said, and slid both hands onto her hips to stroke damp flanks. "If I thought I had to give you something *else,* I wouldn't have given you *that*! That's real gold, Jemmy."

"Umm," she said, nuzzling. "Hanse . . ."

There was only so much succumbing that even an enchanted man could do in one night, and this time he did not.

"This bauble didn't come from those two men, did it?" she asked, watching him dress, which was never as interesting as the reverse process.

"What two men," he said, automatically unstraightforward.

"The count and his man Yole." She giggled. "Or Vole!" And she laughed, so that Hanse interrupted getting into his buskins to watch the pleasant jiggle of this and that salient aspect of her anatomy.

"No. It has nothing to do with them, Jemise."

"Good," she said, sort of snuggling into herself. "I don't think they're good men, Hanse."

Hanse made it a rule never to say "I don't think." He had heard it too many times and believed it at once, so he tended not to hear what the speaker said after. Many people did not think, that was obvious. Hanse could not understand why some wanted to brag about it and take the chance of being believed.

Although he had no reason to suspect that Jemise indulged in that underused luxury called thinking, he did hear the rest of her sentence.

"I don't either," he said.

"Well, you be careful, Stud. I'd like to see you again."

He smiled and nodded. Regarding her as she lay sprawled—really sprawled, this time, in inspiring désha-billé, he thought that seeing was not the word for what he wanted to do to and with Jemise.

"I'll be careful," he told her, and added a lie because he was Hanse: "I'm good at that."

He finished dressing, roused Notable, kissed the cat-like Jemise again, tarried for a bit of mutual fondling, and departed.

When he returned to the apartment he and Mignureal shared, she was gone. A brief look around showed him that she had not gone empty-handed; missing were the silver-backed comb and brush set and the beautiful dress-cloak he had bought for her for far more than the one he had bought for himself the same day. That meant that she was not merely outside or walking.

Hanse sighed. He assumed that he knew where she was—with Turquoise and her husband Tiquillanshal and their daughter Zrena, a S'danzo family living near the bazaar along Caravan Way. She had taken refuge there once before when Hanse had angered or disappointed her with an attack of his . . . . recurrent childness. She did not even bother to pretend that it was because she feared to be alone; Moonflower's daughter Mignue was all honesty.

But this time he vowed not to go after her.

Disappointed and hurt, he was using flint-and-steel to bring life into the little brass lamp he had bought, in the shape of a woman's cupped hand, when he heard the diffident knock on the door jamb and turned smiling. The light went out of the smile at sight of the male of the old couple who lived along the hall and had sort of adopted those nice youngsters with their great big pet, so handy as a watch-cat.

Murge looked no happier than Hanse felt.

Hanse pretended nothing had happened earlier: "She didn't come home from the bazaar today, Murge?"

"Uh, yes, she did, Hansis . . . and waited for you. It hasn't been too long now since she left. I could see she wasn't happy." He scratched the scraggly hair just forward of his fat-lobed ear. "Left you this note and asked if I'd stay around in case you found a word you had trouble with."

That was no embarrassment; Hanse had spent many years unable to read or write. He had never felt inadequate about his lack, or self-conscious either. Far more people could not read than could. Mignureal had been engaged in the sporadic teaching of her man to read ever since they were halfway across the desert between here and Sanctuary—the desert made a nice and easily erasable slate. He knew lots and lots of words existed that he still did not recognize and certainly could not write. He accepted the hinged, closed wax tablet, stepped back a pace to catch the lamplight, and opened it.

Yes, he knew all these words, and read slowly but not aloud:

> Sorry you could not trouble to come home or let me know.
> I am staying with Quill and Turquoise.

Turquoise—whose name was Sholopixa, really—and her husband Tiquillanshal were fellow S'danzo who lived behind her booth where she was paid for Seeing. They and Mignureal had become instant friends; the S'danzo seemed to feel part of one big family wherever they were, wherever they met. It was a kinship that Hanse was unable to understand, but he liked them. The couple were eminently likable people. And Quill was a marvelous cook.

"I can read it all, Murge. Thanks."

"Have you eaten, Hansis?"

Hanse nodded. "Plenty, thanks. Good night, Murge."

"I'm sorry, Hansis," the nice old fellow with the hang-dog face said, and went along to his apartment, scratching the hair in front of his ear.

Hanse closed the door before he plopped down in a chair to stare at nothing. After a while Notable ambled over to give his leg a bump-rub and mention food, but Hanse did not react at all and Notable went elsewhere to turn his back before lying down.

Pets were fine here, their landlady had told them that first day, "so long as there's no mess, mind you, and no loud noises, now; everybody else here is older folk!" On two occasions Notable had made a loud noise—loud enough to rattle glass, as Hanse put it—but no one minded. Indeed, he became the hero of the building, since on both occasions he was warning of prowlers, would-be thieves or worse. Hanse had had to go around and ask people not to keep giving the huge watch-cat milk and little morsels of this and that, since he was interested in having a cat that would land on its feet, not roll if it fell down.

Then there had been the night when three other dwellers in the building had given Notable beer, maybe innocently and maybe with giggles, just to see what the cat would do. They had heard that the big red beast liked the stuff, but found it hard to believe. They became believers. What Notable did was lurch blearily home to sleep it off just inside the door. Hanse, who liked strong drink more than somewhat and had proven his strength by giving it up, was not understanding.

After twenty or so minutes of sitting so in morose thoughtfulness, Hanse rose sinuously. Well, if Mignureal wouldn't stay, neither would he. And he hoped she relented and came in to discover that he had been here, but had left!

First, though, he had to check on the continuing mystery.

He went out the window and up onto the roof he considered his. Here lay the oiled-skin packet he was not worried about losing, but wanted to keep out of his and Mignureal's sight. He opened it.

All four hated objects of sorcery were still there; make it four, counting the name. The two flame-stamped silver coins the Firaqi called hearthers, and the fold-over bees'-wax tablet. The tablet's wax was blank save for the single name unknown to anyone Hanse had asked: Elturas.

"One name and two coins," he murmured, solely to himself. "And before she died Rainbow—Shurina— showed us that at least one man lives in Sanctuary. So who is the other man whose life is linked to these triple-damned coins, and why is his name not here?"

He gazed away into the darkness of nighted Firaqi, and sighed, and replaced the objects in their weatherproof wrapper. And swung down off the roof.

"Notable?"

Notable said something best described as a burble with some "m" sounds, and joined him at once. He looked up at the creature ten or more times taller than he, a god-like being Notable trusted implicitly.

Despite his ego-boosting dalliance with Jemise Hanse was in need, feeling guilty, needing to weep but unable to do so; one more helpless victim of what passed for manliness. He managed to feel neglected, put upon, and abandoned, and returned to Jemise.

Jemise was delighted, and never mind that she had just put her bed back in order. He spent the night . . . and snitched the cloak-clasp when he left next morning early. That afternoon he rode the big gray horse out the North Gate and up the long hill, Town Hill, to sit and stare again at Corstic's estate. He did not enter through the gateway that still stood open; not even stupid thieves would try taking anything from this place!

No tree branches came rustle-hurtling at him this time; no

moaning, wailing men stood impaled and aflame. Corstic
was dead. Hanse had come here to scout; all he did was sit
and think, and at last turned the Tejana horse and let it set
it own pace back down to Firaqa, so long as it did not hasten
overmuch. Hanse wore no cloak; his thoughts were wrap-
ping enough.

That afternoon he merely wandered the streets of Firaqa,
City of the Holy Flame. He wore not his blacks but a
russet-colored tunic and stained old buskins—and the big
feather-decorated Tejana hat that he did like. He did plenty
of looking. It had never displeased him that a display of
bosom was in among Firaqa's women this year, while skirts
were long enough almost to hide the feet. As a matter of fact
in the case of women of wealth and/or station, their skirts
covered their feet utterly and even swept the ground. We,
they silently bragged, have the wherewithal to buy more
fabric than we need, and to have it washed, too.

Only a few women of Firaqa wore their hair loose, as so
many did back in Sanctuary. Mostly it was done up,
sometimes ornately, and decorated with pins and combs and
ringlets. He and Mignureal had already remarked that seven
in ten women's tunics showing as blouses above tightly
belted skirts were in some shade of yellow, and two of the
remaining three in ten were white or that shade called
natural. They assumed that the yellow had to do with Flame.
"Natural," most likely, had to do with lack of finances.

Of course he saw plenty of red hair. Scarlet tresses had
been all the rave the past couple of years, since the
consecration of the newest priestess called Hearthkeeper,
who happened to be a redhead. Red dye was a big seller in
the bazaar. And more than a few Firaqi of both sexes wore
a string of the square copper coins called sparks on thongs
or bits of wire about their necks, so that numerous people of
both sexes seemed to be wearing the same necklaces. At

least the number of coins strung thus varied from one wearer to the next.

Hanse did not emulate the example. The Holy Flame had not helped him. He had given it those damnéd coins, all of them. And they had come back, reappearing like an abandoned cat in the apartment. Besides, gods were gods and Shadowspawn respected them . . . but a flame? Just wavering dancing yellow and orange fire?

Let it try standing up to Father Ils, he had secretly said to Mignureal. Or even one of those Ruman gods!

And he kept his money in a purse as a careful person should, and inside his tunic as well.

6

THAT NIGHT IN soft-soled working buskins and clothes the color of the darkest shadows, he went like a great black cat again up the alley wall of a certain building. He was very wary this time, for he well knew that people once shocked by the territorial infringement of robbery felt violated, and always watched more closely thereafter, as if the thief might be so stupid as to come back to risk arrest or death by trying to take a little more . . . or perhaps, ridiculously, to return the spoils.

This time the thief did indeed return, and his self-appointed mission was to perform the ridiculous.

Easing quiet as a ghost into that same dark bedchamber, Shadowspawn replaced the so-handsome and obviously costly cloak-clasp on a small writing-table in the apartment of its owner, proving himself to himself.

He also narrowly missed being caught—or wounded, or killed; whatever the outraged owner of the bauble had in mind. The man was not in bed but across the room, waiting in darkness, and he was nicely armed to face an armed man or stop his fleeing. A voice yelled curses and threats and a crossbow quarrel sang, but Shadowspawn was not there.

"Disappeared into the shadows like they was a doorway to the First Hell," he heard the man's voice loudly telling someone, but already it was from a distance: the object of the tirade had ghosted one roof away and was moving fast and a bit more quietly than the crossbow shaft.

It was Shadowspawn in black came down off that building breathing hard with his heart doing that thrilling thing and his skin all prickly the way he couldn't help but love and who cat-footed it along the streetside so that a pair of young lovers approaching him stepped well aside in a semicircle to let him pass; it was a calm, cool Hanse in green tunic over natural leathern leggings and big plumed hat who a short time later ambled over to the Bazaar, and to the home that was the rear of the business place of Mignue's S'danzo friends.

His change of clothing was incidental, done after he went back to the apartment on Cochineal Street in the hope that Mignureal had returned to the apartment; to the nice little place they had made their home.

She was not there, and she had not been there.

Quill and Turquoise welcomed him with what he read as restrained heartiness and thought was false; their cute daughter Zrena peeped shyly or perhaps coyly/wistfully at him from behind a drape only a little less multicolored than her mother's skirts. Hanse felt anguish: this was just as Mignureal had once peeped at him in the home of her parents, years ago and far to the south.

"Why . . . no, Hanse, she isn't here."

"Come on, Quill, I'm no stranger. Where's Mignue?"

The couple exchanged a glance and Quill's sigh mirrored Turquoise's. *They don't want to tell me,* Hanse thought in some surprise, and he was right.

He was not pleased to discover that she was attending a drama written by someone local and celebrated and supposedly famous; attending it in company with Arcala.

Damn! Arcala! The man was an attractive widower, practically all-powerful in this city, and not too old, either. He was also, damn it, likable. Hanse well remembered how the mage and Mignue had liked each other at once, and how taken she was with his children. Since the death of Corstic, Arcala was supreme practitioner in Firaqa, which made him

Chief Magistrate; city boss at a level above merely being mayor, although not quite ruler. Not, Hanse knew, that Arcala could not be if he wished, with his unmatched abilities.

"Might as well stay and talk a little," Quill said amiably, obviously working to be casual about it now that the agony of breaking the news was behind him. As if nothing had happened; as if nothing had changed. "She'll be home—*back*," he corrected embarrassedly, "before long. You know, I made a two-dove pie this afternoon that's enough to make a statue's mouth water!"

"Thanks, Quill," Hanse said, pretending not to have noticed the gaffe and forcing a pleasant look—as if nothing had happened; as if nothing had changed—but he turned down food and the opportunity to wait for Mignureal to come "home." He was just able to maintain the decent face until he had left the obviously concerned couple.

They don't like me as much as they did, he thought morosely, with no evidence whatsoever. *She's told them what a rotten untrustworthy dog I am, never home when I should be like a settled man so that all she does is wait and worry.*

He walked along the pave without seeing it, forgetting even to swagger. Nothing was about to interfere with his determination to remain unhappy and self-accusing this second consecutive night. It was repeatedly difficult for him to keep his vow to stay away from something he had decided he loved too much and so had ceased to use: strong drink.

Still . . . being accosted by a footpad just at the edge of the sprawling Bazaar area did make him happy.

Hanse stood and stared, his knees bent only a little. "Well? You want something, fellow? A trip to visit Theba, maybe? Come and get it," he said, in a way so cold and deadly that even without his black working clothes he affrighted the accoster off.

In fact the poor devil fled with such haste and abandon that he actually dropped an earring. Shadowspawn picked it up with a half-smile, turned it over, and his eyebrows rose. He swiftly adjudged the gold-and-topaz bauble to be valuable and therefore stolen, and his was not an unpracticed eye.

"Thanks For The Nice Earring, Rot-peter," he bellowed, and came very close to making himself laugh.

With a little smile he set out to take the pretty topaz-set bauble to Jemise, and he walked more purposefully now, and his customary swagger returned with every step he took.

And when he had knocked, and then confidently, proprietarily opened the door for he was after all welcome here and brought a gift besides, he saw that her hair was disordered just as he liked it but beyond the embarrassed woman he saw too that tonight she had other male company doubtless for the rumpling of her bed: Count Cathamarca.

Hanse left without a word, but with the earring.

Dawn came up on Shadowspawn, sitting atop the flat red roof of a pink "redstone" building, arms locked around upraised knees, staring at nothing as he had been for hours.

He believed in very little except Hanse, and that was ever a shaky matter. Therefore he truly was always ready for anything, particularly the unexpected. It was a trait that had served him well, even before he saw his mentor and father-substitute—and mother-substitute—hanged as a thief. Because he had to be a pragmatist, the orphan called Shadowspawn was a pragmatist. Through the quiet night his thoughts had turned eventually from self-accusation to the poor-Hanse feeling that Cathamarca's presence with Jemise gave him excuse for, and then to business, and at last to a pragmatic decision.

He accepted that he would do it: he would return to that awful place. And now he wanted to get it done with and have it behind him.

That meant the sooner the better. He descended and headed for Cathamarca's lodgings without thinking that the count might still be with Jemise. He bought a half-loaf and an overripe plum from a woman and child—already dirty, so early in the morning!—on the street and resisted giving them the nice earring lest its possession get them into trouble. He ate as he walked.

It was no happy or very polite young man who accosted Cathamarca in his own two-room suite:

"Let's go do it."

"I, uh, Hansis, ahh, about last night . . . when you saw me with, ah, um Jemise . . ."

A bitter Hanse waved a hand and cut the older man off: "It doesn't matter, Count. She's just a whore. You and I both know there're plenty of those to go around."

At that a screech sounded from the other room and here came a tousled Jemise, charging in with a lot of jiggle and an upraised dagger. Hanse's brain froze but automatically his body went into a ready, poised crouch. Cathamarca was not with Jemise—she had nighted with the count!

Cathamarca noted with interest that his . . . *partner* drew no steel. Hanse did not have to regret that or cope with the angry female, however: the handsomely clothed count simply extended a handsomely booted foot to trip her. The half-clothed Jemise had hardly splatted to the floor, dagger skittering away, when Yole grasped her from behind/above and bustled her roughly out of the room.

She kicked air and made plenty of ugly noise, but Hanse noted that she wasn't really trying all that hard to tear free.

"Women," he muttered, shaking his head.

"Indeed," Cathamarca said, with a wise nod. "But *that*, my friend, is not one. *That* is a girl."

Hanse only shrugged, knowing that while Mignureal was younger, she was indeed a woman. Suddenly without thinking about it he was looking past the count, calling out,

"Don't you hurt her now, Yole! She wouldn't really have stuck me."

Yole and Cathamarca took that as mighty strange sentiment and behavior on the part of this *boy* they knew only as a thief and killer, but refrained from saying so. Hanse and his employer began to plan tonight's mission.

7

ONCE AGAIN SHADOWSPAWN in black rode out of Firaqa's northwall gate on the big gray Tejana horse he called Ironmouth.

This time he wore a half-sleeved jerkin of boiled black leather over his tunic and leather leggings. And this time he rode in company of two others. They paced their mounts up the long hill to the sprawling wooded estates of the wealthy, and to Corstic's. The handsomely landscaped place still loomed huge and scary, a dark and demon-haunted keep. Just the sight of it flooded the mind of Shadowspawn with memories he'd have traded away for a millet seed.

Now the mansion was dark and deserted and, he believed or sincerely hoped, harmless. Only a big empty house, its windows dark as the heart of its former owner.

"Wait," Hanse said, as Cathamarca started to pace his mount through the open gateway.

The count and his retainer turned questioning looks on their black-clad professional.

"Just wait a moment," Hanse said quietly, giving his horse a stroke under his mane, where Ironmouth was hot and damp with sweat. "Notable and I had really awful experiences here—and we were far from the first! Just . . . wait a few seconds . . ."

At sound of his name, the big red cat riding the horse before him gave his tail a slashing movement and looked alertly up at his beloved mother—for surely so did Notable think of Hanse, bestower of food and beer and strokes and belly-rubs and even the occasional pick-ups.

"The place is harmless now," Cathamarca reminded, "for we know Arcala removed Corstic's spells."

"Uh-huh."

Cathamarca and Yole exchanged a look; the count shrugged.

Hanse sat his horse for several minutes, just staring at that lofting, handsome manse that had been such a place of evil and horror. The ornate ring, gold with its odd double setting of gray-blue he secretly took from here That Night, was with him still, inside the flap within his tunic.

When he had entered Corstic's palatial home that other time, he had found it protected by spells—illusions—and by real horrors as well. But he had with him the particolored tortoise-shell amulet given to Mignureal on the road up here, by that strange not-what-he-seemed man named Strick. Mignureal Saw its purpose just as Hanse—no, Shadowspawn—had started on the mission here: Strick's amulet enabled the wearer to deal with illusions; to see them for what they were, to see *through* them and will them away.

Sorcery, good and bad, ever contrived to work both ways: the amulet's power had nearly resulted in his death in Corstic's entry hall when Hanse had decided that every attack was illusion. Wrong; Corstic had believed in mixing his warders. One of those impossible attackers had been real.

Although that bore out his sternly held belief that nothing of sorcery could ever be good, Shadowspawn wore Strick's amulet tonight, on a doubled leather thong around his neck. He touched it now, as he and two impatient men sat their horses and stared at the big dark mass of a building without life. He also wore those things he considered more reliable: on one hip the sword with the fancy hilt and twisty guard; scabbarded down his other leg just under two feet of the guardless sword the men of the Ilbars hills called a knife. The sword he had taken as spoils of combat back in Maidenhead Wood after that thieving, murdering highwayman Sinajhal the flamboyant made his attempt on the lives and possessions of Hanse and Mignureal and failed.

And as usual Shadowspawn wore his knives, several of them, as well as several throwing stars with six razor-edged, needle-tipped points.

At last he clucked to his horse and rode easily as Ironmouth paced into the estate. The others were not unhappy to trail as they paced their mounts up to the multistoried mansion. Hanse waited while Yole tied the reins of the three horses, and the three of them mounted the steps onto the porch.

Notable was notably not anxious to go in. He did not run, but crouched, as if to weld himself to the floor when Hanse squatted to stroke the red fur before picking up the cat. Carrying him in his right hand like a limp but heavy sack, Shadowspawn swallowed, hesitated a moment, and tried the door. His emotions were mixed when he found it unlocked.

Knees bent and ready, he entered with trepidation and wariness—and without incident.

He smiled when he passed beyond the entry hall where previously he had been so savagely and sorcerously attacked; why, this was as easy as slicing pie!

"You can handle it, Notable," he said, and bent to put the cat down. "You can see a lot better in this darkness than we can, too."

Notable went into an ears-back tail-at-attention crouch in a clear statement that he believed not a word of that. Notable remembered this place very well.

"Here are candles," Yole announced.

"Good!" Cathamarca said with an overdone joviality. "Light three, Yole, but bring more."

Hanse wondered whether candles found in the keep of such an inhuman human monster as Corstic might not be

made of corpse-tallow, but he kept that less than pleasant
thought to himself. Yellow light made Corstic's grim den
seem almost handsome, almost like a home.

Now in a casual manner Cathamarca told his agent
something he knew and had *neglected* to tell Hanse: the
manse had a cellar.

"I am sure that is where we will find the baubles."

Hanse gave him a long look.

"Is that something you . . . *forgot* till now, *partner*?"

Cathamarca only smiled and shrugged, charmingly.

Shadowspawn was un-charmed. Neither red cat nor
black-clad man liked this cellar business, especially as a
last-minute revelation, but after a bit of wandering in the
eerily candle-lit dimness they found the door. Only Yole
had stumbled, when his knee rammed a huge hardwood
armchair with enough noise to awake a dead man.

Apparently it did not.

The door was thick and heavy, with great iron bracings
and handle. The moment they opened it to a chill draft, a
strangeness, an evil seemed to flow out of the place along
with the cool, stale air. The men exchanged a look; Notable
stared down the steps from green eyes with pupils grown as
big as Hanse's thumbnails. His ears went back and he stayed
close to Hanse's legs.

"Ahhh," Shadowspawn said in exasperation at his own
trepidation, and descended.

Instantly a terrible, unreasoning fear assaulted him, skin
and bones and mind and heart, as an almost palpable Thing.

And then it became palpable.

Despite the fear he felt and could do nothing to dispel, he
tried to take another step, and trailing tendrils of wraithy
stuff like cobwebs writhed over his face as if alive. He
shivered and shook his head, raising his hands to tear his
way clear.

His fingers touched nothing.

Nothing was here to touch; no cobwebs or anything

tendrilly; nothing at all. Yet the eerie feel of them persisted. Fear laid Nordic fingers upon him, tightened them about his heart. Again he shivered. He began to shake and clamped his teeth against their rattling. This palpable evil born of Corstic's dark talents dragged from that otherworld of apparitions and divinations and things a man could feel but not see . . . these things never ceased to make Shadowspawn shiver in fear when nothing else could.

With his mouth invaded by hot water and the taste of bile, he turned away, whimpering, to flee.

That showed him the surprising sight of Yole and his master staring, apparently wondering at the delay. Obviously they felt nothing untoward.

Then, even while his knees shook and his hands had gone chill and wet, Shadowspawn realized what was taking place. Twice before in his persistently adventurous life he had experienced this same Sending from the shadow-world of necromancy and spectres. There had been that wand in Sanctuary, one black long-ago night black and thick with terror; the fear-stick. And again years later but not at all long ago, that night in the entry hall upstairs, when first he invaded Corstic's keep.

"Try taking a step down and you'll feel it," he told his companions. "It's a damned fear spell!"

Yole probably had another motive, but he proved the truth of Hanse's word in mere seconds; he stepped past the man in black. And began to shake, the moment his booted foot came down on the topmost step. A most unmanly noise crept up from his throat. After a moment Hanse tugged him back, gave him a long look directly into the eyes, and eased him aside.

Yole and Cathamarca watched him step into the doorway and grip the amulet, pressing it hard to his chest.

He fought the spell with mind and amulet, knowing even as he shivered and thoroughly embarrassed himself with his babbling that it could not be real; it must be a spell left behind by Corstic—or perhaps recently planted by Arcala. The amulet seemed recalcitrant or weaker, not so swiftly effective as before, and Hanse muttered that news to the men behind him.

"Perhaps this is an Arcala spell, and your talisman is Corstic-specific," Count Cathamarca suggested. "This is one of the reasons I want those rings; one of them creates illusions but another prevents such nasty illusions as this from gaining control of a man's mind. You must believe that it is only a spell, Hansis; believe, believe it . . ."

Go to hell, Cathamuckface, Hanse thought, but he tried. He closed his eyes. *It's only a spell . . . it's only a spell . . .*

At last the amulet seemed to come alive, to glow and shimmer and pour strength into his chest where it lay; into his heart. The mists vanished. The ghostwebs ceased their invisible twisting. The fear that ensorceled him dissipated like dew in the bright sunlight of morning.

"Done! Come along," he said, in good strong voice.

And after his embarrassment Shadowspawn just had to prove himself by trotting down into darkness as if he had been doing it every night for years . . . as if real fear were not nagging at him with every downward step.

Damn, he was thinking; *the son of a bitch neglected to tell me about having to come down here, and he lied to me about just why he wants those rings—it's sorcery we're dealing with! Father Ils forfend—can't I ever get away from it?* He even wondered whether it might have been Catha-marca who sent the attack night before last; the birdheaded men.

But if so . . . why?

They searched, with Notable stalking about the dark old chamber with tail either high or lashing. With Yole's flint-and-steel they lit more candles and set them on shelves draped with dusty cobwebs. They spent time proving that there was nothing behind a wall-hanging that was obviously a warning left by Corstic: the skull of a long-dead human, imaginatively mounted on the wall by an arrow through each shadowy eye-socket.

"Nice," Hanse muttered. "Just what every man's house needs."

Cathamarca was not above joining him in that whistling in the dark: "Aye. Is there a better price for two?"

At last it was Notable's attentive staring and sniffing in an area well away from the warning skull that attracted their attention. What they found first was a slight stirring of air, down near the floor. That led to a flurry of excited activity that discovered the secret door.

A tunnel lay beyond that narrow door, behind the false wood-shored wall, an extremely dark underground passageway walled in dull old gray stone and floored with earth that had long since settled almost into the firmness of wood. The tunnel was not wide, and yet the ceiling was some seven feet above the earthen floor. Trying to will his pupils wider, Shadowspawn stared within at nothing but blackness while Notable pressed against his leg.

Hanse glanced around. "Well? Are we ready to go?"

Cathamarca shook his head. "Beyond here Yole and I cannot go."

"What?" Hanse fixed him with a look. "Why?"

"We cannot," Cathamarca repeated firmly and with that maddening arrogant *coolth* of his, looking as if his agent should have known it all along. "It is the reason I was forced to find and pay you."

Hanse turned away to hide a look mean enough to make babies cry. This damned noble was even less honest than he had already assumed. Cathamarca must be a mage, but none so strong as Corstic or Arcala!

He wants those rings to help him gain power, Hanse mused, *and . . . what else?*

Well, the last person I'll give them to is him!

Yet he was here, and he was after all a helpless addict of danger/excitement. The thief called Shadowspawn was

incapable even of considering not going on. Thinking that
he would find the rings and take them to Arcala for study
and identification, he demanded that Cathamarca describe
each.

"A gold band intagliated with a serpent and set with a
caged ruby," the count said, staring past his agent's head as
he brought the baubles to mind—and incidentally avoiding
the dark-eyed look from under those daunting black brows
that came so near to touching above the youthful thief's
falcate nose. "A double band of silver, plain but twisted
together into a knot on top and set within the knot with a
dull black stone. A plain though broad gold band, set with
a large slate-colored stone. Because it is bifurcated with a
strip of gold, it appears to be a double setting. Those are the
Rings of Senek, Hansis."

Hanse was nodding, keeping his face impassive and his
manner calm, although one of the rings his employer had
just described was the one he had taken from here; the ring
Corstic had worn That Night. Certainly Shadowspawn did
not mention that fact. His eyes showed nothing.

"Well," he said, "you'll soon have 'em, Count." He
swung back to the open doorway. "Come along, Notable,
let's take a little walk."

Shadowspawn stepped into the tunnel with the same
assumed confidence as he had spoken so casually.

Just inside, Notable halted, crouching, ears back. A very
slight sound burbled in his throat. Uncharacteristically the
big cat turned and bolted back out of the passage, where
he meowed pitifully like a scared kitten. Hanse turned in
some exasperation—and discovered that Notable was wiser
than he.

An iron barrier crashed down with enough noise to
disturb a slumbering deaf man, cutting Shadowspawn off
from Notable, Cathamarca, and Yole.

It did not take long to discover that the barrier was

immovable and without any hidden means to open it; none that Hanse could find.

I'm stuck in here, he thought, and knew a niggle of fear. *Maybe you have to have all three rings to get that damned iron wall open!*

At last he turned back to face the tunnel, steeling himself to what he must do. True, he wore a sword and the long Ilbarsi "knife" that was pretty much a shortish sword without a guard, and an assortment of rather more than four or six throwing knives and death-stars. On the other hand, and very likely to become more important, he had no food, no water, and only an inch and a half of candle. And no flint-and-steel; they had agreed that Yole would carry that.

Unless Shadowspawn found another way out of here in time, he would wander in darkness, hungry and, more immediately life-threatening, he would grow increasingly thirsty. Hunger was painful, but slow to kill. Thirst was an important murderer that killed quickly.

Waiting with those unpleasant thoughts while his excellent night-vision began to penetrate the darkness, Hanse decided to slip on the ring of Corstic the mage . . . one of the Rings of Senek.

Immediately the darkness was lessened by half. Black became gray. All remained dim, but now, through what seemed a few minutes past sunset rather than moonless midnight, he could see ahead through the gray-walled tunnel to a point he judged to be twenty or so feet.

"Well, much as I despise sorcery," he muttered, "it does come in handy now and again."

With a nod and increased spirits, Shadowspawn began to advance.

8

WITH HIS USUAL gliding gait he moved confidently along a narrow passage that curved steadily downward. And wished he felt as confident as he tried to seem; tried to tell himself he was. The assault of the fear had come and gone. It was only a dark and unknown passage that lay beyond the keep of a sadistic monster he had slain. Why should he fear?

He soon discovered that he was in no cellar, but a pilgrim in a subterrene warren. All, all was dull old gray stone, hard-earth floored, and about seven feet high by seven wide.

He rounded two turns, made tense but at last shrugging choices along side passages, and descended steps, a lot of them. At last he came to a heavy metal door. Its hinges opened silently, without the expected squeak—and Shadowspawn froze, crouching. Both hands were instantly full of deadly steel.

The wildly particolored serpents had heads the size of his fists and were decorated as garishly as any S'danzo in her skirts and scarves. Both eye-offending snakes were long, with slitted snake-eyes in the big broad-snouted heads staring at him from a point a foot above their coiled bodies.

"You are in the wrong place," the red-and-green-and-purple-and-black-and-pink one said. Oh, and yellow.

Hanse's mouth dropped open.

"You had better think about this again," the leftward one added, in a ridiculous high tenor.

Although fear grasped his guts with cold hands, Shadowspawn made a disgusted face. "Now this is a pale damned illusion! Talking snakes! How damned silly!"

"Pass us and you will be prodigiously sorry," the brown-and-red-and-black-and-blue-and-calf-shit-yellow one told him.

"Nice word," Shadowspawn said with sarcasm, for he assumed that he faced illusion and was only nervous and cautious, not afraid. Not *very* afraid, anyhow. "You sound like Cathamarca. Best that you both crawl away or the two of you are going to be four and maybe more," he told the reptiles, when what he wanted very much to do was turn and run like hell.

"sssssss!" the rightward snake said.

"Well, at least that's more like the talk a man expects from a pair of damned ugly *snakes*," Shadowspawn said. "Likely that's Cathamarca's *real* language, the lying snake"—and he slammed a long, flat, leaf-shaped sliver of steel directly into the mouth of the leftward one just as it started to speak.

Somewhere far down the passage the throwing knife clattered and skittered. Although he had seen it go into that wide lavender-lined mouth, both unlikely guardians had simply vanished.

"Hmp," Hanse said with satisfied smugness, and stalked through the doorway. Nothing assaulted or warned him as he walked. He took fifty-three paces before he reached his knife. "Nice throw," he told himself. It was good to hear the sound of a voice. A human voice. *His* voice.

He bent to pick up the knife—and threw himself down beside it as the horizontal pole, thick as his thigh and seven feet long, rushed over him with a pronounced *whish* sound, at a level of about two feet above the floor. It banged loudly into the gray wall opposite the leftward one that had released it, having passed over him at about the speed of a good runner.

Shadowspawn stayed flat. His heart hammered. Twisting

about in his prone position, he was on the point of rising when here came the deadly thing rushing back. He resumed his flat worm imitation. The pole thumped almost gently into the wall to his left. Remaining prostrate, he looked at it warily.

He gave it several minutes, but it stayed where it was, ready for next time.

"Some kind of spring-release," he muttered. "Or a counter-balance. Must be released by my stepping on . . . the last place I stepped." He took up the knife he had thrown at the serpent that was not there, returned it to its sheath on his upper right arm. Warily he snake-crawled for a dozen feet along hard-packed dirt before he dared stand—slowly, and with caution.

After that he proceeded the same way. Fifteen or so paces beyond the place where he had retrieved his knife and was supposed to have had both legs broken before he was swept into stone wall at unbelievable velocity to become strawberry preserves decorated with white bone-shards, he came to a fork. One way looked as good—or as bad—as the other. Everything was dull; walls of gray stone and floor of earth.

He was Hanse; he turned left.

Fifteen or so paces beyond the fork, more steps led down. Stone steps, this time. He paused long, listening, looking in every direction. At last satisfied that he neither saw nor heard a thing but his own breathing, he nodded and descended. Alone and in dimness; slowly and with care.

Nothing untoward happened, probably because he had kept close to the wall. At the foot of the long flight of narrow, little-worn stone steps he paused, tapped the floor ahead with his swordblade, and advanced along a short corridor.

It led him to another metal door with a small, barred window. He walked boldly to it, reached for its handle—and pounced back with a swift agility that might have made Notable envious.

Through its grille of a window came a hand at the end of a serpentine arm of glowing green. The fingers at the end of that seemingly boneless arm groped for him like tentacles, as if each was individually alive and possessed a mind and will of its own.

Hanse struck at it, thought he saw his blade glide through it as if that groping, seeking hand were only smoke. But this time the menace did not simply vanish; it kept coming, and the arm behind it was lengthening. Already it had to be a full yard long. And still coming for him as if it had invisible eyes that saw just where he was!

Hanse considered only briefly. He decided not to try to dispel this new outré menace with steel or words. Who needed to go through that door, anyhow? Shadowspawn ran fleet as a cheetah and as a startled house-cat did: at speed, and without looking back.

His buskin-shod feet making soft scuffing noises in ever-present twilight between gray walls, he was to be besieged and almost constantly assaulted by guardian horrors he could never be sure were real or illusory. He rounded a corner to face a slavering red wolf with red eyes like smoldering coals. They glowed like torches to surround the creature with an eerie dark-pink illumination. It stared at him, a slavering red wolf—walking on hind legs and wielding sword and buckler. And wearing a nice gold ring in its left ear.

Hanse froze, staring at new impossibility. His face was like chalk and his teeth chattered. Fiery red eyes stared into his black ones. The wolf advanced a half-pace, with a lurch. Of course; canines, with those strange crooked hind legs, were never meant to walk erect! With a speed approaching that of summer lightning Hanse slammed a throwing star at it left eye—and watched the animal interpose its green-and-red shield with seeming ease. The shield caught the deadly star of steel with a heavy thud of impact that was no illusion.

After a moment of thought, Hanse used his right hand to

draw his sword with a deliberate swiftness to make the loud, scary *wheep* sound of steel cleaving air. Staring into the wolf's eyes, he took a step.

"Go away, wolf. I know illusion when I see it."

Lupus erectus matched his step, turning its side to him now, with its shield before it and sword carried at mid-level almost behind, in the pose of a practiced weapon-man.

"Damn."

With that weaponish ability given him by those gods who also granted his request that he forget—Hanse feinted right and struck left. The long blade banged into the shield the animal interposed with unbelievable speed. And the throwing knife shot from his left hand into the wolf's throat.

Both red eyes and black widened; Hanse's because this time his blade went into flesh and stayed in, and blood poured.

"Illusions," he muttered, backing warily, sword up and another throwing knife ready in his left hand, "don't bleed!"

The wolf did. Impossible or not, this incredibility was no illusion! With its sword-hand—sword-paw—it reached up to tear the knife out of its throat and sling it aside. Even as it rang off the stones of the wall a cataract of crimson sprayed under pressure from the throat of the animal. Nevertheless it kept its shield and sword up, staring at this supposed prey become formidable assailant. Its hairy legs began to tremble as blood poured from its severed artery.

Hanse merely stood where he was, watching. Waiting. In less than a minute its ferocious red eyes were only guttering flames. The wolf sank to its knees.

With a judicious wisdom born of some fear Shadow-spawn waited until the eyes looked as if they were beyond seeing and the pool of the unnatural wolf's blood could not have been covered by three prostate Brimms. Then his pounce forward and chopping into the creature's throat was met with no attempt at resistance on its part. Another blow was required to separate head from body. Jerking manically, the headless body flopped with a clang of sword and buckler on stone floor, and kept flopping about.

Shadowspawn, who had thought he knew illusion when he saw it, also knew death-throes when he saw them. That did not stop him from giving the twitching, kicking body another good chop anyhow, just to be sure.

He wiped his blade on long red fur and retrieved his knife—and turned to see three more red wolves, all walking erect and wielding sword or axe and shield, coming for him. All bore shields painted red and green. The wolf on the right was drooling most untidily.

These were impossible odds. Again wisdom ruled: Shadowspawn turned and ran as if he were chased by demons. He assumed that he was.

He rounded a corner and a disembodied fist lunged out of the wall, bashed his upper arm with hammer force, and vanished back within the stone that had extruded it. Hanse heard a whimper escape him. The cold fingers of rising terror gave him a tweak. He ran.

Fleeing blindly through dark, narrow corridors of age-darkened stone two or three minutes later, he was hit in the face by a jet of something like gray fog from the wall itself. Uncharacteristically he stumbled over his own foot and fell headlong. He made a three-point landing on hard-packed earth: an elbow, a hip, and one knee.

As he lay gasping sobbily, all confidence gone in the face of consistent sorcery, a section of stone swung out from the wall behind him. A wiry young woman emerged; a woman whose body was covered with the close-packed irruption of her own long, scarlet hair. Without a sound she slammed the short camel-whip she bore in her left hand down onto the prostrate interloper's back, once, before pouncing back into the passage.

The wall closed with his ever knowing it had opened.

But he knew about the terrifying blow from nowhere, the

pain that was like ice and then just the opposite. His vocal expression was reduced to the sound of a baby kitten whimpering down a well.

With a groan that demeaningly threatened to loft into a shriek, Hanse struggled up in bafflement heightened by the confusion of fear. The little cloud of fog had settled to the floor. Suddenly fearing to let it touch him, he fled blindly more twilit minutes through dim, narrow hallways of stone. Many minutes. He had no way of knowing that he doubled around and ran the same corridors, twice. He had no way of seeing the slender lead pipe slide out of a small hole in one stone, about a foot above the passage floor, just around the sharp turn he was nearing.

Panting, trying to still with both sweat-damp hands the maddeningly joggling, slapping sheaths of his blades, he scraped his upper arm as he rounded the turn. That brought a yelp and new whimpers as he lurched on—and slammed his shin into the lead pipe set to trip him.

He screamed and fell in biting red pain, down in agony in the dark with no knowledge of what had happened except that his leg felt as if it had been bashed by a splitting maul.

As he sprawled on rough, chill floor, ripping cloth and abrading skin, the pipe slid or was pulled back into the wall without his ever seeing it.

He was lying there writhing and trying not to weep when he heard the harsh voice that surely emerged from the throat of some hideous and hulking demon set to rip him into quilting patches:

"I think he rrran down this way! Hurrrry!"

His thought was instant identification: *It's those wolves!*

Despite his flaming leg he hurled himself to his feet and ran. His scabbards swung madly and banged his legs through his leggings ripped by the fall that had also torn his tunic. He tried to hold the plaguey empty blade-holders as he ran, in pain from his leg and stumbling. He was not about to sheathe his sword, but the Ilbarsi "knife" was more torture than value. On the other hand, how possibly could he discard it, or anything else? Something might happen to his sword.

He nearly ran past the narrow door in one wall opening into a side passage. He managed to stop and duck into that even darker subterranean corridor.

Rounding a corner into utter blackness, he stopped. He pressed his sweaty self flat against the chill stone to listen. His pulse pounded hard in the growing swelling of his shin. He tried hard to suppress his loud, gaspy breathing.

A three-inch needle emerged silently from the wall he leaned against and slid through cloth and skin and flesh into the back of his right thigh.

With an unmanly cry he lurched forward—and his knee found the toothy plate set into one of the stones a foot and a half above the floor. Another cry tore from him and he jerked aside—tearing open several shallow trenches in his right arm. His fingers flexed open and the sword dropped.

It did not clang, on a floor of hard-packed earth.

Whimpering on the point of hysteria, he reeled about, grasping that wounded arm with his other hand. After a moment he was able to pick up his sword. Shadowspawn was no creature of fiction, to drop a weapon and leave it!

His staggering body banged into the leftward wall and then the right. That only added new bruises to his tormented flesh. And his hand on the wall slid into nothingness. He caught himself as he started to lurch into the blackness of—a room?

He was debating whether to consider entering such inky darkness when he saw that which approached him along the corridor. His eyes went wide in shock and terror at sight of the un-demonic demon hurrying toward him. The man's face was a hideous and horripilating ruin, with tatters of skin and flesh hanging like ribbons that stirred and flapped loosely as he moved toward the intruder into this underground madhouse.

9

IT WAS THE former master mage of mage-ruled Firaqa. Corstic, dead Corstic.

Swift as thought itself, panic fed reaction and Hanse sent a throwing star directly into the face of the dead wizard, the face ruined by Notable's manic attack That Night. The deadly star remained where it struck. No blood appeared. Corstic came on.

The dead don't bleed, Shadowspawn told himself— silently, for his chattering teeth would not have allowed him to form the words. Then he did, and in a shout:

"No! It's only a damned illusion! Corstic is dead, dead, dead!"

Those words were effective; instantly Corstic was not there.

Swallowing hard, trying to still his shivering, Shadow-spawn elected not to go and see whether his death-star lay somewhere on the floor of hard earth where the illusion had stalked him. Instead he eased into the unknown of the tomb-like darkness of the chamber he had found.

Even as he peered cautiously within, staring hard, pupils widening still more in an effort to pierce the pitch blackness, a light flared into existence on one wall of the same old dull gray stone. Hanse squinted and trembled. More sorcery. No one had lit that glim. He had just seen a torch, set into an old iron cresset standing aslant from the wall, come alight of itself, of sorcery. Under his tunic, a thousand or so ants seemed to be hurrying up and down Hanse's back. The flickering light of the glim, faded from white to yellow, was quite enough to illumine the smallish, square chamber. Hanse stared; the Shadowspawn part of him remembered to flinch back, to conceal himself in deep shadows out of reach of that torchlight. He felt the prickling of the hairs on the back of his neck, and all those ants were still there.

The room was chilly and did not smell good. An oddly pearl-colored ground-fog shrouded the floor and shrouded was an appropriate word. In this stone-floored chamber far below the manse, six coffins were arranged in a rough circle around a stone dais topped by a great stone rectangle. It appeared to be another coffin except that it was of unusual width. Its lid was a stone slab over an inch thick.

The slab began to slide aside.

Accompanied by a worse than unpleasant grating sound, the widening crack liberated an unequivocally unpleasant odor.

The hairs on Shadowspawn's nape stood straight out. He stared in a sudden weak-kneed panic. He heard himself make a little moaning sound, and felt demeaned; diminished by his own reaction, his fear. His legs trembled, but could not otherwise move. He was frozen in dread fascination, the mouse staring at the weaving cobra. His limbs were locked. His feet were glued to the floor. Sweat broke out on him, all over, even though he felt cold. The ants crawled up his back now, struggling against his sweat. He watched helplessly, feeling fear and yet detached from the horrific scene, as the inch-thick stone slab that lidded the unusually wide coffin on the stone dais was pushed completely aside. From within.

A naked woman sat up slowly and reached up to push back long, glossy and intensely black hair.

She was beautiful, sensuous; she defined seductiveness. Her pale, pale face was long and pointed, with handsomely pronounced bone structure, thick black brows, and a long, straight nose. Large and almost snowy-white breasts moved restlessly with her movement. Terrified or not, Hanse was male: he noticed that they were slung low on the chest of this richly attractive woman, who looked about thirty. She glanced around, then down at the six rectangular boxes of wood that were arranged in a rough circle around her dais.

"Time to rise and shine, children."

The face of a helplessly staring Shadowspawn had gone chalky and his brow dripped the sweat of pain and fear. He stared. Huddled in deep shadow, cowering like a chicken when the fox was near.

Around the naked woman the wooden lids of the other coffins began to creak upward, pushed from inside. Hanse stared. He saw a slim hand, pale as new-bleached cotton, pale as the desert under the blinding sun . . .

Then his entire nervous system was flashing hot messages into him, and Shadowspawn came alive. Silent as only the finest cat-thief could be, he turned and fled that chamber of wakening dead. His arm stung, and running hurt the back of his punctured thigh. That was not enough to deter him from running.

10

"THANK ALL GODS for letting me be strong enough to overcome whatever force held me there," Shadowspawn muttered, merely because he needed to hear the sound of a voice and was grateful for the sound of his own, and a sand-white, glowing hand shot out of the very wall to clutch his throat.

His gagging sound was succeeded by a new shriek of terror and his attempt to use his sword at such close quarters struck sparks from the stone wall. Flailing with both hands while his head roared, he succeeded in pulling away.

Shadowspawn ran blindly. His feline grace had left him. He loped blindly through post-sunset dimness, flailing, racing. His heart was a series of booming explosions in his ears and felt as if it was about to come bursting through his chest. Once again he was reduced to something less than human that fled blindly and in terror through dark and narrow corridors of stone darkened by the ages.

He discovered the half-open door by running into it, blind in darkness and whelming terror.

He cried out, terrorized and terrified and hurting and now hurt still more, in still another area of the twilight unknown. Falling backward was a severe jolt and new pain, for *something* had jabbed nastily into one unpadded buttock.

He shoved his shivering, panting self to his feet—gasping a sobby sound as the needly little spike slid out of his rearward flesh—and cautiously peeped through the doorway.

He was gazing at a narrow stairway. Steps. leading up! "*Up,* by all gods!"

Giggling in an unabated terror-induced lunacy, he slipped through, pulled the door shut behind him, and hurried up the steps—painfully, because of the lemon-sized knot on his shin. Sweat streamed.

On almost silent buskins he ascended many steps, amid puffs of dust.

They brought him to a very narrow and grievously dark corridor. Since he had been able to see well enough, thanks to his extraordinary night-vision and the ring, he had paid no attention when he lost the candle, long since. There was no way to keep a candle lit while running, anyhow. Straining his eyes now, he moved along the narrow passage for many steps before he realized that the wall on his right represented a dramatic change from the ever-dull sameness of his surroundings: it was of wood. He tapped it.

That brought a hollow sound.

He began to feel around, heart pounding and his breathing still accelerated and hard-found because of his exertion and his terror. Mostly by accident he found a stud, and heard a tiny click.

He dropped into a squat, at once, fearing a sweeping horizontal pole or worse, and gasped when a narrow section of wall opened. He waited a few moments longer, in his crouch, but apparently he had triggered no traps.

His heart pounded and he was chill with the sweat of fear as he stepped cautiously through into a room—a handsomely decorated and furnished bedchamber! He was pleased to see no tenant. He took a step, two—and a hand whipped out from under the bed to grasp his ankle. With the hoarse, grunting cry of a beleaguered and terror-struck animal he lurched forward to topple bouncing onto the bed . . .

. . . which immediately tilted up at the foot . . .

. . . to send him slithering helplessly, whimpering in terror, toward the ornate carving of the headboard. He saw it open inward to reveal a rectangle of black yawning before him—and with a pitiful howl he slid into the blackness that threatened to be his permanent home. This time he did lose the sword, even when his elbow banged into the edge of the aperture and his fingers flexed open automatically.

With a humiliatingly high-voiced grunt he struck a smooth, narrow-walled chute and went hurtling down, down into demon-haunted darkness.

A curve in the chute tipped him up and over, flopping and unable even to yell out his terror, and still rushing downward at what seemed terrible tobogganing speed in the blackness. Suddenly his slide terminated and he was falling, falling into a stone-walled chamber dimly lit by a guttering torch in its wall-sconce.

He had just time to realize with despair that he was all the way back down in the dungeon he had just left when with an enormous loud splash his sweat-streaming body plunged into a huge vat containing four feet of icy cold water.

He was gibbering when two sets of hands dragged him up and out.

He saw nothing. His thick black mop of hair had become a heavy waterlogged mass whose strands plastered themselves to his face and neck. His stomach and lungs seemed to burst into flame. Forced, propelled by four hands, he lurched forward, mouth wide. Now he could see what awaited: a tall post of rough wood lined—positively festooned—with scores of needles that he realized were the points of nails. Driven in from the other side, they stood forth like teeth on this side. His side. Steel teeth, waiting for the gibbering victim propelled toward them by the rough hands of invisible captors.

The haven of unconsciousness tugged at him like an importuning whore, beckoned as a welcome retreat from constant horror, the conscious endurance of further pain and the vicious transcendent terror that *something* was so barbarically inflicting on him. Corstic's spells, laid long ago, he had to assume. He rejected the seductive beckoning of that haven of unconsciousness—or rather his hysteria did.

In a sudden burst of flailing, manic action, he hurled one still-unseen captor against the post intended for him and slammed an elbow into the flat but soft belly of another. The yell of pain he heard was deeply satisfying. Clawing hands opened gashes down his hip as he struck out and heard a strange *splutch* noise followed by a small, puking outcry of pain.

Again he raced for a dark doorway into dim subterrene passages . . .

And ran . . .

(a blue and pink and puke-yellow snake lunged at him from high on the wall and he lurched aside)

And ran . . .

At last, huffing and wet with sweat, he had to admit it. He was lost. He was never going to find his way out. He had left no kind of trail and had not thought about doing so. How could he have had any idea of the circuitous, amorphous vastness of this monotonously walled maze?

And he was thirsty.

Setting his back to a wall, he slid slowly down to think. Soon he was bending forward, stripping off his leather mail-shirt and tunic, and re-concealing its two knives and three stars here and there on his person. Then he sat and systematically sliced and tore his good black tunic into useless shreds and ugly pieces of fabric.

Except that they were not useless; he would leave one here, now, and every time he came to a stair or door or fork in the maze that entrapped him.

He slipped back into the body-protector of boiled black leather and resumed his way to . . . wherever he was going.

Not twenty paces farther along that corridor a thirsty Shadowspawn entered a tiny chamber and brought up short to stare at a shelf: on it rested a small stoppered bottle of clear liquid. He was thirsty but wanted to pass it up just the same. This was a place of evil, assaults and horror, and it was only sensible and logical to suspect poison.

But he was thirsty.

At last he took up the bottle and shook it gingerly. That produced a normal enough sloshing sound that heightened his thirst. He saw no color, no bubbles, no gas formation. That was a good sign, but the liquid—and for the matter of that its container—was still suspect. Holding it well away from himself he uncorked it, waited, slowly approached his face with the bottle. He sniffed. His tongue went even drier when he smelled only water, and not even musty from being long corked in this too-small bottle. With considerable trepidation he dipped in his right little finger, withdrew it wet, and waited.

He felt nothing untoward.

At last, very tentatively, he touched that wet fingertip to his tongue.

"Water! It *is* water!"

Nevertheless he was still tentative and cautious when he sipped—and tasted water, good water, sweet water as if it had just fallen from a bountiful sky. He drank, waited, and not only felt no ill effects, he felt much better.

Seconds later he discovered that he was unable to see his own hands and, when he looked down, anything else of himself, including clothing and weapons. Yet he could see everything else as well as always, which in this unending twilight was not very.

"It was water of sorcery at that—the damned stuff has made me invisible!"

He proved that, only a short time later, by standing pressed close to the wall while the three sword-and-buckler-toting red wolves lurched awkwardly by on their crooked legs. Since they were continually looking this way and that, each of them looked directly at him. And saw nothing, and went on.

Smiling, Hanse waited until he was sure they would not hear his buskins on the earthern floor of this foul hole before he continued on his way.

It happened also to be their way, but now he was behind them.

He soon realized that his invisibility was no curse, but blessing. Unseen and unseeable, he was able to elude several menaces, including a thin young woman all covered in red fur and carrying a short whip in her left hand. Invisible, he considered toying with her, teasing and terrorizing as he had been, but decided he had better leave well enough alone. Yet as he started to go on here came more insanity: an outsized blue-feathered rooster, waddling importantly along on foot-long legs while most un-roosterishly muttering to itself:

"Got to find Hanse. Got to find that damned little Hanse. Got to find . . ."

That was too much. In a blazing burst of anger the invisible Shadowspawn sent a throwing star to slam into the fat side of the ridiculous and impossible creature.

"You found him, shit-pecker!"

The rooster raced away squawking its normal fowlish sounds of pain and terror, dribbling red droplets and blue feathers as it went.

Smiling grimly, Hanse collected the feathers as he paced on. He took up seven. He felt good about having struck a blow, even against a mere rooster no matter of what outré size, and he eluded another menace by standing against a wall while it passed—looking directly at him at least once—and felt really good about that, too, until he entered the high-ceiled, round chamber and leaned against the wall to pant.

He was instantly assaulted by bats with enormous ears that heard his slightest move.

In terror and under continuous attack he swung the Ilbarsi knife forty or so times against that squealing black throng. He killed one bat and knocked two others many feet—three attackers out of eighty or so. Another flopped limply to the floor when it touched one of the blue feathers. Meanwhile Shadowspawn took many wing-buffets, a few scratches, and two bites before he managed to get out of there, by hurling himself through the same doorway through which he had entered.

Since no bats followed but only chittered as if the open doorway were a leaden wall, he was careful to mark that entry to terror by leaving a large patch of black cloth in front of it.

He felt very good about that, despite the nagging pain of too many wounds, all small but painful . . . until the gigantic dog trotted by, click-click-click, snarling and sla-vering in a mouth set with two-inch canines . . . a gigantic short-haired dog trailing several ragged streamers of black cloth from its drooling mouth.

It would have been nice to weep.

Shadowspawn did not. He knew he already had, and feared that he would again, but he was well on his way to forgetting that fact.

I've wasted my tunic, he mused as he trudged warily along in twilight that seemed eternal. *If I find no pieces of it, I'll know that dog collected them all. But even if I do come onto one or some—how can I know whether they're where I dropped them or it did . . . carelessly or . . . deliberately to mislead me?*

So much for marking his way; so much for his tunic.

His speed and agility remained; not many could have hurled themselves out of danger when a patch of floor opened beneath his foot. Shadowspawn did, and felt even better about that. He had simply eluded another trap, but all was horror here and he needed encouragement, and this was another blow against dead Corstic's empire of evil.

The exertion, however, set up a throbbing in several wounds.

Pacing along on hard-packed earth between the boring but depressing sameness of walls of gray stone, he made two turns before he stopped short. Again he flattened himself against the wall: using one yellow foot, the blue rooster was tapping at a wooden inset low in the wall a few feet from Hanse, and eagerly drinking the viscous liquid that action brought forth. Hanse stared, forgetting to breathe as he watched still more of the incredible that had become the commonplace. The ants were amove on his back again . . .

Suddenly the throwing star dropped from the cock's side with a faint clinking sound and a little puff of dust. A shiver rocked Hanse, hard, when the blue feathers he had collected for no reason suddenly departed his belt and rushed like thrown knives to rejoin their fellows on the body of the creature.

They tucked themselves neatly back into his plumage; into his skin, presumably.

The creature straightened as if just alighting from its perch at dawn, raucously crowed its jubilation, shook itself and ruffled its feathers, and emitted a long, satisfied "Aaaah!" A moment later it added, "That's better! All healed! Now to find that nasty Hanse!"

As the foul fowl strutted past, Shadowspawn saw that it bore no wound.

He collected his death-star, strangely unmarked by blood, stared at the section of wood, looked both ways, and squatted. A few taps and a few sips and every wound ceased to bother him. Those that he could see, for instance the nasty scratches in his forearm, spent a couple of minutes scabbing over, a few more minutes shedding the scabs, and presented an arm unmarked save for pinkish new skin.

"Corstic must have arranged this here for his own rescusci—resci—himself," he muttered, liking the sound of his own voice, "in case he was trapped down here with his monstrosities and needed a quick healing. Damn! How I wish I had kept that bottle—I could fill it here and have instant cure for everything!''

True, *if* he had kept the bottle. He even considered trying to milk some of this wondrous elixir into one of his scabbards, but discarded the idea.

The problem was that drinking the thickish, healing liquid left him thirsty again.

He chose one arm of a fork in what he was coming to think of as the Forever Tunnel. Soon he was pacing into a large chamber—of the usual dull old gray stone. It contained three other doors and, just to his right, a long, broad staircase. He glanced up . . . and felt a sudden new panic that made him weak-kneed. A gasp somehow escaped his very dry mouth as he stared up the broad, open stairway.

He stopped, frozen in mid-step, voiceless with fright. New fear struck him like a physical blow.

She stood at the top of the steps, as if just about to descend. An unusually tall and unnervingly pale woman in a floor-length and blatantly low-cut gown of black velvet.

She was the embodiment of the oft-dreamed but seldom-seen voluptuous image of many, many men: a tall, busty woman with that pale, pale skin set off by large, dark aureoles, and a haughty, gaunt-cheeked beauty. Above full, scarlet lips, her almond-shaped eyes were black as Corstic's heart but alight with an inner fire; the coals were live and hot. Her piled hair resembled his, and her dress: so black that it shone. A thick black belt of sueded leather circled her voluptuous hips. From a snap-held leather loop dangled a length of chain, its links about the thickness of Hanse's little finger.

She was staring at him just as if she saw him. Frowning, he lifted his hand. He looked at it. He saw it. Damn. He was visible again. Of all possible times, it had to happen now!

And he recognized the woman who stood gazing down at an untimely visible Hanse. She was beautiful, sensuous, she defined seductiveness. He had seen her unclothed. He had seen her sit up, in her coffin. She was in the business of collecting souls.

"Hel-lo." Her voice was a throaty alto.

"Who are you?" he demanded, hefting two feet of Ilbarsi steel even while he felt response to the powerful attraction of her, the raw and urgent sexuality.

"You know." Her voice defined seductiveness.

"I do not."

"You have met Theba before, Shadowspawn." She extended her arms. "Come to Theba."

The hair on the back of his neck was high again. "You tell me you are the goddess of Death herself, and you want me to *come* to you? Not likely."

Her voice was casual, conversational: "You have always known that you will die, Hanse. All creatures die."

"Not just now, thanks," he said, standing his ground.

He thought he did; his legs were following his stare up the steps.

She stood waiting, just at the top, with the tiniest hint of a smile only toying with her sensuous mouth. She was a magnificent sensuous candle, watching the approach of the moth.

Shadowspawn stopped two steps below her without knowing how he had gotten there. He stared up into dark, oblique eyes. She stood impressive and menacing and tall, gazing down at the youth on the stair, his clothing as black as her own. Ils, O Father Ils but she was magnificent—and desirable. Beyond merely desirable. She was irresistible; she who had been called the Ultimate Irresistibility.

Resist, he told himself, unaware that he had ascended the stair.

"Well?"

"Well yourself. Would you like to make love with me, Shadowspawn?"

"To make lo—" His eyes flashed and his mouth twisted. "Where, in your *coffin*?"

Her eyes flickered at that, but she gestured and said as if uninsulted, "Here. Right here."

"No thanks."

Her dark eyes went worse than cold. "You mean you choose not to make love with me—*me*?"

"You cannot be Theba. But I did see you open your coffin from inside, and sit up. I have already seen your naked body, witch. We both know it's beautiful. Lots of others know that too, don't they! Now you choose to toy with me for some reason. Any man would want to lie with you—and no, I don't! All I want to know is just wh—"

She sighed. "Well," she interrupted, "die then."

Her hand came up from the folds of her skirt. The shining chain clinked sinisterly as she detached it from her belt of black suede. She swept it up and brought it down faster than most men could have drawn a breath. Yet for Shadowspawn there was time to whirl on the broad step to run.

He did not run. He could not. The steel weapon came rushing down. It thud-clinked across the small of his back. His body shook violently at the impact. Ugly purple-black welts rose the size of walnuts on his back, and swelled.

Somehow he was held on the steps. He could not flee; could not even fall. In grim silence the woman—witch or revenant or that death-goddess worshipped by a few acolytes everywhere—by those Hanse could only consider mentally astagger—slashed at his back, again and then again, and again, with ruthless energy and an obvious intent to maim. Steel links dug into his flaming back. Welts rose, cracked, popped. Two of them oozed blood.

Her voice did not change even the slightest from that calm and conversational tone: "This is only the timid hint of the suffering you can endure, little man."

"Stop!" he heard himself yell. "I'll do it, I'll—"

Somehow Shadowspawn found the strength to break off

that new self-demeaning. It was only that, and certainly of no avail; protests or promises might as well have been the wind.

His body jerked, twitched, shivered. And bled. The flogging of the length of chain over his back left a rash of welts, cuts and bruises all over his skin. Its terrible links burned his back into a sheet of flaming pain from buttocks to the base of his neck. He ground his teeth against the shrieks that wanted to tear from his throat as the hard-flogging chain jolted his body again and again. Pain flowed and lapped at him in strong currents. As if he were above and looking down at this scene of pain and sadistic horror, he had a dreadsome mental picture of his back being turned into a crushed and mangly chopped mess of meat and blood.

Then he could not hold out any longer. He did cry out at the agony of increasingly painful blows on ruined skin, and it was as if that scream was the key that unlocked his legs. He jerked himself about and hurtled forward off the stairs, still in horrible flaming agony, and this time he knew that he would make no cat-like Shadowspawn alighting; he was going to be splattered all over the floor.

He was not. He erupted another throat-tearing yell when the floor silently opened just before his falling body smashed into it, and in a fleeting moment filled with terror, he hoped that what lay below was not the coffin-chamber.

Then he was hurtling down into new darkness.

11

In terror Shadowspawn dropped into impalpable black ink, sure that he was going to fall forever, or into an oubliette whose narrow, slippery bottom allowed no escape; at the very least onto some stone dungeon-like floor where coffins rested.

Instead he plunged onto a bed—a bed!

He actually bounced, unharmed. He lay dazed for several minutes after he had hurtled through the trapdoor. He knew he had fallen onto a nice straw-ticked mattress, but he was too disoriented to think, much less move.

It took the wretched Shadowspawn far longer than usual to gather himself.

He was just recovering, pulling himself together when he realized that he had fallen *down* and yet lay sprawled on the same bed, and in the same bedchamber, as before. The folding bed! As he started to scramble, he froze. A flood of light from above made him blink. He glanced up to get a glimpse of a falling body with loosely flailing legs and arms before the trap dropped shut.

He squirmed, trying to slide out of the way, but the other falling form slammed onto his legs, hard. He groaned.

In inky darkness he groped a cold and lifeless body for a full half-minute before he discovered that it was headless. Shrieking and shuddering, Shadowspawn slid off the bed, leaped to his feet, and ran. Despite his fears of the new unknown of this new area of the warren that had become his home, he feared more that the witch might be following, might at any moment come swooping down on him like a great black bat. With her horrible length of chain.

He banged into a wall, discovered that it was a door, and jerked it open. He fled, but forced himself to slow and observe caution. Bereft of dignity and bravery and pride, he went creeping along another narrow passage walled with stone. Or maybe one he had already traversed.

Well ahead was a dim light.

It occurred to him that he felt neither pain nor blood. He paused to check, gingerly and fearfully putting back a hand to his chain-beaten back. He felt the familiar smoothness of his deep-tan skin; he felt a wisp of sweat-pasted straw. He was unmarked.

Suddenly he sat down. He had not thought about it; his legs merely decided to do that and neglected to advise him.

"Maybe because I drank that cure-stuff just before I was *so-o* fortunate as to run onto her," he muttered, and licked dry lips with a dry tongue.

Then, "Gods, what next—a dragon?"

12

Madness flirted with Shadowspawn, played hide-and-seek with his mind. He *knew* he was not dealing with reality, and yet the attacks hurt and some left marks. Some of the attacks and attackers had to be real. He sincerely hoped Theba/the revenant was not. He had fought and run, run and fought, terrorized by the consistent assault of grotesquerie.

Carefully he made a mark with the point of his dagger—he would never dull a throwing knife—at the top of a flight of many stairs, and descended. His buskins whispered on hard old steps strangely short on dust. It occurred to him that he could not remember seeing any cobwebs.

Nothing is alive down here, he thought. *Not even an insect to keep a spider alive!*

He counted nine and thirty steps of seemingly carven and well-set stone before he set foot on level again; and again it was a floor of hard-packed earth. Here there was no dust. He had one choice as to direction, and started to walk—before turning back to make a mark at the foot of those thirty-nine steps.

The passage snaked along with more curves than the street called Serpentine back in Sanctuary. He walked it with caution, half-crouching at each new curve in dread anticipation of what might await or be approaching, just around the turn. And then a door slid back in the stone wall

111

a few feet ahead and out stepped an ugly man with skin the color of sun-bleached straw.

He stood staring at the approaching Shadowspawn, who halted. The fellow—in tunic and apron of leather over dun-colored tights and medium brown boots splotched with a darker brown like old rust—held a slender, gleaming knife in each hand. Neither was dagger and neither was throwing weapon. They were the tools of a surgeon, and with a new prickling of gooseflesh Shadowspawn recognized his accoster.

The man was Kurd. Kurd the vivisectionist, whom Hanse had called Kurd the Turd and put knives into . . . and who was dead, long ago in Sanctuary.

This could not be. This had to be still another eidolon; another illusion wrought by Corstic before his death.

Yet . . . how could Corstic of Firaqa have known about Kurd of Sanctuary far to the south?

Was there some after-death link among men of evil?

Hanse recalled his earlier meeting with Corstic, dead Corstic in this foul hole of never-ending twilight and gray stone, and what he had said to that seeming shade. He pointed now at Kurd, and said those words again:

"No! It's only another damned illusion! Kurd the Turd is dead, dead, dead!"

Kurd nodded. "That's true. I remember as well as you do. But, obviously, I came back."

Shadowspawn sighed. Oh damn, damn . . . sorcery again. Gods, how he despised sorcery, and how it did ever rear like an unshakable disease or a menacing monster to stand in his path! Would he never be free of it?

"That's stupid, Kurd. I'll just have to kill you again."

"What makes you think a dead man can be killed again, Hanse, you rotten little Downwind bastard and meddler?"

Hanse's temper rose. True, he was a bastard, but it was simply a fact of life and not something he relished being reminded of. He pondered the words of the deceased monster only briefly. He stared levelly—while ants wandered around on his back.

"Well, we can avoid this," Shadowspawn said. "Just step back through that wall and go back where you came from, you dead pig."

"Not until I have carved off a finger or three," Kurd said in an equable tone. "And maybe that ugly nose of yours. I'd like to have that. Not, you understand, to wear. Perhaps I'll find a beakless vulture someday and we can strike a bargain for a new beak."

"I think," Shadowspawn said, "that I will just go back the way I came."

"I think that I will just follow," the dead man said.

In a blurred movement Shadowspawn sent a slender leaf-shape of steel eighteen or so feet and into the chest of the dead man. He watched it go in, and with force; saw that it stayed and so did Kurd. The revenant did not so much as stagger or grunt in response to the impact and impalement. In horror Hanse watched the vivisectionist transfer one scalpel to his other hand and drag the blade out of himself. He looked at it speculatively, shrugged, and tossed it aside. The scalpel's blade glinted as he re-transferred it so that he held one in each hand again. His eyes rose to stare at Hanse.

Shadowspawn watched and heard his throwing blade strike the floor, bounce, spin a little. The blade shone, as always. It was unmarked by blood.

Kurd the vivisectionist began walking toward the younger man who had once foiled his plan for the never-ending torment of an immortal named Tempus—and incidentally brought about the demise of the surgeon.

Hanse's heart pounded, but he stood his ground, poised, knees and elbows slightly bent, two feet of Ilbarsi knife now standing from his left fist and ten or so inches of dagger griped in his right. Staring dispassionately, moving as if he were on a stroll along a safe street, Kurd came at him. His manner was the same as if his prey were the way the vivisectionist was accustomed to victims he approached: unarmed and bound.

Half-crouching, Shadowspawn stood waiting . . .

When the revenant was close enough Shadowspawn pounced easily leftward, slashing with the long blade as he did, and half-pivoted to slash again, on the backswing. The first stroke had to have opened up Kurd's throat; steel from the Ilbars hills kept a good edge and Hanse made sure it stayed sharper than the mind of a hair-splitting arguer. The second slash struck the dead man's right arm just below the elbow and removed most of that arm. The fingers flexed open and the scalpel dropped to the floor with a muted *ting*.

The arm hung, swinging loosely, on a few scraps of flesh and fabric.

Kurd stared down at that arm gone suddenly useless, waggling it and watching the lower half swing loosely in air. He seemed passive enough about it, and in no pain. Then he gave his attacker a nasty look, and turned toward him. Shadowspawn's nape bristled when he saw that Kurd now had two mouths; his throat was sliced open in a gash several inches long. But the rip was not red, or even pink. It was as if he had sliced open a rotting old grain-sack.

Once again Hanse saw no blood. The scalpel in the dead man's grayish left hand was up and ready.

Shadowspawn was caught up in tremors of horror and covered in gooseflesh. And yet he was sure of his own agility. He let the revenant strike, danced aside from the sweeping, gleaming sliver of steel, and in two swift hard blows struck that arm completely off. It flopped to the floor with a little soft sound, but without any hint of wet noise.

Again, he saw neither blood nor lymph.

Ah gods, all gods . . . the dead do not bleed!

But damn it, damn it all, they aren't supposed to walk around, either!

"Now what, slicer of the helpless living? Are you going

to try biting off a finger or three until I send your head rolling, or will you just go back where you came from?''

Kurd cocked his head with its bloodlessly slashed throat. ''Do you hear how your voice quavers in your fear, Hanse the bastard?''

''It may be quavery with horror, Kurd, and disgust too . . . but who could be afraid of a dead piece of slime with no arms?''

One arm gone—bloodlessly—and the other hanging limp as wash on the line, Kurd gazed at him as if considering carefully. ''I suppose you're right, Downwinder. It's only another damned illusion.'' And Kurd vanished.

So did his severed arm, complete with fist that still held his surgical tool, and the other one that he had dropped.

Once again Shadowspawn's legs decided that he wanted to sit down. At least this time a wall was handy, and he slid slowly down it. Thump.

13

His MIND TOTTERING, his mouth dry, Shadowspawn rested a while before he rose, retrieved his throwing knife—handling it as if it might turn on him—and continued along that passage. His stomach petulantly and noisily advised that it was empty. His throat was dry again, and the inside of his mouth seemed to contain sand. Madness beckoned like a beautiful whore who promised to charge nothing. Then he came to the edge of a flight of stone stairs leading down, and stared down at the wound in the earth just in front of his buskinned left foot.

It was the mark he had cut there before descending these thirty-nine steps just a little while ago . . . and since then he had not ascended from the level below.

He sank down loosely, overwhelmed. He tried to think about it, and his mind heaved and reeled. He had gone down nine-and-thirty steps of smooth stone. He had walked along a level passage. He had met Kurd. Kurd was gone; Kurd had never been there at all. After a short rest during which he had definitely not slept, Shadowspawn had walked to this place—all, all on level ground.

He muttered his confusion aloud. "How could I go down and be up? I couldn't have. That's impossible. All right, then I didn't. So . . . maybe these are different steps, and someone or something has copied my mark here from the other flight?" He wagged his head loosely. "Gods!" he suddenly shouted. "How can I be sure? How ever can I know what's real and what is not?"

His sanity shuddered and writhed, considered departure.
He heard the rising note and the catch of a sob in his
voice, and clamped his mouth. No matter that there was no
one to hear his humiliation; he could hear, and he had pride,
and he could not handle the humiliation.

I wish Notable was here, he thought, and a moment later:
*No, no! I'll never get out of here, not ever, and good ole
Notable is safe and alive—and with water and food, too!*

After a long, long while he rose again, and turned, and
walked in some direction, with no idea which point of the
compass lay ahead or whether he had already been this way.
No longer did he walk as Shadowspawn did, light as a cat,
gliding. Nor did he swagger as Hanse did when he wanted
to impress. He slouched along, miserable and confused and
nearly broken. And came after a time to a blank wall with
passages running to right and to left.

A scrap of black cloth lay at the rightward fork.

*Either that means I went right last time and have circled
and so should go left this time,* he reflected, *or . . . the big
dog dropped it there by accident and maybe I've never been
here before. Or I went left and that damned hound moved
my marker to confuse me.*

To confuse *me! Gods! The word is* to keep *me confused!*

While he tried to decide which direction to choose, he had
the intelligent idea of using his dagger to make a mark on
the wall. Once he had made his choice, he would scratch an
arrow on one end. He scratched a horizontal line—and a
small section of stone wall slid back to reveal a foot-square
recess. Within it was another bottle of clear liquid.

Hanse smiled all over his face. "Aha!"

Almost immediately a little frown chased the smile. Lest he
reach in and have his hand trapped or worse by a suddenly
slamming door, he braced a knife in there, removed the bottle,
and tapped the wedged knife out with his Ilbarsi blade.

A steel plate leaped across the aperture with a clang and
the stone slid back into place.

"HA! BEAT YOU, YOU SLIMETRACK!" Shadow-spawn yelled in celebration of at least one victory, however small, and he lifted the bottle in a silent toast of mockery to the failed trap and its author, whoever that might be. Might have been. Corstic?

Nevertheless he went through the same careful testing routine as before, and when at last he sipped, he tasted only sweet water. Again he smiled. Again he lifted the bottle mockingly to the blank wall, and winked.

Then he took the second sip, and went blind.

Shadowspawn staggered about, banging into stone walls, grasped at by hands from the walls, pecked at by a rooster over two feet tall while his heart pounded and he gibbered, pouring tears from unseeing eyes even as he sliced and cut with his long Ilbarsi blade—hearing it swish ineffectually—ran into a wall and fell backward, and at last sank down trying not to whimper.

He slumped there, and stayed there, and stayed there, blind and slumped and streaming tears . . .

Like the invisibility, the blindness at last went away. Sight did not return gradually. One moment he was blind; the next he was blinking, seeing—seeing even better than before in the dimness of his labyrinthine underground prison. He had no idea whether he had been blind for minutes or hours or days.

When he came upon the wide, wide corridor entry guarded by what at first appeared to be a cow but that he soon saw was a rat the size of a cow, he knew he had not been this way before. And the ants were amarch on his back again.

The gray-tan monster was *leashed*. A chain ran from its collar to a steel plate set in the wall to its left. Its leash left it full access across the mouth of the corridor, which was fully fifteen feet wide . . . and beyond the unnatural and intensely ugly beast Hanse could see a table. An ordinary table, well beyond the limits of access allowed the prodigious rat by its leash. The table was spread with a nice white cloth bordered in pale yellow and on it rested temptation that made Hanse's stomach rumble and even brought a bit of saliva into his desert-dry mouth: a pitcher, a drinking mug, a plate, a leg of something that certainly looked like lamb, and a wheel of cheese.

His stomach gurgled and positively snarled. He vented a bubble of gas. That did it. He *had* to pass, despite an ugly pointed snout with foot-long whiskers and set with teeth that looked no shorter than his dagger.

Illusion, he thought, and since the creature stood near the leftward wall staring at him from nasty red eyes, he started to its right. That was a test, to gauge its speed. He learned that it was fast, and no illusion. It lunged with no less speed than that possessed by Shadowspawn. He threw himself back, but the snout struck his leg with a loud clash of enormous teeth. It hurt no less than a blow with a club and knocked him several feet backward to sprawl in pain. The only good part about it was that the creature's leash brought it up so short it was tugged upward onto its hind legs while its eyes bulged and crossed.

Then it took a step backward and dropped again onto all fours. And bared its fangs, and glared with malice laced, Hanse thought, with hunger.

He considered, gathered himself, and made another try—this time with a bit more seriousness and care. He faked a leftward dash and twisted smoothly to run right. The Brobdingnagian rat lunged right and was there to meet him. Shadowspawn hastily aborted his charge. He had the range of a cheetah; so had the unnatural guardian.

"Damn! Fast, aren't you!" he muttered, and tried the same tactic again. The result was the same. The great head was there to meet him, mouth open for a good chomp of the small, black-clad interloper.

He tried faking right, running left, and then swerving right to pass. So did the huge guardian of the repast. Again, it was there to meet him, and this time he actually felt its fangs clash at his arm—brushing it without harm.

Frustrated and angry, he knew he had better let himself

cool a bit. Accordingly he peeled down his leggings to inspect his leg. A large colorful strawberry was spreading there on his thigh, where the pointed snout of the impossible rodent had struck on that first testing charge.

"When it leaves a bruise, it's real. That's not possible, but neither were a lot of things Corstic did while he was alive. *He* set this thing here, the rotten slimetrack, with that food just beyond to make a man try and try and try . . ."

He tried and tried and tried again. Each time the monster was there to meet him, and on that third try Shadowspawn took another bruise and worse; a fang slashed legging and left a red line on the leg within. Fortunately he had almost gotten away; the wound burned, but was not deep. The fact that he had made good a slash of the Ilbarsi blade was little more significant. It did prove that the outré creature could bleed, and squeal in pain, but Shadowspawn had cut no deeper than its daggerish fang had cut him.

And somehow, somehow damn it oh damn sorcery anyhow, that thing knows what I'm going to do—it must be reading my mind!

Yet he had to keep trying. Sight of food made him feel weak with hunger. He made a new decision, gathered himself, and charged still again. This time he feinted left, swerved abruptly to the right and was starting his leftward swerve preparatory to a rightward pounce again when he slipped and fell down.

And the guardian had gone right, his destination! Only an accident had confounded the ugly thing's apparent telepathic ability and thwarted its attempt to kill and presumably eat him!

Small muscular butt high, a desperate Shadowspawn scuttle-crawled past, fast, on hands and toes. Teeth clacked behind him and the rat squealed with a sound like metal scraping metal. But it had missed; its prey was past and headed for the food. Hanse's mouth was too dry to water, but it tried.

A thick wall of iron dropped from the ceiling to impact the floor just in front of him with a crash, completely blocking off the food-laden table—and a trapdoor dumped him painfully into another passage, this one walled with dirt. And considerably darker once the trapdoor closed a dozen or so feet above.

Shadowspawn lay hurting, trying not to weep.

Once he was capable of movement and had stopped his whimpering at being denied the sustenance of that beautiful meat and cheese, he learned too swiftly that this was no passage, but a doorless chamber fifteen or so feet on a side.

He went round and round, futilely chopping in frustration and anger at earthen wall. And around again, chopping in a madness of frustration.

On his fourth circuit the substitute sword chopped deep and stopped short with a clacking sound. Panting, Hanse dug out enough dirt to reveal that it masked a stone wall. He made a sobbing sound and bashed the earthen floor with his blade. He did that three times, on the point of hysteria, when once again the blade made a clacking sound on something under the hard dirt of the floor—and amid a grating noise a shower of dirt from the wall fell over him.

Despite the filth that coated him he pounced, for a section of the stone wall beyond had proven to be a door. The grating sound had been its opening.

He emerged astagger, filthy with a wall of dirt clinging to his sweat, into a passage just like all the others. Not ten feet away was a stairway, leading down. At its lip was the mark he had scratched there hours or days or an eternity ago.

Hanse sank down and sat, slumped with his back against the wall, for a long, long time.

He had walked for ten or so minutes when two vomit-green snakes came slithering out of the wall to drop onto him. He pounced back, flinging them off himself, and with pounding heart and soaring joy—and borderline hysteria—Shadowspawn chopped them into many pieces, each. They bled, too. Gratifying, very gratifying.

He was reaching for a nasty-looking morsel, definitely going to force himself to eat it, when he spotted the *manifestation,* well down this passage. With a sigh he straightened to his feet, transferred the long Ilbarsi blade from left hand to right so he could flex and swing his left arm a few times, and transferred the substitute sword back.

He was staring at a single fist-sized something—it looked very much like an eye—that glared at him out of the eternal twilight dimness of his ever-gray prison. The . . . eidolon was about eight feet above the earthen floor. But even as he watched, the apparition grew. It was not fist-sized, but larger. Seemingly staring at him. Unblinking. Hanse realized that it was not growing, but approaching.

Closer, and it had become about the size of an infant's head.

And now he was sure that it was not just that it resembled an enormous, unblinking and disembodied eye; it *was* an eye! A great green orb, centered with black—a pupil the size of Shadowspawn's fist.

"Whatever is above or below that eye," Shadowspawn said quietly, "you'd better stop. I'm armed, and I know how to use these weapons. Stop or you're going to be pouring blood."

"Nothing is above or below this eye," a voice said, a low tenor or highish baritone that spoke so rapidly Hanse could only just catch the words. "I am simply what you see: an eye."

"That's ridiculous," Shadowspawn snapped back instantly, once again whistling in the dark.

"So are you, and rude besides," the fast-talking voice snapped just as swiftly, with definite petulance.

"Me rude! You're the one coming straight at me out of the darkness!"

"It isn't dark, it's only dim. And besides, I am not 'coming at you.' I have stopped. You can walk right under me. I'm not one of the guardians of this scummy place of the damnéd. As for coming at you out of the dimness-not-dark—are you so stupid as to think a bodiless Eye can carry a torch?"

Hanse was so affronted that he snapped back a reply before he had time to consider how ridiculous it was: "No, and not stupid enough to think one can talk, either."

"That, my sneery friend, is where you are wrong. I am an Eye, nothing more and nothing less. Since you hear me and I hear you, it is obvious that I am an Eye who can hear and speak."

Hanse did not quite stamp his foot. "That is impossible!"

"And you are bor-r-r-innng!"

Hanse bristled, but stared. He could see the impossible. He was able to make out dull gray wall above the great green eye, and he had clear vision below it, and on either side. Nothing was there but an eye. A talking, seeing, and apparently even cerebrating eye.

"But," he stumbled out, "how can you be just an eye?"

"Well, I am, and a poor wandering one besides."

"What?"

"You heard," the impossible Eye said, impossibly. "Everyone has heard of a wandering eye, and I am just that: a Wandering Eye. Pretty lonely down here, don't you think?"

"Yes," Shadowspawn said, very, very quietly.

"So? We could keep each other company, don't you think? Or are you too damned militant?"

"Milit—I've been nothing but attacked and worse since I came down here."

"Dumb thing to do, coming down here. But . . . yes, I know. This is a bad place. Any interloper is not supposed to survive. Shall I call you that?"

"What, interloper?"

"Do you have a better name?"

"Hanse. My name is Hanse."

"Hello, Hanse. You may call me Eye."

"Just . . . Eye?"

The disembodied apparition bobbed in air. "Yes. With a capital letter, if you don't mind."

Shadowspawn could find no answer for that, and so he simply nodded. Like it or not, impossible or not, ridiculous or no, the eye—the Wandering Eye—bobbed or glided in air along beside him, having become his instant chatty-chattery, sarcastic-petulant, coy-insulting, fast-talking companion.

14

Soon Shadowspawn could not help liking his impossible and consistently disconcerting new companion, or at least accept it without minding; the accursed thing was company.

It even helped him fight off an attack by two Brimm-Mitras, or two oversized someones who looked just like that big dead barbarian from Barbaria who appeared to be so much better at fighting than he had proven. The Eye helped by diving disconcertingly at the grim Brimm-twins like a big wingless bird trying to frighten snakes away from the nest. That prompted them to make wild, wind-noisy slashes with their swords, and enabled Hanse to get them with his Ilbarsi knife and dagger.

The huge sphere of green even followed when he plunged through a trapdoor and fell and fell and fell . . . and landed almost softly—in a sub-dungeon that was a blank-walled chamber about twenty feet on a side without a sign of means of exit.

"I can't get out of here," Shadowspawn said morosely. "Guess I'll start beating on the walls."

"Now that's as brilliant as anything I've heard since the theory that you and I and the rest of the world are borne on the back of a giant turtle."

"Damn you!"

"That, Hanse, has been done," the low-tenor/high-baritone said softly and, for the first time, not rapidly.

Hanse blinked, hearing sadness and wondering at the

meaning of the words. While there were obvious advantages to being able to fly and talk without a body to feed or feet to get sore, he could see that being nothing more than a discorporate eyeball could be a curse; a form of damnation. He assumed that some ugly story lurked behind this new impossibility—the first not to be inimical!—and that it was a sad one, just as the story of Notable's enchantment was.

Shadowspawn was curious, and he did dislike being callous or at least seeming so, but he was sure he did not want to hear the Wandering Eye's story.

"I guess we're both damned. Do you have a suggestion, Eye?"

"As to getting out of this particular part of Hell, you mean."

That was a question Shadowspawn saw no reason to answer, but when the Eye remained silent for second after second that stretched into a minute and more, he nodded. He even managed not to be petulant about replying:

"Yes. Might you have a suggestion, O Eye, as to getting out of here?"

"Try not to be so sarcastic. Try to emulate my even temper, Hanse. Wisdom is patience, you know. I have been here far longer than you. Yes. I might have a suggestion as to how you can get out of here. I, you understand, could merely float out at any time? With admirable and almost infinite mercy I have stayed to keep you company."

"I . . . thank you," Hanse said, and it was an effort.

The Eye rocked in air, a sight beyond disconcerting. "I should think so. It's an effort."

"Eye . . . about that suggestion. About my getting out of here?"

His impossible companion abandoned its coyness. Hanse watched it diminish in size and realized that it was backing away from him, still suspended seven or eight feet above the floor.

"Walk this way."

Shadowspawn followed, and within two minutes obeyed the injunction to press on this stone, this one right here. He watched the wall open to reveal a chamber from which one flight of steps led up and another down. He headed for the up-staircase at once.

"You do want to get out of here, Hanse?"

Shadowspawn paused with his foot on the bottom step, thinking he was being chastised; he was so excited he had forgotten to thank his incredible benefactor.

"Absolutely, Eye, and I thank you four times!"

"Well, that's better than two or three times, isn't it! Positively effusive. However, believe me, Hanse . . . you will thank me more if you go over there and walk *down* that other flight of steps to leave this hole."

"But . . . Eye . . . we fell *down* into this, uh, hole, and—"

"*You* fell. I but followed. In mercy and a true spirit of camaraderie."

"Uh, yes, and I do appreciate it! I fell down, *down,* into this trap, and these steps lead up. It seems to me that—"

The Eye said nothing, and the incredulous youth's words slowly petered out. He glanced at the other set of stairs. The suggestion was so ridiculous, so . . . nonsensical. So? What was there down here in the unending gray-walled dimness beneath Corstic's keep that was not nonsensical?— what did make sense?

He took his foot from the bottom step and walked over to set it on the top step, and he descended the short flight of steps . . .

. . . and was back up precisely where he had been before he fell into the hole.

The Wandering Eye was right there. "Very, very good," it said. "You pass!"

Hanse stared into that enormous unblinking orb of black set in green. "Wha-at?"

"Wisdom," the green eyeball said without a mouth, "is taking nothing for granted."

And then it fled, for Corstic had appeared once again, dead Corstic the monster in a handsome mauve tunic broidered with cloth-of-gold, and now Shadowspawn became prisoner and suffered torture.

He tried to shout that Corstic was dead and this was not real, but the demon had stolen his voice. His mouth gaped and worked and no sound emerged. He shrank and tried to fight, but he seemed to have the strength of a child and he had nowhere to go and no hands with which to resist when long, cold fingers forced him onto the rack and strapped him down.

The wheel creaked and the chain rattled and Corstic chuckled. The stretching of his body brought fire into the joints of his victim; the lash of a barbed whip replaced fire with ice. Hanse groaned and sweat gushed. Corstic struck again and his victim gritted his teeth and began to make little sounds in his throat. Then he was writhing and quaking in agony, as claw-like nails raked long trenches in his flat, whipped and empty belly and long, slender fingers plopped and squished in and out of blood-dripping welts and channels. Despite his efforts to remain stoic, his eyes had commenced to leak salty water. He was leaking elsewhere too; his bladder's sphincter had failed. His world had disintegrated around him. His existence and the world that housed it had come apart like torn paper. He was suffering and he could not get his mouth closed or stop moaning and whimpering and saliva was starting to ooze out of his slack mouth.

And suddenly he had voice again.

"Corstic!"

The sorcerer chuckled. "Ye-esss?"

"You're dead, sorcerer. It's only another damned illusion! Corstic the Turd is dead, dead, dead!"

Hanse lay on the floor with no rack in sight, and no blood or pain. Better still, with dry leggings. And better still, no Corstic. Even as he sat up, slowly and gingerly, fearful of what terrible wounds and pain he might discover, the Eye returned.

Hanse's face, tone, and voice were accusing: "Why did you leave?"

"Only you can stand up to Corstic, Hanse. True wisdom is the maturity not to bother trying to deal with the impossible."

Very quietly Shadowspawn said, "oh."

"I thought he was dead," the Wandering Eye said.

"He was. Is. That was illusion, only illusion. Darkest, ugliest sorcery, Eye, and it's all I have known down here. This place is madness and I am joining it in madness, because I never know what is real and what is not."

"Are you testing yourself for some purpose?"

Hanse stared at his bodiless companion. "What? Why— what do you mean?"

The Eye eased lower to hover a foot or so before the seated youth's face. "You keep creating one illusion after another, and I just wondered if you—"

"*I* keep creating!"

"Of course, you. Do you take me for stupidity itself? Only you are wearing the ring!"

"The . . . ring?"

The Eye shot straight up to hover an inch or so below the ceiling. "Hanse? Do you notice an echo in here?"

Worse than befuddled, Shadowspawn held up his left hand and extended the finger that Corstic's ring fitted best. "This . . . this ring . . . ?"

"Of course that ring," the Eye said testily, "and I do *not* appreciate the gesture."

Hastily Hanse folded the finger down, saw that he was aiming a fist at the Eye, hastily extended all his fingers, didn't like the looks of that either, and slowly lowered his hand.

"I'm sorry, Eye. I . . . do not understand."

"You actually mean to tell me that you put that ring on without knowing its power?"

Shadowspawn sighed and looked away, unable to meet the eye of the Eye. He nodded. "It was Corstic's. A certain Cathamarca mentioned a ring that fought illusion, and I supposed this was it."

"Oh, Hanse! You are *not* wearing the illusion-fighting ring this Cathamarka mentioned; that is I mean was one of Corstic's *protections.* The ring on your finger—no no, don't hold it up again!—is one of Corstic's *weapons.* It creates illusions out of the mind of the wearer."

"*Whaaat?!*"

"Absolutely. Friendship is never having to question your friend's statements. In this case, that ring has been creating illusions out of *your* mind, Hanse. Hmm. Yes, I see . . . you are no mage, and—"

"Definitely not!"

The eye bobbed up and down. "Sometimes you make me want to chuckle, did you know that? Unfortunately, anyone knows an Eye cannot chuckle!"

It paused. Shadowspawn thought of several replies and decided against all of them.

This time, after a moment, the Eye went on without being prompted: "Anyhow, since you have no ability, no training, no talent—sorcerous talent, I mean; do stop bristling!—you do not know how to *direct* the illusions, as Corstic did. And that amulet you're wearing—that's only a bauble when it is worn by the same person who wears the ring."

"You . . . I . . . you mean I—" Hanse's voice was only a croak but he was not able to maintain even that.

"Yes. Oh, make no mistake: Corstic did set many traps and guardians here, and they are most definitely real. But yes, I mean that you have been creating all the illusion menaces yourself, from the deeps of your own mind and fears, through the ring.''

Hanse was glad he was sitting down. He knew that his legs had gone to no more than thick oil and had he been standing the act of sitting would have been sudden, involuntary, and painful.

"Damn! Sorcery! Me!'' He was removing the ring. "So that's how that father of rats knew which way I was going to swerve and really go! It wasn't reading my mind—it *was* my mind! I mean it was from— And those other things! They came from my own mind and and and so they knew exactly what I was going to do!''

"Exactly. What a mind,'' the Eye said.

"Damn! Sorcery!'' Shadowspawn dragged off the ring and started to throw it from him—and thought better of that, and stowed it away in the little pouch on his belt.

"Well,'' said the Wandering Eye, "I'm really sorry about all this. Too bad you didn't run onto me earlier, or try thinking a little.''

Uncharacteristically, Shadowspawn did not even bridle or consider violence. He was that shocked, disconcerted, and . . . demeaned.

"So, Hanse. Ready to do a little walking?''

Walking beside/below the Eye in gray-walled twilight, Shadowspawn slowly regained a semblance of his wits, and mind, and with it came the ability to think. Eventually it occurred to him to ask whether the Eye might perhaps know about any treasure hidden down here: "trinkets, gold, rings, jewels, that sort of thing.''

The green sphere bobbed in air in what its companion had come to think was its version of laughter, or chuckling anyhow.

"So that is why you're here? Looking for sparklies? You came down here *voluntarily,* Hanse?''

"Uh . . . in a way . . .''

"All right, all right, I don't need the whole sordid story that is doubtless too long anyhow. Corstic's dead, so I am free to answer."

Shadowspawn had no opportunity to question that statement. In its medium-voiced fast-talking babble, the Wandering Eye was advising him that Hanse was the ninth to try for the trove of goodies everyone knew the master mage must have down here somewhere.

"When Corstic was alive, his sorcerous mind-warders killed seven of those other seekers, Hanse. Two others prevailed or nearly, but would not accept my advice to walk *down* steps to get to a higher level."

"That—that's what you meant when you told me 'You pass.'"

"Exactly. I had to do it. I was under a sp—I am under a spell, but at least that one is broken. You passed. I can talk and even help."

"I'm glad. I wish you had come looking for me a little earlier."

"Sorry. Couldn't."

"Oh. Part of the spell."

"Right. And you are really the man who killed Corstic?"

Hanse's head was already nodding automatically, but he realized that for once he could not lie. Ridiculous that he could lie to anyone on earth, including himself, without half trying and without compunction, but felt compelled to tell the truth and even exceed it, to this—this thing that was nothing more than a floating, browless, bodiless eye. Yes, he had slain Corstic, but only because Notable's attack on the master mage had diverted his attention and broken the spell of paralysis he had laid on Hanse.

"Actually my cat did," he said.

The Wandering Eye bobbed up and down.

"That's a good one. A cat! A good sign, too. Being able to joke shows you are getting yourself back together, coping. A cat, eh!'' The Eye bobbed its mirth. "Well met, Hanse, well met. Ready to come along?"

More than ready, Hanse thought, with vehemence, but he only nodded. "Ready."

"Walk this way," the Eye said, and floated off.

Shadowspawn did not try. He followed, walking his own way.

The Eye led him to the trove. That involved quite a bit of walking and quite a bit of doing, complete with some old Corstic-set traps that involved true nastiness and might at last have settled the career of Shadowspawn but for his new ally and guide. At last they came to a metal door with a small, barred window. Shadowspawn gasped, staring at that grille-set door, and something like a sob caught in his throat.

All that wandering, and this was the door he had come to so long, long ago . . . so early on in his odyssey through Corstic's diabolical maze.

"Just stand to the side and chop it off," the Eye said.

"Chop what off?"

The Eye stared. Without another word Hanse nodded agreement. He stood to the left of the door, with his back to the wall. The Wandering Eye swooped close to the grille. It hovered there a mere instant before it backed away. Out rushed the serpent-like green arm with its tentacularly writhing, reaching fingers, and with a stroke Shadowspawn lopped off the hand. It flopped to the floor . . . and every finger shattered into rattling pieces, like broken glass.

The arm withdrew like a frightened snake. Without blood.

The door was unlocked. Hanse swung it wide, but peered about warily, his long guardless sword—its blade unstained— at the ready.

"We're there," his unlikely companion said mouthlessly. "This is the place. Going in?"

"What about that arm?"

"What arm?"

There was no arm.

"Oh."

Still wary, Shadowspawn went into the smallish room. There was no arm. He gazed at shelves empty but for dust and cobwebs, a comfortable-looking chair done in beige and dark blue, a blue-painted table empty except for a realistic carving of a serpent done in green glass, and a stairway.

"Don't step here," the Eye said, gliding down to hover above a spot of floor no different from any other. "Knock the glass snake off the table, Hanse. You'll be happy you did. No no—don't touch it. Knock it off, I said. Wisdom is an attentive listening that is the key to a long life."

Hanse used the Ilbarsi blade. The glass serpent shattered all over the floor, but his interest was instantly distracted from it. The true burden of the table was now revealed. On it lay a number of weapons including a nastily curved short sword or long dagger, an amulet carved so intricately from scintillant crystal that looking at it hurt his eyes, a small round box, two clear jugs apparently full of water, and a large oilskin bag. And a sword. His sword, with its ornate hilt.

"Leave that box alone! Trap!"

Shadowspawn nodded. His eyes were for the sword. He touched it. It felt real. He picked it up, whished it through the air.

"Here, careful there!" the Eye said.

"It really is my sword."

"Oh."

Tentatively Hanse sheathed the sword; it dropped in and was at home there. With a nod and a pleasant expression he sheathed the long knife from the Ilbars hills and drew the sword again. He raised it.

"I wouldn't chop that bag, Hanse."

"Oh." Hanse regarded the box with a mixture of curiosity and apprehension. "Would you open it?"

"I'd have to. Curiosity doesn't kill us—it makes us human, rather than dumb cats."

Shadowspawn felt it wise to make no comment. If ever he got out of here, he did not think that the Wandering Eye and Notable were going to be friends. The disembodied green eye had proven itself to be his valuable friend. If it considered itself human, he saw no reason to argue. He laid his sword on the table, reached for the bag, felt a warning qualm of nervousness, picked up the sword, and sheathed it. The mouth of the sack was drawstrung and knotted.

"How about cutting the knot?" he asked.

"Sorry," the Eye said with a note of petulance. "Can't. No hands."

"I mean suppose I—"

"Oh. Good idea."

Hanse sliced through the rawhide drawstring and opened the big sack—gingerly. Cautiously he peered within. His stomach rumbled.

"You—you think this loaf of bread is safe, Eye?"

"I've never known a loaf of bread to attack anyone," he was advised snippily, "even in Corstic's keep."

Again uncharacteristically, Shadowspawn withheld a retort. "I mean safe to eat."

"Oh. Definitely. This is Corstic's keep of keeps, his final retreat. Here he would have fled if he were attacked by anyone or anything that proved strong enough to make him seriously nervous about his health. *He* knew how to open that box without spraying the poison into his face. The amulet and blades are for his emergency use, and probably ensorceled. I strongly advise that we leave them alone. The bread of course was for him to eat. But I'm sure you'll find it stale."

"The bag," Hanse said, withdrawing the golden-crusted loaf, "is damp inside. This feels soft enough."

"Ah. That Corstic! Clever son of a demonbitch, wasn't he!"

Stomach rumbling and roiling with the gas of emptiness, Shadowspawn sliced the loaf and in two seconds had a mouthful of good, gloriously un-stale bread that tasted as good as anything he could ever remember having eaten.

"It's nut-bread! Good!"

"How nice," the Eye said tonelessly.

"What about the jugs, Eye?"

"It is a habit of yours, is it?—talking with your mouth full?"

Hanse shook his head, chewing, his face cherubic. "No no," he said mouthfully. "I'm not often starving, either."

"Oh. Good. Politeness is the mark of a good companion. As to the jugs—one is water and the other is poison. Acid, as I recall."

Shadowspawn poised in mid-chew, shivering. He looked askance at the jugs.

"Going to ask?"

Hanse was breaking off a palm-size piece of golden-tan bread crust and arranging it carefully on the table. "No. I'm going to dribble a little from this jug on this piece of crust."

"Ah! That's quite intelligent, Hanse! I'm afraid I don't know which jug is which."

Hanse did as he had said. The bread moistened, but nothing else happened. Before he made an assumption and drank, however, he opened the other jug and dribbled a couple of drops of its contents on the bit of crust. The bread bubbled and smoke curled up.

"Gods!" Swiftly he restoppered that jug, swigged from the other, emitted a long "aaah!" and treated himself to another outsized bite of bread.

"It's nice to know I'm going to live," he said a few moments later. "One thing I don't see is any sign of, uh . . . sparklies."

"Oh. Under this floor are two chambers. One is floored with spikes a foot long. Lots of them. You'd have found that chamber if you stepped on that area of floor I warned you about. In the other chamber Corstic hid his *real* valuables. I would bet that it's trapped in some way, but I'm afraid I don't know. I do know how to get to it.''

Hanse heard the teasing tone of those last words, and his mouth opened to ask the question. He closed it. ''Let me try a guess.''

''Oh,'' the Eye said in that same toneless voice so eerily devoid of emotion, ''what fun.''

''The room is below us—down. To get to it I go up those steps.''

The Wandering Eye bobbed and soared, swooped, bobbed some more. This time its voice was definitely not without emotion: *''Right!''*

15

SMILING, RESUMING A bit of his customary swagger, Hanse approached the stair. It was narrow, about two feet wide, and was contained within a wall of the room and a separate one that seemed to serve no purpose other than to enclose the steps.

"Wait."

Hanse froze. Slowly he turned to look back at the Eye, but it was just floating past, on its way around to face him. Facelessly.

"The chances are excellent," his companion said in a conversational tone, "that Corstic equipped one or more of these steps with a trap. Think about Corstic—he probably trapped *all* of them."

Hanse nodded. He glanced around. After a moment he decided to make use of something that had been plaguing him for—however long he had been down here. He unbuckled his weapon belt, slid off the sheath containing the Ilbarsi blade, and resumed the belt. He poised, staring, and tossed the sheath, two-foot knife and all, onto the first of eight two-feet-wide steps.

He was holding his breath, staring with narrowed eyes, when the scabbard clattered.

That was all it did. Clattered, and thunked down, because it had not landed flat and thus did not fit. Thinking that the sheathed knife's total of five or so pounds might not be heavy enough, Shadowspawn extended his right foot and, like a cat testing water with a careful paw, pressed on the step. Nothing happened except that his heartbeat had stepped up. He lifted his foot, set it down on the floor, picked up the scabbard, and measured a little more carefully with his eyes before he dropped it onto the second step.

Nothing happened. Again, he tested with his buskin-shod foot before taking back the sheath. The moment he dropped it onto the third step a whole covey of foot-long darts shot from the leftward wall so fast that they made zinging, bee-like noises. They sped across the step some three feet above it, to imbed themselves in the other wall with a rattly little bundled sequence of thunks.

"Nasty, nasty," the Eye commented, while the armpits of its human companion flooded. "Finding the first two steps untrapped was supposed to allay your suspicions so that you'd step right up for a multiple puncturing. And every one poison-tipped, no doubt."

Hanse swallowed and said nothing so that he would not hear his voice quaver. He used his sword to wipe the scabbard off the step and tried dropping it there again.

Nothing happened.

With a nod, he positioned himself on the first step and tested the fourth. It did not react to the scabbard. He ascended to the second step and tested the fourth with his foot.

Nothing happened.

Thoughtfully Shadowspawn put to work the practiced eye of one whose safety had often depended upon noticing little details. His eyes widened, then narrowed at sight of a horizontal line of six small holes lining the riser between the fourth and fifth steps. His face was grim as he nodded. It was a bit more than a hunch that told him to flatten himself against a stairway wall before tossing the long sheathed knife onto that step.

Nothing happened.

"Good!" the Eye commented with enthusiasm, and then, "Why are you hesitating?"

"I think something triggers something from the riser under that step," Hanse said. "See the little holes?"

"Seeing is something I'm really good at," the disembodied Eye said, and settled onto his shoulder to peer at the suspicious riser. "The holes are low, shin level, and big enough to hold more darts. Can you try a chop onto that step and keep your legs out of line with that leftmost hole?"

Good idea; Hanse could. He drew his sword and chopped. The blade bit well in, surely generating at least the illusion of weight on the step.

Nothing happened.

He considered. Thoughtfully he backed onto the first step and chopped the third. The holed riser coughed forth six darts. They flashed past and rattled off the stone wall across from the steps.

"Aha! *Really* nasty!" the Eye said. "Quite clever of you, Hanse."

"Fear," Shadowspawn said in imitation of his companion's habit of making pronouncements, "is good food for making a man think."

A moment of silence stretched before the Eye said, "That's pretty good. 'Good food for feeding thought' might be better. I'll remember."

Without comment Shadowspawn tossed the scabbard onto the seventh step, which promptly upended from the right end and slammed up diagonally against the opposite stairwall. Hanse realized that it had been propelled by a spring mechanism so powerful as to have slammed him into the wall in the same way. Only when the step started to drop back into place did he note the spike that had emerged from the leftward wall of the staircase. It would have given him a new navel, several inches deep.

The Eye hovered. "Why not the sixth step?"

"I *was* going to step over it," the disgruntled Shadow-spawn said. "But I can't step over two. So—"

Several tests indicated that the sixth step was safe. Minutes later, Shadowspawn had established that so was the eighth and last, and he stepped across the seventh. But froze there, realizing that his first pace onto this new floor was likely to trigger still another trap. Nothing happened when he dropped the scabbard directly before him. He tested further by extending one foot to exert more pressure—and triggered another of those horizontal dead-fall mechanisms such as he had narrowly avoided when first he descended into the warren. This one swept across the space where his waist should have been.

Thus, in a chamber seven feet high by only about four on a side, he gazed at the narrow, eighteen-inch-high wooden door on his left, and shook his head. He made his cautious way to the wall straight ahead, squatted, and used the scabbard to rap the wall above his head. With a click and the sound of a released spring followed by a high-pitched multiple humming—bees, again—the wall opened in a long vertical slit that spewed darts.

Every one of them bounced off the wall four feet away—except for the two that actually imbedded themselves just deeply enough to hang there. Imbedded themselves in stone!

"The monster did understand the facility and felicity of strong springs and good steel," the Eye commented.

Shadowspawn did not rise from his squat. "What do you see?"

"A smallish leather-covered box resting on the floor of a little niche," the Eye reported. "How did you know not to try that little door?"

"It's got to open onto a down stairway or chute," Shadowspawn said, quietly.

"Ah. Perfect logic. Except since when has logic had

anything to do with anything down here under that murdering swine's keep?''

True, Hanse thought. "Well, I was right." And he added, with a grim imitation of a smile, "For once."

"Ah," quoth the Eye, "modesty is an integral part of wisdom and maturity!''

"Would you just stop with those pronouncements—you sound like a priest or an official," Hanse started to say, but got no further than "Would you just st—'' before he broke off and clamped his mouth. He had an ally, no matter how outré and impossible a . . . being it was. He could stand its sententious pronunciamentos for now at least; getting out of here was a lot more important than expressing his displeasure unto exasperation.

"Would I what?" the Eye responded, in the accommodating tone of a friend and ally.

"Sorry," Hanse forced himself to say. "Bad idea." Slowly and with considerable nervousness he rose.

Nothing happened.

He pushed his sword into the eight-by-eight-by-six-inch niche. Six spikes leaped up from the floor of the aperture to impale its ceiling. By coincidence they missed the sword, only one scraping its blade. At least one and likelier two, however, would have impaled his forearm. Probably poisoned. Hanse's armpits were sticky. Never mind his unwanted over-familiarity with sorcery and bad men doing bad deeds; Corstic had an uglier mind than any Shadow-spawn had ever encountered or even dreamed of.

He withdrew the sword. The spikes leaped back down out of sight.

He tried it again. One spike made a *ting* sound off his blade as they all leaped upward again.

"Damn. There isn't enough room between the spikes to drag the box out."

"So. It can't be done, then," the Eye said. "So much for the baby-eating swine's treasure. Ready to go?"

"No!" Hanse replied instantly, his voice rising. "No," he said more thoughtfully and manfully. "There has to be a way. The baby-eating swine wouldn't have made it impossible for him to get to his own stash."

"Oh. Of course. Right. I just don't like this place. Fear interferes with thought, which is the essence of wisdom."

"I don't like it either," Shadowspawn assured it.

He experimented. Nothing happened, then something did, then nothing did, then something nasty did, then . . .

It took the better part of nine minutes clad with sweat and grunts, grunts and expletives, gasps and curses for him to discover that when he set his left hand against the wall beside the niche and poked within, the spikes were not triggered. Nevertheless, even as he smiled happily in triumph, he used his sword to wipe the handsome little gold-tooled leather box out of its hidey-hole.

Immediately an ear-splitting shriek ripped the air and an eight-foot gorilla appeared in the room—necessarily hunched into a half-squat, since the shaggy black and chocolate-brown thing was higher than the ceiling.

"Hanse!" the Eye called, in a true soprano. "Look out."

Shadowspawn was thoroughly tired of all these damned manifestations. "Oh *stop*," he snarled. "You can't exist down here, so go away."

The gorilla obligingly vanished.

"Hanse!"

"I took care of it, I took care of it."

"No no—it's the ceiling! It's coming down!"

Box in hand, Shadowspawn looked up.

"Oh no."

Oh yes. The ceiling was descending and he had no doubt that it was designed to come all the way to the floor. With irresistible force, of course. Probably had a mountain made from sorcery on top of it. That made it time to throw caution to the cliché and yank open that little door set low in the wall, which made him suspect that if he did he would find a final trap, the hard way. He sheathed his sword and sidled along the wall and around the corner, while the ceiling descended. The Eye came down with it, hovering just below the downcoming menace.

Standing beside rather than before the slim, low wooden door, Shadowspawn gave it a chop with the Ilbarsi knife. The door cracked. Hanse had to waggle the blade to get it out, while the ceiling continued to descend. At the next such blow a hinge snapped and dropped to the floor.

Wanting very much to kick the little door in, Shadowspawn remained where he was, while the ceiling came down at him. Not, unfortunately, quite noiselessly. The scraping was maddening, threatening, and made his teeth feel itchy.

He swung the long blade again, with strength.

The door collapsed and a niche in the wall beside it opened to spit another of Corstic's clever dart-coveys, the brevity of their *zinnng* sound a scary indication of their great velocity. Hanse felt the ceiling touch his head and squatted. That wasn't so good; it put pressure on a squirmy stomach and pounding heart. He peered into the opening behind the ruined door.

"What do you see, Hanse?"

"Danger," Hanse muttered, in a voice that clearly indicated the unspoken words: "What else?"

He threw in the Ilbarsi knife and heard only a clang followed by a clatter and a series of clang-rattle-thunks, on a descending note. He tossed in a throwing star and listened while it, too, bounced down steps.

The ceiling touched his head again and Shadowspawn, already squatting low, decided it was time to bow to clichés. He thrust Corstic's box into his mail-jerkin. Away went caution as he crawled through the little doorway, watched a torch come sorcerously alight, and looked down eight steps. They were not walled. He merely lay down, wiggled his legs and then body over the side until he clung to the landing by his hands:

And let go.

He landed in a crouch . . . in the room with the table and shelves, bread crumbs and acid. He glanced up to see the Eye emerge from a unbroken and seemingly solid ceiling, and shook his head.

"I hate this stuff!"

The Eye rocked from side to side, in air. "I can't say that I enjoy it, myself." Then it hastened to follow the lean young man with the odd accent, who was leaving that chamber at speed.

In the corridor, Shadowspawn sat on the floor. He kept the front edge of the box faced away from himself while he experimented, applying pressure here and there. He was not even sure what he had done when he triggered the mechanism: the lid sprang open and a puff of dust or gas shot forth. He dropped the box and crawl-ran, on hands and toes with tail high, many feet before he stopped and turned to look.

He saw only Corstic's box, covered with handsomely tooled leather. No smoke, no gas, no gorilla, no bipedal wolves, no giant blue chicken. He jerked at sound of the voice from just above and behind him:

"You run like a cat!"

"On all fours, you mean? I was in a hurry."

"No, I mean first you run as if you are being chased by lions or worse, and stop a long way off to see whether you're being chased. Humans and dogs usually keep looking back while they run."

"Believe me, I fall into the human category."

"I never doubted it for an instant. I just meant that sometimes even imitating an animal as stupid as a cat can be a very good idea."

"I think so, thanks."

The Eye meandered a bit, then: "Anyhow it's all right by now, Hanse. That little quantity of verian dust is harmless in open space, and even this accursed tunnel qualifies as open space. If you'd opened the box in that chamber where we found it, though, you'd be a dead man already.''

Hanse ignored the ''where *we* found it'' and muttered, ''Glad I didn't. If that ceiling hadn't started coming down I probably would have. Corstic outsmarted himself! But— only I would be dead? What about you?''

''I really can't say what effect the dust of the death-flower would have on me,'' the Eye said, ''but whatever I would be, it would not be a dead *man*.''

''Ah. Uh . . . are you sure it's safe now?''

''Hanse, we can't be sure of safety so long as we're anywhere near Corstic's keep. But I can be sure you're safe from that verian dust.''

''Ah. Let's see what we've got, then.''

''We? Nothing *I* can use, you can be sure of that!''

16

THE BOX CONTAINED two rings—*the* two rings—along with a malachite pendant on a relatively heavy gold chain, which was promising; three tiger-eye rings fit for the fingers of a slender woman; and a pair of silver-and-onyx-and-jade earrings. Far less interesting were the tiny bag of sand, and the three small white pebbles.

Not bad, Shadowspawn mused. *This other stuff far outweighs the silly insult of sand and little rocks!*

He was making glittering objects disappear here and there in his clothing. He decided, just in case, to leave the box where it was. On second thought, he decided to chop it up, to make sure he didn't miss something else that might be concealed in some tiny secret chamber.

No. All his chopping accomplished was to destroy a handsome teakwood box covered with gold-tooled leather.

"Now to get these to Arcala, and if this other stuff isn't sorcerous, I've got something."

"Arcala? He's still alive?"

"Alive and well, yes."

"I'd have thought Corstic would have killed him by now," the Eye said, and added grimly, "or worse."

"Arcala is more powerful than you thought, then. After that, I've also got something for Cathamarca—his ears, after I chop them off!"

"Poor Catha-what-you-said. I've seen how handy you are at chopping!"

Shadowspawn twisted his head around on his neck, very
slowly, to peer at his companion. "Eye? You don't, ahh, by
chance, know, ah, how I get out of here, do you?"

"I might," the Eye said, and Hanse sighed, recognizing
the thing's return to its coy mode.

"Well . . ."

"I'm just not sure that you deserve any more help," the
Eye observed with unseemly petulance.

"My friend! How can you say that?"

"You, with your personality like a battle ax, have not
even asked me why I am only an Eye, and why I am here."

Hanse sighed with resignation, and asked.

"I'm glad you asked. You see, I was a handsome young
man, really, everyone told me so, and there was this big ugly
fellow named Thulsa Doom, a cousin of Corstic's, I believe,
and a matter involving his wife, his daughter, and his
mistress."

"Whose?"

"Whose who?"

"Whose wife, daughter, and mistress?"

The Eye's voice went testy. "Does it matter?"

"Not to me. I'll bet it did to the individual, though."

Suddenly the Eye was bobbing up and down. "True!
True! How tragically true!"

It proceeded to relate an involved, exciting, and woefully
windy story that involved individuals named Thulsa Doom,
Corstic, Satella, a knight marked with red crosses, The
Punisher, a thrice-wicked witch named Taramis, a faceless
being called the Iron Lord, another bearing the ugly name
Oglan the Un-mage, someone named Rollan the Child, a
wonderful kind sensible innocent man named Aphorislan
who was so superb an individual that Hanse suspected
he was now called Eye, a battle that did not quite come off,
a duel of sorcerers that did and was distinctly un-
entertaining to Hanse of Sanctuary, and others he had never
heard of and was not likely to and did not care to either. The

tale meandered about like a scent-seeking hound and was ridiculous besides. It went on and on without coming to the finale: by what dark sorcery man had been transformed into Eye.

At last Shadowspawn was so unwise as to say so.

Without comment the Eye angrily/petulantly departed his company, at speed.

Never had Shadowspawn felt so ridiculous as he did in calling apologies after a disembodied eye.

It relented and returned only after it had soaked up enough of that to persuade three average women. "Wisdom," it advised sententiously, "is knowing when to apologize."

How well I know, Shadowspawn thought, and again mentioned the possibility of taking leave of the subterranean warren of the dead sorcerer.

Having received abject apology and a second, politely-put request, the Eye agreed without being condescending.

"Just a moment," Shadowspawn said, and dared return into Corstic's keep of keeps to fetch that jug of acid. He had a sort of premonition: had Mignureal been available, he thought, she'd have advised him to take it along, sure.

The Wandering Eye showed its new friend the way out, which involved a good deal more walking and the *de*scending of two more flights of steps. All while Hanse must be extra careful with his chosen burden: the cumbersome and heavy jug with its deadly contents.

Shadowspawn could hardly believe it when they opened a filthy and partially rotted door to be assailed by cool fresh night air, and emerged almost at the foot of the long Town Hill of estates under the luminous glory of a full moon. He glanced about, wondering just how much of the area under that hill Corstic owned and had mined—and how many miles Shadowspawn had covered tonight. It seemed to him that he had endured about a month of horror and insanity and pain in that awful warren, but judging from the moon's position, he decided that it must have been something over three hours.

"Note well just where we are," the Eye instructed, "and close the door."

Hanse glanced around without questioning, fixing landmarks in his mind, and heaved shut the wooden door set into the side of a low hummock at the base of a long hill. Immediately the door disappeared to be replaced by earth and a low, broadly branching, and unpleasantly thorny bush.

"It is not true," the Eye told him unnecessarily, "that all of a sorcerer's spells die with him."

"Uh," Hanse said, looking thoughtful and nodding slowly. "I admit I like the fact that only we know where this door is."

On the other hand he was horribly thirsty and ravenously hungry all over again. And of course it occurred to him that there had been no need at all for the jug of acid he had lugged all this way. So much for premonitions. They were better left to Mignureal . . . wherever Mignureal was. He set the jug down beside the sorcery-created thornbush.

Suddenly the Eye was bobbing in air as if caught in an upward draft. Hanse needed no sorcery or powers of Seeing to recognize jubilance, even in a bodiless giant eye.

"I have to say it, friend Hanse: thanks to you I am now free of Corstic and that awful, dark place, and you, Hanse, are now a young man with a wandering eye."

Shadowspawn did not laugh.

He ascended a huge and beautifully gnarled old roanberry tree as easily as if it were equipped with steps, and gained the little natural enclosure some twenty feet up where the tree branched into three.

"You . . . do . . . *climb* well!" the Eye said, rather gaspily.

Shadowspawn said, "uh."

In the niche of the tree, in his belt-purse, he deposited the contents of Corstic's leather box along with the illusion-creating ring—which naturally he considered rightfully his.

Keeping out only the two rings that interested Catha-marca but would first be seen by Arcala, he descended and turned to stare back up toward the estate of the master mage.

He decided not to climb back up there; the count and his man would wait only so long, and he did not think they'd have left Ironmouth or Notable—assuming that Notable would have agreed to leave with them.

I'll just go over to Cathamarca's lodgings and confront the son of a bitch about tricking me, he decided. *Either they'll be there or I'll wait.*

Maybe the Eye wanted to go along. Hanse supposed he could stand that. He looked up, then around in every direction. The Wandering Eye was gone.

"I guess it wandered," Shadowspawn muttered, and started walking.

17

No ONE COULD have expected to find what Hanse discovered when he entered the second room of Cathamarca's suite. He had thought he was done with horror. He had a right to be.

He could smell it even before he stepped through the open doorway: blood was splashed everywhere. It had splattered onto two walls and an area of ceiling where an artery must have spurted its crimson fountain. Little streaks of it ran across the floor like snail-tracks done in red. In the approximate center of the splashes and sea of red-brown lay Jemise. She was naked. She had been mutilated. Horribly. The eye she had left was open, wide open but seeing nothing. That she had not been slain quickly but had suffered torture was obvious; her wrists were still tied behind her, under the sprawled mess that was her cold body, which bore the signs of having been both beaten and carved.

There was no need for Hanse to touch her to be sure that she was dead. He swallowed. The ants were in his stomach, now.

"Oh damn, Jemmy, I'm sorry I didn't leave you that earring," he said in a very, very quiet voice, and he stared, just stared, with his lips compressed while his stomach rumbled and roiled.

"This is not illusion, Hanse," a voice said.

Hanse jerked automatically, although he recognized the voice. The Wandering Eye had wandered back.

His companion said nothing and did not nod. His lurching belly would not be put off. He barely had time to turn away and heave up its meager contents and too much tongue-burning acid before three Reds arrived, noisily.

The Eye promptly vanished when the trio of grabbers of the City Watch came in, two with cocked crossbows. The quarrels were aimed at Hanse.

"So, the informant was right," the tall thin one with the ugly tricolored moustache and odd fawn-colored eyes said. He was staring at the foreigner as if he would just love to be given reason or excuse to trip his crossbow and puncture the young man's flat belly.

The sub-sergeant in charge pointed. He was not a huge man, but big enough, with a mouth that looked as if he had lost at least one fight. "Turn around and put your hands behind your back for some rope, boy."

"Look," Hanse said, staring into angry eyes above a large tan moustache, "I just came in and found her. As a matter of fact I just finished throwing up—see?" He glanced around. The Wandering Eye had wandered, probably at speed. Hanse realized that he did not dare mention his witness.

"Fascinating," the sub-sergeant said in a flat voice that matched his expression. His mouth was forced to twist oddly with every word. His eyes stared coldly from under brows like caterpillars. "You going to turn around like I said or get yourself punctured?"

Hanse had misgivings about turning his back on a trio of angry men. Uniformed civil "servants" or not, this lot looked as if they would enjoy beating him black and purple. But experience had taught him when it was time to be obedient. Trying his best to look meek, he turned, slowly, and put back his hands for tying.

"Tie those wrists, Neth, and make a good job of it. Then we'll see about relieving him of all the steel he's wearing. Just who are you, boy?"

"Hansis, from down south. Ouch! I respect crossbows—trying to cut off my wrists with rawhide isn't necessary!"

"Not to you, maybe," the man behind him said, and gave the bindings another tug that made Hanse wince and reset one foot.

"Neth enjoys hurting rotten murderers," the third man said.

Hanse considered more than one comment and decided it was wiser to keep them to himself. He was sure the Eye would have an aphorism for the situation and the decision.

"Get on with who you are, boy."

"The name is *Hansis*. I came here—oW!—from down south but I've lived here for months. I've got friends here—Arcala for one. Gaise and Rimizin, among others. I've had the same apartment for—"

"Uh-huh. So you know some us by name, or say you do. Honest people seldom know police. And who is this poor thing—or rather, who was she before you had your fun with her?"

"Her name is Jemise but I had nothing at all to do with this. I just found her. Just now. I swear that."

"Sure."

With his wrists roped tightly enough to make circulation in his hands a mere memory, the three Reds were stripping him of weapons. They were unfavorably impressed with the collection they amassed. At that, they missed two death-stars and a throwing knife.

Then the one called Neth stepped around and punched the prisoner in the belly. The fist bounced back, but Hanse went down, helpless to break his fall or do a thing to stop whatever might be coming next. A booted toe or ten, likely.

"All right, that's enough of that, Neth. Get the bastard up and out of here. Ashes and embers, what a job you did on this poor little girl!" The sub-sergeant's big moustache writhed as he turned to stare at Hanse, working this mouth.

"I *told* you I—"

Neth took pleasure in cutting off that uninteresting expostulation of innocence with a booted toe in the huddled perpetrator's side. Gagging and gasping, Hanse decided to say not another word.

"Tiv? I know about this fellow," the third Red said, the one with the crossbow. "Seems to me he really is a friend of Sergeant Gaise. Maybe we'd better just take him along and be careful how we treat him."

"Oh," the sub-sergeant said, "I just love to be careful how I treat murderers who torture and carve before they finish! And a *foreigner,* too."

"S-sir," Hanse gasped from the floor, "would you please allow me to say something without getting another kick or punch from Neth, here?"

The sub-sergeant looked sour, but did give that suggestion a moment's consideration. "All right, Neth, I said get 'im on his feet, not shine your boot-toes on his guts. Say it, boy."

"Uh, sub-sergeant sir . . . look at the blood. Look at her."

"I'm looking. And it just makes me madder!"

"Me too," Neth snarled. "Maybe I didn't get that rawhide tight enough!"

"What's left of that girl is cold and very stiff," Hanse pointed out, trying not to sound as hasty as he wanted to be, "and look at the blood. You know old blood when you see it—that's brown as old walnut and already hard. Whoever did this did it a long time ago—hours and hours. Would I have done this and then stayed here to be caught and tortured?"

"He's right, Tiv." That from the Watchman who had recommended care with the bound suspect. "By the Flame, this blood is like cold wax. Nothing liquid left about it."

"What do you mean, *tortured*?" Neth demanded.

Hanse worked to keep his voice quiet and matter-of-fact. "That's what it's called when you bully someone with his hands tied. And that's what I'm telling Gaise and Arcala too.''

Neth's face was dark with blood and his voice a snarl: "Let me just rearrange this big buzzard's beak of his, Tiv.''

"Damn it, Neth,'' Sub-sergeant Tiv said, straightening from the ghastly corpse of what had been a more than pretty young woman, "he's right. She's cold. She's been dead for hours.''

"So this *foreigner* forgot something and came back for it,'' Neth said, hopefully.

"Uh, does anything you know about me make you think I'd have tortured and murdered this poor harmless girl?''

"Nothing I know about him, Tiv,'' the tall thin one said. "Say . . . Singlas was talking about this Hansis the other night. Ashes and embers!—didn't you have something to do with Corstic's death, Hansis?''

Damn and blast! Arcala was supposed to keep that quiet! Does everybody in this Flame-ridden town know about me? Hanse went stubborn: "Never heard of him. But by now you three know very well I'm not the monster you're looking for.''

"Maybe not,'' the sub-sergeant said slowly, obviously thinking as he gazed about, "but you can see that you have to come with us, just the same.''

"Uh. How about easing up these cords before my hands turn black and drop off, then?''

Tiv gave him a direct look. "Don't push your luck, b—Hansis.'' He turned away and waved a hand. "Neth, you stay here and keep everybody out till we sent the *other* cart for her. Arlas, come on, let's take him to headquarters and let them deal with him.''

"Why in fart do I have to stay with . . . *this*?'' Neth demanded.

"Because I wouldn't trust you in the cart with *that*,'' his superior said grimly, with a gesture at their prisoner.

Hanse was more than ready to leave that room of horror

that was not illusion. Since Neth looked ready to chew up an
anvil, it was both gratifying and fun to wink at him in
passing and show him a cutely boyish grin. The Red's face
twisted in fury and he started to move; Sub-sergeant Tiv
snapped his name; Hanse followed Arlas out of the room.
He was happy to precede Tiv down the steps and out, while
Arlas led the way. So long as he kept his back straight,
Hanse discovered, descending steps with his hands bound
behind him was not too difficult. He told himself it was a
good lesson in balance, and his self sneered right back.

The trio of Reds had materialized so conveniently and
ready for action, he learned as he was loaded into the cart
and taken the several city blocks to Watch headquarters,
because an anonymous someone had advised by note that
something awful was taking place in the inn.

Along the way other things they said brought him to a
revelation that left him unable to speak while he pondered
it: Shadowspawn had been belowground not three hours,
but twenty-seven.

18

NEITHER GAISE NOR Rimizin was present when the sinisterly dark-clad prisoner was brought in. Singlas was. Babbling away on Hanse's behalf, the doughy-faced grabber looked ready to burst into tears. Naturally he was not able to keep the suspect from being locked up. At least that meant that the ropes came off Hanse's wrists—after he was walked down the echoic corridor and assisted into the ugly little cell. He wished the walls were different. He had had quite enough of gray stone.

From behind bars, Hanse the criminal requested a visit from Arcala.

"Only the master mage of Firaqa!" the very jowly guard said. "Don't want much, do you?"

"No, I don't. He and I are friends, and I did not murder anyone. You heard Singlas. Besides, the girl was killed hours and hours ago. And," Hanse hurried on when the guard smiled and opened his mouth to speak, "if you say 'That's what they all say' you'd better kill me right away, because once I'm out of here I'll remind you of that snotty smile. Physically."

The jail-bound Red's expression changed to one of anger. Before he could speak it, however, those piercing black eyes held his and the dark fellow in the cell spoke further:

"Better find out whether what I said about being Arcala's friend is true before you do anything unwise," he said.

"You can ask my friend Gaise, or my friend Rimizin, or . . ."

"Ahhh!" the guard snapped in exasperation, waving a hand. "I'll bet your eyes was blue before you got so full of shit it's right up to your brows!"

But he turned and departed, presumably to check with his superiors. Hanse gazed through the bars after him, chewing the inside of his lower lip.

Arcala owed him much for *removing* Corstic and thus making the lean younger mage the prime practitioner of Firaqa, and thus its prime citizen. Arcala was director of the FSA—Firaqi Spellmasters' Alliance—and Chief Mage, which here was the same as Chief Magistrate.

After an intolerable wait that had to be tolerated—Hanse did check the bars of his cell's small window, which were of hard, unrusted and well-seated black iron—Arcala came, wearing a handsome tunic picked out with silver, and a corrugated frown.

Of average height and rising thirty-five or so, Arcala was balding around a center lock of gold-red hair that made him look high of forehead. That hair was a bit darker than his moustache, which was of the droop-tip variety, but well and carefully trimmed. He was slim and small of bone though not thin as he must have been a few years back, a man who had been thin but ate well and did not labor. Hanse did not miss the excellence of the fabric and superb color of the obviously very good tunic Chief Mage and Magistrate Arcala wore over dove-gray leggings and tall black boots. His very long cloak was as black as Hanse's working clothes, but again, fine; lined with deep red.

The master mage of Firaqa wore no weapons, not even an eating dagger. Only a thin staff or rod, white and about a foot and a half long, was tucked through his loose belt of soft white leather. That loop in the belt had been made there, Hanse saw, for the round-tipped rod. It did not resemble a weapon.

His large eyes were intensely blue and looked right at Hanse, almost as if into him.

"Hanse! What*ever* are you doing in here?"

"Someone framed me," Hanse said, "and if you say 'That's what they all say' I swear to come back and haunt you after they hang me."

Arcala neither smiled nor looked affronted. "I was not thinking any such thing, and would not, when you are concerned. Besides, we don't hang murderers in this city."

"That," Hanse said drily, "is encouraging. What does happen to them, then?"

"Impaling them in front of the Temple so they're a while dying has proven the best deterrent to murder here," Arcala said. "But that has nothing to do with you, surely. Tell me what happened."

Shocked by the penalty but now considerably cheered because his mind needed to be, Hanse stated his case, accompanied by a subtle reminder that Arcala owed him.

Arcala made a gesture. "I am not *ruler* of Firaqa, Hanse, and can't just order you freed. I can and will *strongly suggest,* though, that the Reds send Malisandis over to that apartment."

Hanse was not cheered. "Who's Malisandis?"

"Police work in a citystate that is, uh, governed by mages is a little different from elsewhere," the mage told him. "People may leave no tracks or odors but they do leave *prints* behind, Hanse; the prints of their auras. Malisandis is the mage assigned to the Watch, on retainer. Here in Firaqa many crimes are solved with his aid—providing they weren't committed out in the open air. Auras do dissipate as rapidly as odors."

Hanse was unthrilled to be told of more sorcery. Somehow it was worse when it helped him; it was demeaning. He said one word, low-voiced:

"oh."

Arcala smiled. He well knew this very youthful-looking

man's impatience. "For you, Hanse, I will see to it that Malisandis goes *at once* to the apartment where that poor woman was murdered. Do please be patient, Hanse," he said, and broke off when Hanse shot him a look like a glancing blow.

Arcala made a gesture that was almost pleading. "Please, Hanse. Malisandis is the best."

"I thought you were."

"At what he does, I mean."

"oh."

Uncomfortable despite his power, Arcala turned to go.

"Arcala, wait. I need another kind of help—I'm hungry enough to eat the Temple!"

The mage turned back. He nodded.

"If cheese and bread will do, I'll have some sent."

Contrary to the opinions of some, Hanse did possess some virtues. He would have been among the first, however, to admit that patience was not one of them. Counseled to be patient while Firaqa's forensic mage did his work, he sat in his cell, brooding. Singlas came with food and Hanse ate, brooding. After a time he rose to pace, brooding. Thoughts like furtive shadows scurried willy-nilly through his head. He thought, considered, reflected, cudgeled the memory and resourcefulness of his good brain. And he brooded.

Someone had killed Jemise and someone had notified the police—knowing that he would be there to be caught supposedly bloody-handed? Someone, hell—who could it have been but Cathamarca and/or Yole. And if Yole, it didn't matter and was not an action of him alone; he was Cathamarca's man.

Why had they killed her?

Because she had found out something they couldn't allow her to continue to know? That would be something incriminating about something; something that made them unsafe. Unsafe from whom? The Reds? The law-upholders of some other city; Suma, maybe? Unsafe from the man they had a bargain with; Hanse?

Me? What would I be likely to—oh.

Maybe whatever she had learned, if she had learned anything, would not have made *them* unsafe, but their business arrangement with Shadowspawn the thief. Something that would have angered or affrighted him, provoked him to abort the agreement. That would be costly to them and they could not allow it to happen—not knowing, of course, that the agreement was already aborted, and had been the moment he discovered that he had been tricked. Long before he found the rings (found? Well, in fairness, long before the Eye had led him to them, then) Shadowspawn had decided that the very last person in the world he would give the sorcerous rings to was Cathamarca.

Maybe that was the explanation and maybe it wasn't. Maybe they were criminals, plain and simple, and wanted for all sorts of bad things here or somewhere else or both or all, and somehow Jemise had learned that and been stupid enough to confront them with her knowledge, and . . .

But why do it so horribly, so messily?

Because they had *enjoyed* doing all those ghastly things to her?—to giving her such pain over such a long period of time? That thought gave Hanse the tickling sensation as hairs moved on his arms. They had certainly been in no hurry in their gory work of paring off her earlobes and one of her nipples and four digits, no two side by side and therefore not at once . . . not even to mention slitting her tongue and nostrils and perpetrating that lower-body mutilation too horrible to contemplate or mention but that made the sensuously appealing young woman look as if she had birthed a fifty-pound mountain cat, and done it alone and unattended at that.

Hanse's stomach made noises and writhed restlessly. He swallowed, several times, but a little hot fluid came right up his throat and into his mouth just the same. Staring at nothing, trying to think, he swallowed it back. It was his; let it stay down there where it belonged.

Wait a minute. Maybe it wasn't that she had found out something, but that they wanted some kind of information from her. In other words maybe they had been slowly and systematically torturing her for the time-dishonored reason of getting her to talk, to admit or confess something.

What?

"Something about me," the incarcerated Shadowspawn heard himself mutter.

Suddenly he was staring at nothing, head cocked, eyes narrowed. A smile flirted with the edges of his mouth.

Then he was in action, calling the warder, discovering that it was a different man, meaning he had been here long enough for a change of shift among the guards. Hanse held up a coin as he requested good beer, and while the Red's eyes followed the twinkling coin Hanse neatly snitched the man's purse from his belt.

"Sure," said the lanky fellow with the nice face, and went for some beer.

Hanse watched him out of sight before he extracted a broken cloak-clasp from the purloined purse.

"Nice of him to keep this worthless thing," he muttered, and went swiftly to work making it useful. He was picking the lock on his cell door when he heard the familiar voice from behind him.

"Greetings and transmutations."

He turned slowly to face the speaker, except that technically he could not face the faceless; it was the Wandering Eye that stared at him through the bars of the window. It was floating just outside his prison, Hanse realized, and he considered the considerable benefits of being able to float.

"Easier just to come out this way," the big green orb assured him. "You do climb well, I remember."

"Greetings yourself," Hanse said, but he really hadn't time for petulance, which was the Wandering Eye's specialty anyhow. "Those bars may not stop you, but they're too close together for me to squeeze between and I sure can't break them!"

"Yes you can. Wisdom is the ability to believe only what you have to."

Hanse managed not to roll his eyes. "oh. What am I supposed to believe?"

"That you can get through these bars, and quickly. Bring that sack of water over here and slosh it on these two."

The Eye pressed in so that it indicated the designated bars by being mostly between them.

Hanse stared, sighed. "Water. On the bars."

"Right."

Hanse sighed, stared. "I think I'm not going to like this."

The Eye replied with irrefutable logic: "You're going to like being out of there, aren't you?"

Hanse heaved a new sigh, and went to the corner of his cell for the sack of water. Feeling silly, he used it as he had been instructed. And while he watched, smoke or steam began to rise from the water-sloshed bars.

"That's uh, not illusion," the Eye pointed out.

"Thanks."

"In which case I suggest you cover your hands with the bedclothes, Hanse. And come on out of there."

Blinking in surprise and more, Hanse swathed his hands in the coverlet from the skungy little bed provided for denizens of this skungy little cell, and laid hold of the bars of black iron. Tentatively, feeling silly, he exerted a little pressure. His mouth dropped open when iron bars yielded! He applied himself, feeling the heat. He grunted with some effort . . . but relatively easily, the bars bent away from each other as if they were made of unalloyed copper rather than iron.

"Aha!" the Eye said, dancing in air. "Come right on out of there, Hanse!"

Instead Hanse hurried back to throw the guard's purse

well up the corridor so that the man would think he dropped it. And Shadowspawn went out the window, with only a small "ow" when his elbow touched one still-hot bar. Rather than jumping or descending as anyone else bent on escape certainly would have done, he climbed.

The Wandering Eye floated up beside him, just at his shoulder.

"Thanks, Eye," Shadowspawn said, as he made his way up the wall with less effort than it had required to bend iron bars made both hot and soft by—by that which Hanse hated.

"Pleasure," the Eye said equably. "We're friends, after all."

"I suppose there's something to be said for sorcery after all . . . sometimes . . ."

"Actually it was alchemy," the Eye told him, "but never mind."

"Oh," Hanse said, wondering what alchemy was, "well then."

Shadowspawn the consummate roach easily reached the roof of Watch headquarters, and went up its tiles as easily as a cat. The Eye soared right along with him, riding the air.

"You seem to have had a lot of practice climbing walls and walking on rooftops," it observed, in that same equable, conversational tone.

"Uh . . . yes."

Only when the much-practiced wall-climber and roof-walker was three roofs away did he descend—into an alley. He dropped into it with a lightness to make a cat envious and straightened just as swiftly and sinuously in the dimness. Again the hint of the shadow of the ghost of a smile just touched his lips. He was free, with knowledge that his impatience—and the Wandering Eye!—had made him a fugitive.

"The trouble is," he muttered to his rescuer from durance vile, "I thought of something and didn't feel like waiting for Arcala and Malawhatever. It would be so *demeaning* to be freed on the words of two—'' he paused to spit—*''sorcerers!''*

The Eye said: ''Hmp.''

''Eye . . . how is it that I was down there in that maze for over a day and a night's worth of hours, and I wasn't all *that* hungry or even sleepy?''

''I'm not privy to a dead monster's spells and elixirs,'' his floating companion said with asperity, ''but it must be another effect of that elixir you drank . . . the healing stuff.''

''oh.''

Shadowspawn skulked his way to the Bored Gryphon, accompanied by a floating manifestation that kept having to duck away to avoid being seen by others, but there Hanse entered boldly on the assumption that word of his escape could not have gotten here before him. The closely-planked floor was clean except for grease spots that were here for the long haul, and the place had no patrons.

The same well-fed innkeeper looked up from his mopping.

''Ah, Hansis from down south, ain't it?'' The fat man's face broadened in a smile. ''Good to see ya again. I'm Gulapherolias, but everybody calls me Smoky.''

With a name like that, I can understand why! ''Uh, all right, Smoky.''

''Something for ye today?''

''This afternoon,'' Hanse said, ''I made a certain arrangement with one of your regulars—Darry. Now I need to—''

Smoky beamed. ''Ole Darry'll likely do what he says,'' he said, pouncing despite his weight to the conclusion that this young fellow wanted reassurance and/or recommendation. ''Just, uh, you know . . .'' Smoky lowered his voice and put on a confidential face that made him look more ludicrously dolorous than conspiratorial. ''Just don't pay him till your business is did. Otherwise he'll be in here. Ole

Darry does think his mission in life is reducing Firaqa's beer surplus."

Hanse nodded. "Thanks, Smoky. The trouble is I need to see him tonight. I mean, the trouble is I don't even know his real name or where he lives."

"His name's Darnarislas." The innkeeper twisted around to gaze at a water clock. "He has a room over on Cameltrack Way, but he'll be here in a few drips of that clock. You can put money on that."

"Oh. Well. Thanks, Smoky. I can't wait right now, but I'll be back."

"Glad to have you, Hansis! Come on back and have one!"

19

IT WAS SHADOWSPAWN who lurked outside the Bored Gryphon in waning sunlight, waiting for the advent of the smallish fellow with sadly thinned hair and a tunic that looked old enough to have been inherited from his grandfather. He passed the alley and a black-clad arm appeared from nowhere to wrap an arm around his throat from behind.

Thus Darnarislas did not pass the alley at all, but was yanked backward into it, heels skidding on edge.

"Be loose now, Darry," a voice murmured, close to the trembling man's ear. "I'm no enemy and don't mean to hurt you a bit. I just need your help. Listen while I remind you of something you said the other night, after all the excitement when the Reds and that rich foreigner and his man were here: you said it seemed to you that one of those Meditonese mercenaries said they'd got some work."

Darry said "Gl-gl-gl-l-l."

"Oh." Shadowspawn was kind enough to loosen his arm. He felt the thin-haired man's adam's apple move in a hard swallow.

"Maybe I was wrong," Darry whispered. "I'd had a mug or two . . ."

"Or ten!" Hanse snapped, and reached his other hand around to show the fellow a smallish but twinkingly sharp dagger.

Darry's memory returned in an instant. "Oh, yes, uh-huh,

sure, right, yes sir, I was just about t' tell you. I'm sure they was talkin', joken really, about bein' on the side of the law—they had plenty of coin, good coin, because they had been hired by a mage, as bodyguard or escort or somethen like that.''

Hanse considered that, thinking, nodding. *Plenty of coin, hmm?* Then: "What's that have to do with the law? Oh, you mean because they were to be somebody's sort-of personal police?''

Darry tried to nod, found that the arm around his neck wasn't *that* loose, and gave it up. "That, but also because they'd just been hired by the Reds' tame mage, that Malisandis fellow.''

Hanse stared at nothing over the other man's half-hairless head, pondering the information.

And he paid them plenty of money in advance? Why?

To kill someone?

Why would they attack Cathamarca to rob him when they had plenty of money . . . unless they had plenty of money because they'd been paid to attack Cathamarca not to rob but to kill him?

"Thanks, Darry. Sorry I was so rough, but I'll stand you to a mug.''

"Sounds good to me,'' Darnarislas said, happy not to have been murdered and still without having seen his accoster/benefactor. "No offense took,'' he added, with the prospect of a free mug hanging before his eyes like a vision.

Hanse *aided* him to emerge from the alley only to find several waiting Reds. Every eye was staring at him.

At least this time none of the grabbers was aiming a crossbow quarrel at him. They were led by a pleasant-looking sergeant with sun-lines etched into his young face. His pale eyes stared into the dark ones of Hanse, but they looked weary, rather than laden with menace or malice.

"Hello, Gaise,'' Hanse said, to his first and probably best Firaqi friend.

The sergeant attacked with his mouth at once:

"Damn it all, Hanse, you and your impatience! All you needed to do was be a *little* patient for a few minutes more and we could have been saved two perfectly good bars—well, not perfect but they *were* perfectly good, and now . . ."

Seeing that he was not to be arrested again, Hanse chuckled.

When his arm relaxed, Darry twisted round. "Oh. It's Hansis." He turned back to face the police. "Me an' Hansis here was just about to have a mug or two . . ."

Everyone ignored him.

"I'm sorry, Gaise," Hanse said. "I didn't mean to escape. I mean I didn't intend to. It just kind of came over me when I thought of something that needed fast attention, and . . ." Hanse spread his hands, trying hard to look young and ingenuous. He had been doing it for years. It would serve him a while longer.

"Well, we won't impale you this time," Gaise told him, without smiling. "But damn it, Malisandis is already back from that room where Tiv and his boys arrested you. To our expert practitioner it's obvious that poor girl suffered the attack of two men, two who stayed there long enough to imprint the rooms with their auras. Neither of the two is a Firaqi, but neither of them is you."

Hanse affected his wide-eyed boyish look. "I knew that."

"Uh. Well, you're clear. Here, Neth, hand Hanse his weapons."

Hanse stared into Neth's eyes as the Red proffered a good-sized cloth bag that clinked interestingly. Neth looked down. Hanse accepted the sack, which was not light.

Sergeant Gaise raised his eyebrows and both hands. "That's, ahh, quite a plenitude of sharp steel," he said.

Hanse considered it wise to make no comment.

As he was strapping on his knives he said, "Hmm. I suppose there's something to be said for sorcery after all . . . sometimes . . ."

"Sorcery?"

"I mean Malisandis's evidence."

Gaise nodded. "Oh. Sometimes I forget. I mean I take it for granted. It's just a part of police work."

"Only here in Firaqa, Gaise, believe me!"

He shifted his shagreen belt, situating sword and Ilbarsi knife, noticing how passersby were giving the clot of grabbers a wide berth and never considering that they might be rather leery of the wiry young man with all the sharpened steel. He motioned Gaise aside.

The sergeant maintained his large-eyed, open-faced demeanor while they stepped away from the others and against a pocked building wall that was not, oddly enough, pink.

"Would you like me to tell you who it is you want for that murder?"

"No need to," the sergeant said. "Two Sumese named Cathamarca and Yole. It was after all their suite. I've had men looking for those two ever since I heard about the body being found, but they've done a good job of disappearing. Nowhere to be found. No one on duty at the gates remembers two such men riding out of the city, either. My boys are spreading the word, seeking them."

"I would wager good coin that they haven't left Firaqa and won't be leaving, Gaise. Not just yet."

Gaise put his head on one side. "Should I ask questions about that cryptic remark?"

"Not if you expect an answer."

"Understand, Hanse," Gaise said, giving him a straight-on look of utmost seriousness, "we're not raving happy with you. If anyone but the man who saved Firaqa from Corstic had damaged city property the way you did our jail, *and* fled detention, he would be in a lot of trouble."

"I understand, and I really am sorry. I'm pretty shaken, Gaise. A few nights ago I was with a woman we'd just met and a man I'd traveled across the desert with. A big, likable fellow and a fighter, and he was killed in minutes. I met two others and even saved them from thieves bent on murder, and those two tricked me and almost got me killed and did kill the woman and have vanished. I don't like the way people I meet get dead.''

And what if I told you what else has happened to me since then!

Gaise's big uniformed chest moved in a sigh. ''Death does seem to follow you around, Hanse. But somehow she misses *you*.''

''Oh, she's tried more than a time or two, believe me.''

Gaise looked straight into his eyes, which had never been blue. ''Oh, you know I believe anything you tell me, Hanse.''

''Uh-huh.''

They ambled back to rejoin the others. Hanse noticed that Neth looked nervous as a rabbit in a stone courtyard full of dogs, and realized that the overzealous grabber undoubtedly thought he had been the subject of the private conversation. Hanse smiled to himself, deciding to let the swift-fisted and slow-brained pride of the Reds stew in his own bigotry.

Another of Gaise's men expressed a desire to know how Hanse ''did that business with those bars.''

''I'm really sorry,'' Hanse told them all, ''but I'm in a terrible hurry. Got held up not to mention roughed up in a false arrest, you know. Interfered with my schedule. So sorry. Maybe I'll explain tomorrow . . .''

''Uh . . . Hansis . . .''

Hanse stared. ''What . . . is . . . it . . . Neth?''

''I'm uh, I . . .''

''You remind me of a bird, Neth, you know that?'' Having delivered himself of that cryptic line, Hanse paused dramatically while everyone gave him full attention, with expectant faces. ''You eat shit, Neth.''

He was making dramatic departure on that note, amid laughter and someone's jovial ''He sure knows you, Neth!'' when a hand caught his sleeve. Hanse was on the

point of coming around to put Neth away for a few weeks
when he saw that the plucker was not the grabber but Darry,
and stayed his hand.

"Uh . . . about that mug you mentioned . . ."

Hanse passed over a coin, added another. "Have two,
Darry. And keep those good eyes open. You're more
observant than most grabbers I've ever met."

"He's met plenty, too," Gaise called, and he and Hanse
exchanged a look, and broke up in laughter.

He was walking away on his business when he heard
Smoky come out to complain that the presence of so many
Reds was keeping his place empty.

". . . except for Darry, of course."

As he was hurrying along Acacia Street, Hanse twitched
at the sound of a familiar voice three or so inches from his
left shoulder.

"Greetings and salivations!"

"Wah!"

"What a clever response! You going back to Corstic's?"
the Wandering Eye asked casually.

"Damn it, Eye," Hanse said, refusing to glance at it,
"it's you who should be called Shadowspawn! You keep
sneaking up on me! And how about moving around on my
other side?"

"No problem." After a brief pause, the voice spoke from
some three inches right of Hanse's right shoulder. "Why?"

"Because I'm left handed."

"Oh. I'd not even noticed! You'd think a Wandering Eye
would be more observant, wouldn't you!"

"I would. By the way—how is it you keep disappearing
and others don't see you?"

"Easy," the voice told him, in that same casual voice. "I
blink."

This time Hanse could not help it: he jerked his head to
the side to stare into that big, green, floating orb with the big

black spot in the center. At its present proximity it looked positively enormous.

"*What?*"

The Eye bobbed its mirth, or delight, or happiness, or something. "Watch."

Hanse could only arrest his forward motion and stare as a lid came slowly down over the enormous eyeball, in a blink. The effect was that of lowering a thick drape at a lighted window: the Eye simply was not there. It proved the secret of its invisibility by "reappearing" directly in front of him.

"I'll be damned."

"I think we've covered that," the Eye observed. "Are you going back to Corstic's?"

"Yes, because now I've got to be worried about Notable. But—"

"Notable? You make it sound like a name."

"It is."

"Odd."

"Look who's talking!"

The Eye bobbed a little, proving that it had the wisdom to take a joke. "Who is this Notable?"

"My cat."

The Eye shot straight up a couple of feet and executed some unpleasant swoops. "Oh. A cat. Yukh. You didn't tell me you were a cat-person."

"I'm not a *cat-person.* I have a friend who is a cat. He is my very good friend," Hanse added, to preclude any further rude comments on Notable or catdom in general. "When Notable is around, just stay high, Eye. *Realll* high up. That cat is quite the jumper and he can climb almost anything."

"I will remember," the Eye said, with asperity and no pleasure.

"Anyhow, right now I need to see Arcala."

The Eye wandered back over to his right and settled onto his shoulder. Hanse sagged on that side and twitched violently.

"I had no idea you were so heavy! How is that possible?"

"Oh, sorry." And immediately the Eye became lighter.

Hanse sighed. "I wouldn't think that would be possible," he said, and his tone was almost plaintive.

"What?" the Eye asked in an equable tone.

"You were heavy but you suddenly got lighter. Doesn't seem possible. I mean, you're floating in the middle of the air."

"Not quite the middle," the Eye informed him. "That's higher up. As for not seeming possible . . . well, it happened. I can adjust my weight. Are we going to start that impossible business again?"

And suddenly its weight increased. Hanse flinched away, lowering his shoulder. "Stop that!"

The Eye's weight lessened. "Just to let you know that it is possible," it said airily, in a conversational tone.

Shadowspawn kept walking. "I will *not* ask."

A street away, he did think to ask at last whether his companion had a name, or would perhaps like one.

"You find something wrong with calling me Eye?"

"No no," Hanse assured it. "Just asking."

"Good, good! Wisdom is knowing when to shut your face."

At least I have one, Hanse thought sullenly.

The Eye elected not to accompany its new friend in to visit Arcala, and either blinked or wandered; after stepping aside with assumed respect to allow free passage to a pair of the severely attired not-quite priestesses called Hearthkeepers, Hanse glanced around to discover that he was alone. He turned completely around, attracting attention as he did not like to do. The Eye was gone.

Shaking his head, Hanse went on. It did occur to him to wonder about Mignureal, who might have wondered about him or even worried. He was mildly sorry about that, but he had always been a loner and this was important.

20

WHERE HANSE CAME from the city was ridden by arrogant Rankan conquerors and the not-quite-human Beysib who claimed not to be conquerors. But Sanctuary was only *afflicted* with sorcery and its practitioners. Thus it was strange to him that a practicing mage had an office in Firaqa's City Building. But so his friend Arcala had, and a nice office it was, too. Pacing in on a heavy, thick carpet of wool in a complicated multicolor design, Hanse said nothing, not even a greeting. He merely walked to the man by the window and handed Arcala the two rings from Corstic's subterrene hidey-hole.

He watched Arcala examine them. Oddly again, Firaqa's Chief Mage was very plainly dressed. His long white tunic topped white leggings tucked into short tan buskins of soft leather. The medallion slung on a chain around his neck and pendant on his chest was his only decoration. And it was not that; the stylized symbol done in gold proclaimed him Chief Magistrate and thus, his disclaimers to the contrary, the city's first citizen, if not quite its ruler.

Hanse had decided not to take the mage to the tree where he had hidden the rest of the stuff from Corstic's trove, or to mention what he had learned about those four Med mercs—and Malisandis.

Arcala half-closed his hand on the rings, moving the hand up and down a little as if he were weighing the baubles. His eyes were very mild when he looked at Hanse.

179

"Are these a present?"

"I'm afraid not," Hanse said, but his face did not reflect the smile that seemed to ride his voice and lighten the words. "I'm asking you to study them and let me know what they are. What they do."

"You do know they're sorcerous, then."

Hanse nodded.

"I know a few things about these rings without, uh, studying them," Arcala told him. He was staring down at the two collections of glitter on his palm. "This one is ancient and I always thought Corstic had it; it makes the wearer almost impossible to refuse."

Hanse blinked at such a concept, which he immediately interpreted as a prospect. "Really! Nice!"

Arcala gave him a look. "For one who wants supreme power, yes. I don't, and I don't want anyone else to have it, either. First I'll set about removing the spell; the ring's power. If it proves too resistant, I'll destroy it."

He did not ask permission; he merely stated what he would do. Had he been anyone else than Arcala, Hanse would have demurred, objected, or worse. Instead he said only, "Terrible waste . . ." in a murmur, gazing at the ring and thinking unworthy thoughts.

Arcala chuckled. "This one, Hanse . . . this other pretty thing is an old, old Nisi horror. It provides power over death."

"You mean like bringing back or keeping alive a man with a tree limb right through him?"

The memory flooded in at once as a picture behind his eyes. It was vivid, a ghastliness that would never, never leave a cupboard of unwillingly stored ugliness in his brain: *The thigh-thick branch cracked loudly amid leafy sounds as of a tree in a high wind. With only a glance up Shadowspawn was somehow able to croak "haiya!" as the branch broke off and came hurtling down at him with a leafy rush. Impaled and swinging hideously from the downrushing bough was Thuvarandis, transpierced by the largest spear imaginable. And yet the man, horribly, monstrously, was not dead. His wound was awful. His eyes were worse.*

And later, inside the manse:

Corstic impelled *Shadowspawn* to walk over to the table, an armless prisoner in his own body. He stared down at the victim strapped there, and shuddered in a mingling of horror and outrage. A closed fist could have gone into the gory hole in this pitiful man's middle. Illusory or no, the tree branch had done that, and Hanse had seen it, for this was Thuvarandis. The transpiercing branch could not, however, account for the fact that the long-legged man had also been emasculated. And still Thuvarandis breathed.

Gooseflesh tickled Hanse's arms now, and as if from a distance he saw Arcala nod, heard Arcala's voice:

"Exactly. You've experienced its power, yes. I vow not to use it, but . . . to destroy it will be difficult. Unless you want—"

Hanse back-paced two steps and held his hands up before him as if in a ward-sign. "No no. I have no use for it!"

Arcala gazed very seriously into his eyes. "Good." After a moment he looked again at the rings he held, and twisted his lips in thought. "You found these in that warren beneath Corstic's house."

Hanse merely nodded.

Arcala tipped his head a little to one side. "What exceptional bravery it took to go down there."

"True. But I was tricked into it."

The mage in white gave him a friendly grin that went not at all with his office and its badge, aglitter on his chest. "Well said. You're showing signs of positive honesty, my friend."

"I'll try not to make it a habit, my friend who so likes my woman."

Hanse was startled to hear his own words; he hadn't intended to say that about Arcala and Mignureal. It had been there in his mind, waiting, and when opportunity came, the words slipped out.

Arcala's smile vanished but he didn't look angry; he looked uncomfortable. "Is she, Hanse? Pardon me, but . . . I know how far you two journeyed together, and what you've been through together. Partly because of that and . . . partly for . . . other reasons, there is strain between you. Is she still your woman? Are you still her man? Or did two large children leave Sanctuary and come up here and become two horror-assaulted adults who, with more maturity, are not as crazy about each other as they had thought?"

Hanse stared. His mouth worked; he closed it firmly only with a deliberate conscious thought. Did this man see these things because of his powers beyond the norm, or was he so wise?

"Hanse . . ." Arcala said quietly, maintaining careful, full eye-contact, "no matter what you think about my interest in Mignureal—she's years younger, you know—I am sorry for you both because I like you both."

Wearing an uncomfortable look, Hanse glanced away. Arcala watched his chest swell and slowly relax in a sigh. Be honest, Hanse was telling himself. He is a friend. Tell him. Say it.

"I . . . we've been through a lot together, Mignue and me."

He paused there, but Arcala, more than other men, knew that something was coming out and it was a difficult birth, and was wise enough to keep his "I know" to himself; to keep his mouth shut and his eyes open.

"I . . . still like her extra much . . . and always will," Hanse said quietly, and broke off. He was hoping that Arcala would speak. Unfortunately Arcala knew that. A very long minute passed before Hanse went on, in an even lower voice:

"But things we've said and done since we came here . . . and thought, yes, I'm sure she's had these thoughts, too. . . . She was infatuated with a romantic figure, down in Sanctuary, when she was just a girl peeping out at me around her mother's skirts. Her mother was very . . . big," he said, in helpless digression amid pain. "Her name was Moonflower and she and I liked each other. Really liked each other. Then a monst—then someone killed her, and I killed the killer, and had to leave Sanctuary. Mignue needed no coaxing to come with me. Since then . . . since then . . . we have been through a lot together," he said lamely, knowing in his pain that he was repeating himself but not finding other words to say what he wanted to say/did not want to say.

And Arcala waited, letting him say it, obviously determined not to speak.

I had to go and bring it up, Hanse thought, in agony.

He made the effort, struggling to say the words, quietly and hesitantly: "Now . . . now I know we . . . we certainly are not meant for each other and our, uh, deeper relationship is . . . beyond just, uh, in trouble."

"I know."

Arcala spoke just as quietly in a voice full of friendship and sympathy and support, but the truth was that he was not really sorry about the difficulties between this troubled, youthful man and Mignureal. How his children loved her and looked forward to seeing her! How she obviously loved them; how good she was with them!

"Anyhow," Hanse said, and forced himself to look into the other man's eyes, "I thought I would, and I would have a while ago, but now . . . whatever you do . . . I don't hold it against you, Arcala."

The white fabric stirred and rippled across Arcala's chest as he heaved a large, long, and quiet sigh. "Now you've touched me deep. I have to tell you that you have nothing to hold against me. Just as I'll tell you that if you two break for good and all, I will try to . . . hold her against me."

Hanse almost smiled.

After a long moment both of them wanted to be somewhere else, and both did the next best thing: they looked somewhere else. Silence made the room seem smaller; after a long minute or so Hanse felt that he could put out his hand and feel the silence.

He was grateful that Arcala was able to break it, and that the subject was dropped.

"There should have been a third ring, Hanse," the mage announced in a new, more official voice. "The Ring of Illusion. I'm sure Corstic had it. A mage could control the images it created, and if he was armed with the counter-stone, those images did not affect him."

"Really?" Hanse turned back to him and forced his eyes wide in an ingenuous expression. "Not this?" He showed Arcala a triangle strung on a piece of rawhide. The amulet was made of pieces of tortoise shell, in various colors. Its border appeared to be gold. He ducked his head to take it off, handed it to the mage.

Arcala closed his hand around it, the dull thong dangling, and soon closed his eyes as well. The man appeared to be thinking. Hanse knew that was not quite all of it, and he said nothing. He knew when a mage was probing, Seeing. It was a good time for keeping mouths shut.

At last Arcala shook his head and opened his hand to peer at the amulet.

"No. This is nowhere near so strong as the Ring of Illusion. Hmm . . . interesting. Its aura tells me that Strick created it to try to fight Corstic. Poor Strick! You know him, Hanse?"

"Strick." Brief vision of a big weapon-man with a big yellow moustache that drooped like the wings of an ex-hausted bird. "Not really. Mignue and I met him on the way up here. He gave us that amulet. Gave it to her, really. So that's not it? So what d'you mean, 'counterstone'?"

Arcala shrugged and shook his head. He looked uncom-fortable again; frustrated, more likely. "I never knew what it was. Never heard or read a description. A stone of some kind. It could be anything. An amulet such as that one, or a gemstone—any gemstone—or even a common rock."

Hanse could only stare at him and try to mask his expression. *Or a little white pebble?*

21

THUVARANDIS HAD BEEN the next to the last name on the sorcerous list of Corstic's. All the men who had so willingly participated in the monster's ghastly punishment of his wife and his young apprentice were dead, save one. According to the last message of the cat that had been Corstic's wife, that man was somewhere in Sanctuary. Until he was dead the last of the ensorceled coins would not disappear for good and all. Hanse had another reason for finding that man, too, whatever name he now bore. Corstic's assistant, who had given solace to the mage's much-abused wife, was neither a man nor dead. He was a cat. His name was Notable. Perhaps Hanse thought by finding that last man—and seeing him dead—he could help Notable back to humanity.

And perhaps back in that secret place in his mind where he kept things he knew but did not like or want to know, he knew that was futile, not possible . . . but Shadowspawn wanted vengeance.

At any rate he wanted to be on his way back down to Sanctuary as he had planned coming on two months ago—and away from this city, and its memories. Still, he would delay the trek a little longer because he thought he must. He was also determined to confront and, he sincerely hoped, to punish Cathamarca and Yole. Accordingly when he left Arcala he headed for the apartment he shared—had shared—with Mignue and Notable. Along the way he

185

bought a pear, and ate it as he walked. It was not a good pear. It crunched.

Neither woman nor cat was there. Obviously neither had been here. Hanse was not happy about that, but he was not worried about Mignureal; she would be with Quill and Turquoise over in the Bazaar.

Notable was another matter. Name of Ils, could the cat be still there on the hill, in Corstic's manse and waiting for Hanse's emergence from behind that iron door? Twenty minutes later he had put still another coin into the dirty hand of the stable boy and was swinging aboard Ironmouth and heading once again for the city's North Gate.

He made two stops: he bought a pint bucket of beer and small loaf of bread, and a little farther along the street found a vendor happy to sell him a cooked, smoked tongue of beef. Hanse watched the severely balding man slice it in two about a third of the way along its length. He paid, muttered something in response to the pure-politeness comment about the possibility of rain, and slid the small piece into the beer. He chewed at the larger piece of tongue as he rode, at the plod. He was headed again for Corstic's manse, this time in quest of Notable, and fearful of what he might find.

Along the way he was rejoined by his sometime new companion.

"Greetings and transmigrations!"

The voice came from the air quite near his right ear, and somehow Hanse was only just able not to jump or turn and look into the single huge eye he knew he would see there. No one else talked so, and besides no one could be so tall. Hanse was not, but he sat astride Ironmouth, and the Tejana horse was tall.

"You certainly spoke true," Hanse muttered in manner surly and accusative. "I do indeed have a *wandering* Eye. How interesting, the way it *wanders* off when police are about!"

The voice came right back, snappishly: "You, ah, think

those men of the Watch would have taken the word of a large disembodied *Eye,* Hanse? Grow up!''

A frown brought Hanse's brows down like hawks on chickens, but as he thought about the words, he could not help a little smile that slowly broadened into a grin.

The Eye disappeared at the gate but joined him a short time later, presumably having chosen to sail over the wall at an area where it was not likely to be seen. They met a trundling old wagon coming off the hill behind a weary and too-thin old horse, but when Hanse thought to shoot a rightward glance, the Eye was not there. And then the wagon was past, and it was.

''You didn't want to be seen so you . . . blinked?''

''I blinked.''

The three of them plodded, rode, and floated in silence for a minute or so. Up the long tree-lined hill.

''We aren't going back to that hellish hole of Corstic's, are we?''

''I am,'' Hanse said equably. ''You're more than welcome to come along.''

''Why?''

''Well, just to keep me company, if nothing else.''

''No, I mean why *ever* are you going back?''

''Cathamarca and Yole are missing. Maybe they know I was arrested the way they planned and maybe they don't. Maybe they know I'm out and maybe they don't. I like to help out people who don't know things.''

Hanse-like, the Eye said, ''Uh-huh.''

''I think maybe they're up here,'' Hanse went on, as if he hadn't heard the satire. ''Besides, I'm worried about my cat.''

''Your *cat!*''

''It's been nearly two days since I went into the warren, Eye. I'm afraid that cat may have been waiting for me all that time.''

''I think you have that beast mixed up with a dog, Hanse.

Dogs are loyal. Let a dog's human die in a closed house and his faithful dog will stay right there and mourn him. Its howls will probably bring people. Put a cat in the same circumstances and soon it's hungry and angry that its human isn't feeding it and soon it's eating its dead human.''

Hanse made a face. He sighed. ''I understand that you don't like cats, Eye. I never did either, until Notable. But Notable and I are friends. Notable would starve before he'd eat me—no, he'd probably just tear his way through a wall to go get help, and food as an afterthought.''

''That,'' the Wandering Eye said, ''is ridiculous.''

''Whoa. Easy there, Ironmouth. Oh Stop, damn it!'' The horse did, eventually and only as if it were his own idea, and Hanse turned to look into the Eye floating a foot and a half or so to his right. ''You and I have been through a thing together and I thought we were friends, Eye. I have told you that Notable and I are friends. Now I want you to stop talking ill of him—and of cats in general, when I'm around.''

The Eye waggled in air. ''Hmp! You didn't talk so mean when you had to depend on me to get out of that warren!''

''And you were a lot friendlier. But stop it about cats and Notable, or we've had a short friendship.'' Hanse held the eye contact for a long moment before turning away to face front again. ''Let's go, Ironmouth.''

Hanse did not glance to either side as the big horse plodded up the hill, obviously ready and more than willing to try it at the gallop. Whether the Eye was there or had gone off in one of its miffs, Hanse did not presently want to know and wasn't sure that he cared.

Then, after several minutes, he had his answer, when the voice came once again:

''I'm impressed. You're right. Friendship means avoiding hurting your friend. And wisdom is knowing when to refuse to take any more shit.''

*   *   *

An emphatically red cat of improbable size greeted Hanse's descent into Corstic's cellar with an emphatic and distinctly accusatory noise. Somehow the animal's eyes looked accusing, too. The hungry, thirsty Notable was right there waiting as Hanse had predicted, reproachful but obviously delighted to see his human—or mommy, as cats were said to think of those who fed them and who they marked with the scent-glands along their cheeks and tail.

Then big-bodied cat spotted disembodied eye. A strident *miaow* became a hissy noise as Notable bristled at the Thing floating in the air. When the outsized red cat bristled he became about twice as big as he was, which was large enough to frighten big dogs and bigger humans. The Eye, well up toward the ceiling, was indubitably impressed but seemed unfrightened. Animal stared at apparition, back up and tail jerking.

"This is Eye, Notable, a true friend. Eye, my friend Notable."

"Big one, too."

Notable kept right on staring. The Eye stared back.

"Sure is a big one, Hanse."

"Uh-huh. Thirsty and hungry, too." Hanse took the lid off the small pail he carried.

Suddenly the big one's nose twitched a few times and his arched back dropped. His emerald gaze swerved from the floating Thing to fix in a stare on the opened bucket. Notable's entire demeanor changed to one of loving cajolery. He went into action, banging his sinuous body constantly against his human's legs while Hanse poured beer into the large and extremely fine bowl of cobalt blue he had picked up from an equally costly table upstairs.

An aghast Eye made clear its disapproval: "I'd say that Corstic spent about the price of a good cow on that bowl, you know."

"Good!" Hanse said. "He sure doesn't mind how it's used now! Here's a bowl you deserve, Notable. Sorry I had

to leave you so long, but I've been in jail. Here you—
dammit, Notable, ease up! You'll spill the beer and me
too!''

He had to hold the bowl up while he squatted to restrain
the cat long enough to get the bowl full of shimmering
amber onto the floor with the other hand. That operation
was no simple one; Notable was large, heavy, and squirm-
ing like a sack of serpents. Released, he attacked the beer
like a man flopping into an oasis pool after a waterless day
on the desert.

The thirsty man, however, would not have made such an
improprietously loud rumbling noise.

Then Hanse plopped the piece of beef tongue into the
half-empty bowl, and the cat's purr rose to seismic propor-
tions.

''That sure is a big cat,'' the Eye said, staring.

Hanse straightened, looking pleasant, and turned his
attention to the iron barrier that had sealed him in Corstic's
maze. Within two minutes, bowl clean and dry and meat
vanished without a trace, Notable took time out from licking
his whiskers, both dripping and greased, to respond to this
and that question and gesture in a way that let Hanse know
that Cathamarca and Yole were on the other side of the
barrier.

''I'm impressed,'' the Wandering Eye admitted. ''That is
no stupid cat—which is normally a redundancy. Sure is
big!''

''Eye? You don't happen to have an idea how to raise this
thing, do you?''

''Not a clue. That sure is a big cat. And *beer*!''

''Uh-huh. Well uh, Eye . . . can you get past the
barrier?''

''Yes. By my way, meaning I can't take you.''

Hanse decided against asking what ''my way'' was. He
considered lots of things better left unknown. Anything
sorcerous was at the top of the list. ''Wel-l-l-l . . . would

you go in and have a look for the two men I told you about?''

The Eye would, but not without a parting shot. ''Wisdom,'' it threw back sarcastically, ''is knowing when to get someone else to go into danger for you.''

Someone? You mean some *thing,* Hanse thought, noting that from behind, the Eye was either invisible or as black as the interior of the tunnel. Then he plopped his little butt down on the floor to give Notable the attention he deserved and to receive plenty of rubbing in return. Rubbing the big red head with force, scratching hard in the way guaranteed to make Notable's eyes close as if he were in a trance, Hanse wondered just what would be too much roughness for this cat's head. An eagle's talons, maybe, or using one of his throwing stars as a brush . . .

After a while the Wandering Eye wandered back. Actually it just seemed to appear, its presence announced, as usual, by its voice:

''I found them. They are both well down in there, and they're lost.''

Hanse nodded grimly.

''Good for them. It sounds as if it's best that we go back in the way we came out, then.''

''We?''

''Notable and I. And you too I hope, friend.''

''The cat will slow us down, going down the hill.''

''Notable. His name is Notable, *Eye.* And no he won't. He rides.''

''Poor horse.''

Shadowspawn stopped at the tree to retrieve the rest of Corstic's trove. This time well-armed and carrying food and water, he, the Eye, and Notable reopened the concealed door and went back into the passage that led into the maze.

22

AGAIN, THERE WAS only dullness of gray stone walls without cobwebs and floor of hard-packed, almost dustless earth. Corstic had of course seen that the dullness of the physical surroundings did not lead to monotony. This time the deadfall involved an upside-down T of oiled wood that swept down from the ceiling like an enormous pendulum. The pole whizzed down the center of the passage, the crossbar at its bottom sweeping the entire width of the passage about a foot and a half above the floor. And it came down behind Shadowspawn and Notable, as they paced into the maze. The Eye saw it, and fortunately did not merely call out, but saved them with specific instructions:

"JUMP! HIGH!"

Notable turned crouching at the shout, saw what was coming, and shot two feet straight up. That was unnecessary; he was not in line with the center pole and the T's cross would have passed above him. Shadowspawn crouched but did not turn; he jumped, high. With a strong hiss as it broke the air, the crosspole rushed under him at the speed of Ironmouth's best gallop. Hanse felt the breeze of the center pole to his left.

Then he was on the floor again, in an alighting crouch, and muttered "Oh, shit!" and leaped again. The inverted T swept back, at reduced velocity now, impacted the ceiling only with a *thunk,* and latched. Man and cat stared at the thing as if intent on revenge.

"Thanks, Eye. *Good* warning! If you'd yelled 'Watch out!' or something I'd have turned, and I wouldn't be standing now or ever."

For once the Eye had no aphorism: "Thanks, Hanse. I'm glad you're all right. Quite a jumper, too."

That was the perfect remark to release the tension. Hanse laughed, squatted, and talked to Notable while he stroked him and rubbed his skull. With force, the way the big cat liked it. He decided that the danger was past and it was time to purr. Come to think, it was time to get his belly rubbed.

"Oh you damned cat," Hanse muttered, and succumbed to the invitation.

"That's disgusting," the Eye said. "That enormous animal, flat on its back with all four legs in the air—he looks like he wants to be mounted!"

Shadowspawn glanced up. "If you had legs and . . . so on, I'd invite you to just try mounting this cute li'l kitten!"

"Whether or not I had legs I wouldn't try that!" the Eye avowed, and began bobbing up and down. Hanse laughed too.

They went on, doing that which Hanse had never expected to do: re-entering Corstic's awful system of tunnels and stairways. A horizontally sweeping blade made Hanse dance and sent Notable scampering up a stone wall like a menaced kitten racing up a tree. Another time Hanse saw a section of floor give, ever so little, under Notable's feet and smiled. Walking carefully around it, he was sure he had avoided another trapdoor. The Eye warned of darts, too, and Hanse squatted to bang a scabbard on the floor in their path. A covey of darts coughed out of the wall to zip across the passage, strike the opposite wall, and clatter down.

But this time Shadowspawn was not wearing the illusion-creating ring, and this time no impossibilities menaced or attacked. He much preferred the real danger of real traps to sorcerous illusions, however physically harmless. Besides, the pain had been real, even though it came from illusion and left no wounds.

The unlikely trio mounted some steps and turned and descended some steps and came upon Cathamarca and Yole. Shadowspawn stopped a dozen or so paces from the two, whose backs were to him.

"Hello, *partners*," he said, with just a little sarcasm edging his voice like a stripe on a sleeve-hem.

Startled, both men whirled around amid a flapping of Cathamarca's cloak. "Thank all gods!" Yole gushed. "We've been lost down here forever and I don't mind admitting it and I'm sorry about any trouble we've had, Hansis."

"Actually it's been two days," said Cathamarca, who was still got up in blousy blue leggings under a full-sleeved white tunic, tucked in and surmounted by a long red jerkin with a line of cloth-of-gold closures down the front. Both men, naturally, wore daggers and swords.

"Two days, eh?" Hanse said drily.

"One thing I have," the count told him as if lecturing to a larger audience, "is an excellent sense of time. Just a bit beyond normal. You know, like your strange heightened abilities in . . . shadows."

"How did you get past the barrier?"

"Almost as soon as you were on its other side and I saw it could not be opened, I went straight up to Corstic's . . . workroom. I think you remember it?"

"I remember it." Hanse's tone was flat as a beggar's purse.

"There I found that which I expected," Cathamarca said in that sententious-pretentious way that not even his mother could love, if he had one. "Another way down here. Corstic's own secret escape route, you see: a passage and a series of ladders between the walls. The entry you used had wards on it, in addition to the barrier. Anyone pursuing him could have spent hours or even days getting past that iron barricade, only to discover the fear spell . . . and the fact that not one man in twenty could survive the . . . other wards there. You see, I knew I was not one of those men, and I was sure you were.''

"Interesting," Hanse said. "How could you be sure?"

"Well, reasonably sure," Cathamarca said, and flashed a smile, and hastened on: "But I found Corstic's route to be perfectly safe. What we had no idea of is the magnitude of this accursed maze! We assumed that we would come onto you in short order. But you know this; you've been here only a little longer than we ha—oh, wait. The cat! How can the cat have got in?''

"Maybe he dug his way in to be with me," Hanse said, glancing casually around. Seeing nothing, he assumed that the Eye had *blinked*. Shadowspawn had not forgotten the "reasonably sure" part, and what it implied: that Count Cathapretentious had been perfectly willing to subject his agent to a deadly hazard he was *reasonably* sure would not kill him. In other words, he had been perfectly willing to risk his agent's life. And had.

"And maybe I've been out," Shadowspawn told them casually, "and come back. For you, of course, because I've *missed* you both so much!"

Yole's face became positively dazzling. "Ah, thank Toolsa," he said, or something like that; he expressed his gratitude not to Hanse but to a god Hanse had never heard of. "Then you know a way out!"

Suddenly Shadowspawn was frowning. He moved a little closer.

"Why . . . both of you are *stubbled*!"

Yole put his hand up automatically to feel his hair-shadowed face; his employer did not bother.

"While one *could* shave with a dagger," Cathasententious said, "one would definitely not do so without water! I hope our unshaven state does not offend your sensibilities, Hansis.''

Hanse hadn't time to bridle at the satire like a trace of red pepper in a sausage. "But . . ." By stretching things a little, he could imagine that Yole might fail to shave, two days running. But Cathamarca? Never! In which case the count would not allow Yole to let his face grow stubbly. But in that case . . . but . . . but . . .

"You really have been down here for two days!"

Both men blinked. Both chins lifted a little—Cathamarca's the more, of course. "Did you have any reason to disbelieve me, Hansis?"

"But then . . . you don't even know about Jemise!"

Hanse watched Yole look past him, as if expecting to see her, and in that instant he believed them; these men he knew he could not trust, and so Cathamarca's "Why, no—did you bring her with you?" was unnecessary.

"She's dead," Shadowspawn said flatly. "She was murdered. Mutilated. It was awful. She was tortured to death, there in the inn where you stayed. Are staying, I mean." Watching them as he spoke, he could not believe that their sagging jaws and aghast stares were other than real reactions to the news. "I found her and I was arrested. Someone had informed the Reds." He spread his hands, palms up. "I'm sorry, partners, but now they're looking for you. A mage who does police work proved I didn't do it, but reported that he found traces of you there; auras, or something like that. Naturally they think you killed her."

Cathamarca was shaking his head, still wearing that expression of horror and disbelief. "Naturally . . ." he murmured. "That poor girl! We never even—Hansis? What do *you* think?"

"I don't know what to think. She was in your rooms and naturally I assumed you had done it. I don't know you all that well, you know. I did see you at her place, of course. Now . . . damn. I can't not believe that you really have been down here all along. Longer than I was!"

"Yes," Cathamarca nodded. "Longer than you, and

assaulted by a series of impossibilities and unlikelies. Jemise . . . moved in to stay with me. I'm not going to castigate the poor girl, or praise her either. She was ready to live with any man with some money, I believe. In other words, if you had suggested that she move in with you she would not have been there when I . . . visited." He shook his head. "I'm sorry, Hansis. This is babbling. Unlike me." He cleared his throat and for the first time Hanse saw Cathamarca look embarrassed. "I . . . like her. She made me feel . . . I liked her. Who would have . . ." He trailed off, shaking his head again.

Hanse stood in silence, as Yole did. Waiting. Hanse felt an uncharacteristic embarrassment, too, because he had seen Cathamarca so. Admit it or not, Hanse understood about wearing a public face and manner designed to cover inner reality. Now he realized that Cathamarca wore one; the man behaved as he thought a wealthy noble should, and in a way he bullied with his impressive appearance and his way of speaking. Hanse had an idea that just saying that he liked Jemise had been a big admission for the man.

He was also one of the best Shadowspawn had ever seen at not answering implied or even direct questions. He knew about that, too.

At last he showed them the sack.

Cathamarca's mien changed. "You did it? Is that the . . . merchandise?"

Hanse jingled the bag. "This is the merchandise, partner. I'll just hang onto it for now, until I lead you out."

Yole looked insulted and angry; Cathamarca smiled. "I . . . understand," he said.

The moment his back was to them Hanse slipped on the Ring of Illusion that had brought him so much grief down here. Not this time. The Eye had told him about it, and the way it worked. In past, sorcery had worked both against and for him, if the strange S'danzo Seeing power of Mignureal's could be placed in the same category with magic. Now, for the first time in his life, Shadowspawn was prepared to use sorcery, actively use it. Thus he turned his back and kept it turned, following his own markers out of the maze; giving the two men behind him opportunity to show their treachery.

How could a mind such as his believe other than that their intent all along had been to get the rings and kill him?

The Wandering Eye did not make an appearance. That was the agreement. Count and retainer had not seen the Eye; therefore it could keep watch on the pair while Hanse kept his back to them. Notable kept close to Hanse; there was little to turn aside and sniff at, down here.

"Trapdoor here," Shadowspawn warned, and a little later, "Careful. Stay away from the center. Darts! Crouch this way." And a little later, "Ah. That's it just ahead. All we have to do is stamp the floor," he lied, "and we come out right beside the road, downhill of Corstic's house."

"They are coming up behind you with drawn blades," a voice said quietly from his right and just above his head.

Grimly Shadowspawn made a mental picture of Jemise as he last saw her, gory and short fingers and earlobes and nipple, tongue and nostrils slit, and the hideous mutilations below . . . but he visualized her as alive, and angry, with talons.

Behind him two men shrieked, and Hanse spun, drawing steel. He stared at two men retreating from nothing, fighting the air with swords and daggers both, wild of eye and slashing wildly. Notable yowled, bristled, and departed at speed.

Shadowspawn did not smile. One of the gemstones or pebbles in the sack he clutched in his right hand was obviously functioning, because he was not affected by the ghastly illusion he had created with the ring. He saw only Yole and Cathamarca—and they certainly were affected! His face set grimly, he glanced at the floor, moved aside, and took off his weapons belt without letting go the bag of stones.

He watched Yole fall, screaming, but roll, come up with sword and dagger still grasped in fists clutching so tightly that the knuckles were bloodless—and his gaze fell on his dark-clad partner. With a glance at the ''demon,'' which was apparently fixed only on Cathamarca just now, Yole rushed at Hanse. His sword was up and out to slash; he held his dagger low and closer to his body. Yole knew what he was doing with weapons, Shadowspawn remembered . . .

And almost calmly he performed the ridiculous act of tossing his belt with sheathed Ilbarsi knife and empty sword-scabbard onto the floor.

Not, however, just anywhere on the floor. Yole was in the center of the passage when the inverted T rushed down to smash his skull and body while its crossbar destroyed his legs. Corstic's trap swept him almost up to the ceiling before Yole slid off to fall with a limp squishy sound to the floor.

As he had done when it came down, Shadowspawn performed an easy hop to avoid the cross on its backswing. *thunk.*

This time Notable was a good thirty feet away and had never glanced back.

Swallowing hard after a glance at the bloody, mangled mess that had been Yole, pieces of red-smeared white bone thrusting out untidily here and there, Shadowspawn turned his attention to Cathamarca.

He lay crumpled on the floor, both weapons dropped and his right hand still grasping his left upper arm. Shadowspawn saw no blood, but Cathamarca's eyes were huge and staring.

''Looks like his heart gave out,'' the Eye said, cruising lazily above the corpse.

Adrenaline high and ready for combat, Shadowspawn showed disappointment along with his amazement.

"You mean I *scared* him to death?"

"I'd say so, Hanse—you and the ring scared him to death. Literally."

Hanse stood where he was, sack in hand, ring on finger, sword in his left fist, and stared down at the crumpled man. Tonight Corstic had performed the first act of good in his life, despite the fact that it involved two more deaths. Cathamarca had come a long way and gone to a lot of trouble to wind up in an underground tunnel, dead of a fear-induced heart attack . . . and without having so much as seen the rings. Hanse didn't feel good about it. Not after the human admission the count had made about himself, when he talked of Jemise. Shadowspawn had to remind himself that the man had been about to kill him from behind.

"Uh . . . Hanse. Hanse? Uh, they're both gone, but, ahh . . . Notable still sees the illusion. Maybe you could take the ring off before all those straight-up hairs start spitting off him like darts?"

"oh," Hanse said very quietly, and dropped unused sword and well-used sack of stones to use his left hand to get the ring off his right. And yelled, his hair standing and gooseflesh breaking out all over his body, as the ghastly Jemise-apparition from his mind came racing for him.

He hurt his finger yanking the ring off and hurling it to the passage floor. The apparition vanished. Jemise, presumably, rested in peace.

"It's over," Shadowspawn breathed.

23

SHADOWSPAWN FULLY INTENDED to destroy the Ring of
Illusion, there in the maze. Somehow, at the last moment he
just could not do it.

Maybe I'll just give it to Ahdio or somebody, he thought,
restoring it to its bag among the other things, *once we get
back to Sanctuary.*

Neither he nor the Eye mentioned or even considered
doing anything about the corpses. Let this place of horror be
their tomb. Let Cathamarca lie here in his finery until it clad
only bones, and then it too became only dust.

The three of them hurried out of the maze, not using the
false directions Hanse had named just before the attack; he
had done that to precipitate the assault on him, and if the
wicked pair had succeeded in killing him, they'd never have
found their way out unaided.

They emerged, man and cat and floating, disembodied
Eye, not back into the manse cellar, but at the base of the
hill. Shadowspawn glanced up at the house that stood on the
very top of the hill. A dark bulk full of memories ranging
from bad through unbelievable to unspeakable; still not an
attractive structure, but no longer menacing—again.

"It's over," he murmured, and neither of his companions
minded the fact that he had already said it several times.

Triumphant, elated, relieved, they untied Ironmouth from
the tree where the bag had been hidden, said nice things to
him for having waited so long, and slipped him half an apple

from the small saddlebag. Hanse swung up and headed down the hill for town. The yawning guard at the North Gate admitted them into Firaqa, and they clop-clopped up Caravan Way on their short trek to the bazaar, and to the booth-and-home of the S'danzo couple.

This time rail-thin Tiquillanshal and Turquoise seemed genuinely delighted to see Hanse, and wondered if that nervous-looking cat mightn't like a little milk. Fortunately Notable did not recognize that word and so did not attack or suffer the same end as Cathamarca. As usual the couple's daughter Zrena stared at the romantic figure, left-handed and so well armed and clad all in black . . . which was no darker than his hair and eyes, at that. She wriggled in excitement. All three noted how much better he looked and acted.

Turquoise—in yellow blouse, particolored vest, trailing red sash, a necklace of multicolored beads and skirt striped in yellow and green and blue and another shade of green, put her feeling into words, however clichéd:

"You look as if a great weight has been lifted from you, Hanse."

"It has. Something I haven't been able to tell anyone about. It's over. Look, I really need to see Mignureal," he told them. "*Need* to."

Quill and Turquoise showed surprise, and exchanged a quick glance.

"Hanse . . . you know she isn't here," Quill said.

"What?"

"I mean . . . she's with you . . . isn't she? . . ." Quill's voice trailed off as his forehead began to furrow.

Now Turquoise's bright smile had faded to a look of concern, and her beringed fingers clutched each other over her particolored apron as if seeking solace from her sudden dread. "Don't tell me you sent her *back* here? But she hasn't arrived—how long ago did she leave you? Oh, oh my . . ."

"Send her back here? Come on, people! I haven't seen her for days."

Turquoise and her husband exchanged a look.

Hanse tried not to shout. "Hey! I'm here! Now you've got *me* worried! Talk to me!"

"Hanse . . . she was here," Quill told him. He swallowed and his adam's apple bobbed like a knife under the skin of that too-thin neck of his. "We were talking about you no more than an hour ago when that nice mage who does good work for the Reds came by with a message from *you*."

More than concerned, Turquoise just had to speak, now: "Mignureal got her cloak and left with him immediately."

Someone had just dropped an iron weight into Hanse's stomach and his heart was hammering. "Malisandis?"

Both of them nodded. "Right!" Turquoise said, looking relieved, wanting to be relieved, as if Hanse's knowing the name of the man made everything all right. Quill said, "That's the name!"

"Right!" Quill said again, considerably cheered.

"He and Mignureal left to meet you at the house he says he just bought, up on Town Hill," Turquoise said, talking rapidly in her relief. "You know the one—"

"Corstic's manse," Quill finished.

A groan of anguish quivered out of the black-clad young man before them. He whirled without another sound. Without so much as a word to alleviate the fear that had leaped up in the couple, he left them there, staring after him, as he ran. That huge red cat was loping along with him, keeping pace.

The two S'danzo exchanged another look, and this time all the worry and apprehension had returned to their faces. Knowing something was wrong but with no idea what, Zrena began to cry.

It wasn't over.

Count Cathamarca and Yole were greedy, grasping men

who had been ready to lie and even murder to get what they wanted. For all that, they had not been villains. Not what people called good men, either, but then neither could Shadowspawn be squeezed into that category. Nor could he be called a villain.

The true villain had come from behind his mask of respectability, and now Hanse must go to him. Must. At that same place of evil.

The worst horrors he had ever seen and endured had been at that place, and now he must go back. Must: *That bastard has Mignue.*

Hanse worked it out as he hurried Ironmouth through nighted Firaqa. Notable rode before him, curled at his crotch, and presumably the Eye was about. Hanse had forgotten the Eye. His mind was busy, trying to work it out:

It wasn't over.

Malisandis was a mage. Malisandis was no boy. Malisandis must have known about the rings the same as Corstic and Arcala—and must have coveted them. With Corstic dead, Malisandis would naturally have decided to have them; must even have considered them his. All he had to do was get his hands on the things. Malisandis knew about Cathamarca, too, and why he was here. The "kind sorcerer" who was so helpful to the police had been unable to see any way that Cathamarca could be of any value to him, but the foreigner and his man could get in Malisandis's way; give him trouble.

Hanse nodded as he rode. Yes, that was probably about the way of it. "So," he muttered, "that nice Reds-helping mage hired four foreigners to murder the count and his retainer."

"mrarrh?"

Without even glancing down, Hanse traced a hand across the limp cat who was trying so valiantly to snooze across his crotch.

The human he owned was still hard at work, inside his head. It Was Not Over.

When the attempt at murder failed, Malisandis went to their inn rooms. Maybe to try to bargain with the count; maybe to do murder. Instead of the Sumese he found Jemise there, and tortured a bit of information from her before he murdered her—slowly. Information about one Hansis, among other things.

How twistily ironic that Malisandis went there again on behalf of justice and the law, and served it!

For he *had* to provide evidence that would free Hanse; he *had* to say that the apartment contained only evidence of two foreigners—obviously the Sumese pair who rented it. Otherwise the camel-humping son of a snake might have implicated himself, particularly if Arcala with his superior abilities came to double-check and discovered Malisandis's lie.

So—Malisandis did not lie. He merely left out mention of another aura that lingered in those rooms, and not a foreigner's. His aura.

So now he has Mignue, and he's there waiting for me. He knows or assumes that by now I have the rings. Either I hand them over to him or . . .

But Hanse didn't want to think about anything after "or."

He stared grimly ahead. "I'll do it."

He would give the rotten swine the rings. Anything to get Mignue free and get both of them out of this horrible city that had been so very, very bad for them and to them.

"She will leave if I have to tie her in a saddle!"

The street was deserted for a good fifty yards. Therefore the voice that replied to his mutter did not belong to a person: "Good thinking. Who?"

Shadowspawn did not glance aside, but stared only ahead, barely seeing. "Mignureal."

"Your . . . ah . . ."

"My woman. *Was* my woman, maybe. But I love her and I am responsible for her."

"You're going to give this other sorcerer the Rings of Senek."

"Yes. I have to, Eye. Have to. And . . . I don't have them. Arcala has them."

"You *gave* them to still another sorcerer. For *nothing*!"

"Yes," Shadowspawn answered dully.

"So that's where we're going."

"Yes."

Silence for a few clops of Ironmouth's hooves, then, "Hanse? You aren't the sort to go and ask a man for help, are you?"

"No." Hanse's face was grim and anger rode his voice.

"Are you going to ask Arcala for help?"

"No."

"You despise sorcery and we all despise that thrice-damned mansion—and you're going back up there. To deal with a sorcerer."

"I don't need to be reminded of it, damn it!"

"Hanse . . . wisdom is not doing the things that are too dangerous to do."

"Uh-huh. No one has ever told me I was wise, either."

"I've seen you *be* wise, though, my friend. Have I ever told you about courage?"

Hanse tried to outwait the silence, and could not. "Do I *have* to answer? I'm awake, believe me."

"Courage," the Wandering Eye advised, "is *doing* those things that are too dangerous to do."

Somehow that new aphorism from the being so positively laden with them tunneled through the roiling mud in Hanse's mind and set off another thought. *Oh no. Now it's courage. I wonder how many of* those *he's got!*

24

As the Eye had observed, Hanse of Sanctuary was not the sort to ask for help. Yet Arcala, already in his house-robe, knew something was wrong, and kept asking, without handing over the rings, and time was passing, and Malisandis was doubtless growing impatient, and Mignue might be suffering . . .

Hanse told the night-robed master mage what had happened. He told him all of it, or nearly.

"Malisandis-s-s! That—that rotten, lying, murdering son of a bitch!"

Hanse blinked. He had never heard such an outburst from Arcala or seen such passion in the man.

"That's a pretty good description, yes. A little understated, maybe. The point is, *I want those rings back,* Arcala! Now."

It was Arcala's turn to blink in surprise. His gaze was directed into Hanse's eyes, but he did not miss the dark hand that had gone to a hilt.

"For Mignureal," he said quietly. "For her you'd threaten even me."

Hanse only stared.

"We're going *together*!" Arcala snapped, and in his own home, hoisting his robe, he *ran.*

Hanse waited without patience while Arcala rushed about, collecting the rings and assembling some other . . . things. Some of the time he was muttering, and Hanse was not sure whether the words were intended for him or not. He caught the mage's comment about how thick Malisandis and Corstic used to be. Then Arcala went rushing upstairs. Unfortunately he took the rings with him. Hanse tried to wait, while every second seemed ten or so minutes. Once he heard Arcala shout a name that sounded like Brandis, maybe, and moments later a nicely put together man in leather leggings and jerkin strode rapidly past Hanse and out the door.

Shadowspawn jittered about for as long as he could stand it, and decided to hell with waiting for the man.

He had the door open when he heard the shout behind him and turned to watch Arcala come bounding down the stairs—quietly. Almost, Hanse smiled: the master mage had changed clothes. He wore black. Just black. That included the soft-soled buskins. The odd thing was that while he carried the little bag of rings and *things,* he wore no sword.

"I never even had a brother, much less a twin!"

"How would you know? You told me your parents were minimally acquainted and you never so much as saw your father. Let's go. We're in a hurry."

With uncharacteristic but admirable restraint, Hanse said, "oh."

He was starting to mount Ironmouth when Arcala, several paces past, paused to shout back at him.

"That animal is tired. Brandis has just bridled and saddled my two best racing horses. He'll take care of your gray. Come On, Hanse!"

Hanse glanced at Ironmouth, gave him a quick pat, and hustled after the other man in black. The horses were indeed ready, and with tight girth-straps. Brandis was just leading them out of the stable. They were nervous animals, nickering and twitching their heads back a little as the two men ran up.

"See to that big gray of my friend Hanse, will you?"

Arcala said, and Brandis nodded, moving away from between the horses.

"There's an apple in the saddlebag," Hanse told him, hanging onto the saddle's high horn and rein while his sleek brown horse played the game of move-the-hindquarters-away-in-a-circle-to-see-if-this-twolegs-knows-enough-to-stop-me-and-deserves-a-ride.

Hanse did, just. Thief and mage swung aboard hastily. then both horses shied as the huge red cat came hurtling at them and seemed to disappear from their view. Hanse's mount acted worse than nervous when thirty or so pounds of airborne feline dropped onto his back. Brandis quickly grasped the horse's halter and muttered into the twitching ear. The animal subsided. Arcala was already ten four-legged paces away; Hanse gave Brandis a look of respect.

"Just a small touch of the heel, sir," Brandis said. "He knows his name: Firefoot."

Oh, nice, Shadowspawn thought, and said, "Thanks several times."

He twitched a heel against his mount, well forward of the flank. He had learned that much, anyhow. That did not mean that he was happy about being up here. His animal trotted after Arcala, who held up a little.

"Have I ever told you how much I hate riding horses?" Hanse said, when they were side by side.

"You may hate this more. We're going at the gallop."

"The gal—isn't that illegal inside the city?"

"We're right at the wall, remember? Besides, where's the fun in being boss in a city if you can't bend a few laws!"

With that Arcala flashed a smile and jerked both heels backward. Suddenly Hanse was looking at the streaming tail of the other man's horse. Hanse jerked his feet and hung on. Notable dug in his claws—only into Hanse's leggings, fortunately, as the horse might have objected.

25

ONCE AGAIN SHADOWSPAWN in black rode out the North Gate, etc.

26

THEY DID NOT so much as see another soul as they galloped at breakleg speed up the long hill of villas.

Not another soul mounted or afoot, that is; abruptly the Wandering Eye was just there. It accompanied them, merely sailing along as always, however it did it. Hanse had to call out to his companion to swerve here, toward that tree at the foot of the hill surmounted by Corstic's manse. Without question Arcala slowed his mount and made the turn.

"Better go up to the house, not this back way into the tunnels," the Eye counseled.

Hanse blinked. After a moment he said, "Wisdom is listening to good advice," and swung his horse again. The animal went up the grassy hill among the trees as if it were on ruler-flat turf.

Arcala glanced up at the Eye. "A friend of yours, Hanse?"

The Eye replied before Hanse could: "Merely destiny's puppet, sorcerer." And then it sped off to the mansion.

To no one but himself Arcala said, "Now that is beyond interesting."

And they were there, and dismounted, and once again Shadowspawn entered Corstic's gods-hated manse. Each time was one too many, and each time was the last. But . . . it wasn't over.

By the time the two men made their way through dark rooms to the kitchen, with Arcala muttering about wards and "dry old spells a child could see through," the Eye was back with them.

"No one else is in the house," it reported. "They are in the tunnels. The mage and a girl wearing enough colors for six."

"That's Mignureal," Arcala said, with a quick smile that was no more than a flash of teeth.

"The tunnels," Hanse said. "Oh wonderful."

The two men looked at each other, moved their shoulders in a tiny shrug, and nodded. Hanse led the way.

A thief all in black, a vehemently large cat, a master mage all in black, and a disembodied Eye descended to the dim cellar, and entered the darker passage beyond the wall. The barrier fell with a crash and Arcala turned with a curse.

"Get back out of the way," he muttered, gesturing, and the barrier obeyed like a faithful dog.

"I'll be damned," Hanse said, and then swiftly, trying to beat the Eye but forming a chorus with it: "We've covered that."

The Eye was their guide; it paused and Notable bristled while Arcala, from what seemed to be a twig from his bag, *created* a nice little hand-light for their way through Corstic's maze. It stretched ahead, a grim dark passage between grim walls of gray stone.

"Nice trick," the Eye observed in a voice dry as dust, and scudded ahead, knowing it would be followed.

"This place is chock full of traps," Hanse quietly advised his companion, in a conversational way.

"Full of *sorcery,*" Arcala murmured, and Hanse saw him slide a ring onto his gloved left hand . . . and then another onto his right. He recognized those rings; a broad gold band with what appeared to be a double setting the color of slate; another gold band intagliated with a serpent and set with a caged ruby. The Rings of Senek.

All the horror those damned rings have caused—and this

one too, Shadowspawn thought, for he wore the third ring, the creator of illusions.

"Some few things can be worse than sorcery," he said, walking as silently as the cat. "Deadfall here. Step around this way."

Arcala did, and quietly Hanse told him about the horizontally sweeping, tree-sized pole they had avoided.

"Nice," Arcala said. "And something like that saw to Cathamarca's man Yole, did it?"

"A worse one, yes. Their bodies are a long way from here." Suddenly Hanse frowned. "I think. This place is full of attackers that are not illusions, lots of turns, side corridors and steps that take you down while you walk up."

"Really?"

"Really," Shadowspawn said firmly.

"Truly interesting," Arcala said, as if he might have been an apprentice mage on an educational tour.

They did not see the being who claimed to be Theba, or Kurd, or sword-armed wolves, or the impossible rooster. Corstic did appear, and Arcala only gestured and spoke off-handedly: "Oh go away." Corstic vanished.

"I wish you'd been down here with me yesterday and last night," Shadowspawn said, with fervor.

The Eye came swooping back. "They're right around this turn. It's a big chamber—a place you haven't seen before, Hanse . . . I think. I'm afraid the excrement-masticating offspring of a canine is ready for you."

The two men exchanged a look and a nod, and took the ten or twelve steps that brought them to the sharp rightward turn in the passage.

"I'm just going to . . . blink," the Wandering Eye said, and did.

As far as the two men were concerned, it disappeared. Notable made a spit-sputtery sound and moved a pace closer to Hanse. Long red tail coiled and looped to caress dull black leggings.

Arcala stopped just before they made the turn in the passage. With another nod in response to his meaningful look, Shadowspawn turned the corner and took two and a half steps into a chamber big as a barn. The Wandering Eye was right: even in his twenty-seven seemingly endless hours down here, he had somehow not chanced upon this huge room. And well-lighted! How enormous was this maze? . . . or did it fold back on itself, warp in and out of another dimension, perhaps . . . or was it even real?

Mignureal and the man he assumed was Malisandis were indeed waiting, some twenty feet away. Although the sorcerer's eyes were not all that dark his complexion was as dark as Hanse's—like a rotting apple, Shadowspawn thought, although he had never thought of himself that way.

"Stop there, won't you," the dark man said in a quiet, agreeable voice, and Hanse aborted his third step to lower his foot slowly, perfectly balanced, ready for anything . . . except what he saw. It was not fear of Malisandis that made him heed that polite *suggestion,* but fear for Mignureal.

Her plight was perilous, but at least apparently not too uncomfortable—physically. She was still clothed, Hanse saw with relief—clothed in red and yellow and three shades of green and in stripes as well, and an alert and bristling Shadowspawn could not see so much as a snag in her blouse or vest or skirts. Her wrists were roped behind her and he assumed that under her concealing skirts her crossed ankles were, too. Presumably to prevent her shouting a warning, Malisandis had seen fit to gag her, and well. Not with a silly kerchief tied between her teeth in a way that allowed all sorts of noise. Instead her elongated face indicated that the swine had stuffed her mouth with something, before tying the scarf around her head so that the large knot he had made in it was between her teeth.

She sat perched on a square platform something under three feet across and five or so feet above the floor. The platform rested atop a stand like a stool for a giant; four slim legs with two rungs connecting each to the other and, for extra sturdiness, an X-brace of slim metal on three sides.

Directly below her, within the "cage" formed by the uprights, seven spearheads stood hungrily up from a thick block of wood the same size as the platform above. They looked sinister, ugly, menacing . . . hungry.

The platform where Mignureal sat was of course hinged on one side. The side opposite was held in place by an iron brace. It formed a very long L all along the edge of the platform, with an inch or so under it and an inch or so standing at a right angle to it. Another iron brace, at a forty-five-degree angle to the floor, held it that way, else Mignureal's weight would have tripped the L and dumped her onto the spikes. The bracing bar of iron was embedded in the little circle of wood on the floor. Her captor stood on it.

The look she turned on Hanse from tear-misted eyes seemed to owe more to sorrow than to fear.

"In the event that it is not obvious," the almost-smiling sorcerer said in a perfectly normal, everyday voice, "she remains safely perched there so long as I stand exactly where I am. If I move—if you move me—the brace pushes the vertical, and the brake under her . . . releases. It is *possible* that she might fall forward and *only* bash her head while she remains stuck there above the spikes. But of course she would remain so precariously balanced that way only for a few seconds."

He shrugged and made a "So there you are" gesture. "You know who I am and what I want."

"I know who you are," Shadowspawn said, slowly untensing and straightening from his automatic crouch. "A liar, a murderer, and worse, a murderer by torture—you *tortured* Jemise to death, you son of a warthog."

Malisandis affected a yawn. "She was a pleasant enough diversion for an hour or so," he said. "Better keep your

tongue in check, little fellow—and that outsized cat, too,"
he added, although his height was no more than Hanse's.

The treacherous mage looked above forty but his teeth
were excellent and his hair a rich dark brown. He wore a
nice blue tunic over well-made green tights that fitted his
good legs as if sewn on them. His soft-looking brown boots
were low fold-tops. He was gloved but a couple of rings
adorned his fingers just the same, and a handsome seven-
sided medallion hung on his chest, in silver set with what
appeared to be a large opal: a black circle of night shot
through with lightning in a rainbow of colors.

A crouching Notable stared at him as if the fellow
resembled dinner. His tail imitated a dying serpent.

"So," Malisandis said in that same pleasant voice.
"About the Rings of Senek, Hansis."

"We have them," a familiar voice said from just behind
Shadowspawn, and he watched Malisandis's gaze swerve
over his shoulder.

"Well, well. Two sinister black-clad visitors, hmm? But
no brother of yours, eh Hansis? An honor, Master Mage."
Malisandis even made an abbreviated bow. His smugness in
triumph was maddening, unbearable . . . but when he
straightened his eyes were as cold as any Hanse had ever
seen this side of a snake.

"Just lay the Rings on the floor there, and go right back
the way you came. Don't even think about a sorcerous
attack, Arcala, or throwing a knife, Hansis."

"My knives are sheathed and you see my empty hands,
sorcerer. If I had considered throwing, you'd be wearing
one in your eye."

"No attacks, Malisandis. I am just as concerned about
that woman as Hanse is. We'll have to give him the rings,
Hanse."

"Aye," Hanse said. "Eye? The way you can make
yourself heavy . . ."

Arcala was working the rings off his gloved fingers.

Malisandis smiled. "Why not just toss the gloves, rings and all, toward me, second-rater? *Toss,* not throw!"

Evidently the Eye had caught Hanse's meaning; it appeared behind Malisandis, apparently having un-blinked. Notable was staring balefully at the sorcerer, tail straight out behind him, fur fluffed and making him look even bigger, his ears almost invisible along his skull. And Shadowspawn was back into his crouch.

"Ready, Eye . . . *Notable!*" he shouted. "*Foe!*"

The cat was more than ready to respond to the signal. He charged flat out, a huge red demonic *thing* imitating a racing-horse with every hair on his back and sides standing straight away from his body. The red streak trailed a straight-out tail like a red bristle-brush.

At a distance of about four feet from Malisandis the cat launched himself. A rushing blur of fiery red sped through the air to hit the sorcerer in the chest—every claw digging in and needly fangs working to eat holes in the pretty blue tunic.

Only the fact that he wore gloves enabled Malisandis to tear the clawing raking chewing horror off and hurl it aside. The impact, however, had staggered the mage so that he stumbled back and off the braking platform. The mechanism creaked, clicked . . .

And the Wandering Eye settled into place on the platform vacated by Malisandis, almost instantly adjusting its weight well beyond the sorcerer's. The brace had begun its fall and the long steel L that kept Mignue safe had just started to slip and dump her onto the spearheads. That process came to a stop under the weight of the Eye. The L-brace clacked back into place. Mignue was jarred and terrified and in strain, but she was safe. And Malisandis was unable to boot the Eye away; what he had in mind was necessary with a considerably higher priority. Mignureal had served her purpose: she had brought the foreigner here. Now whether she lived or died was unimportant. Plenty of time to carve her later.

Merely gaining the Rings was not going to be quite so easy as the sorcerer had hoped. The first step was to dance back so that he could face both Shadowspawn and the enormous, evilly snarling cat.

Hanse saw the opal on Malisandis's chest wink alight like a lantern—and an instant later he and Notable were sorcerously held where they were. He had no feeling of invisible hands or a wall; it was simply that his muscles seemed to have left town. Man and cat resembled statues created by an artist who had perfectly caught movement and frozen it for all time.

Malisandis had no time to gloat or sneer or indeed for anything else at all: from about twenty-five feet away Arcala launched his own sorcerous attack.

It was Shadowspawn's body that could not move; his muscles. His brain was alive and active, and he could see and hear. He liked nothing he saw and heard. Once again he was involved in the bane of his life, accursed and hated sorcery—doubled, for two mages were dueling! This time that which he despised was working for him and Mignureal as well as against them.

He heard the horripilating roar before the ball of fire rushed over his head from behind him, headed for Malisandis. The mage stared at it, his amulet glowing and winking like a bright candle in a little breeze—and the hurtling ball of fire became a large black bat that wheeled around to race at Arcala, squealing like a painfully young youth. An iron spear appeared—from nowhere, of course—and leaped from Arcala to transfix the attacker in flight. Both fell to the floor and erupted into flame . . .

. . . from which rose a green-and-yellow dragon the size of a small house. Under its clawed feet bat and spear—iron spear!—burned on. With a frightful roar the dragon gushed fire at Malisandis.

The hair of both the helplessly watching Hanse and

Notable was standing straight up now, and this time not because the cat was making a hostility display.

At a mere uncomplicated gesture from Malisandis the flame from the hideous dragon's mouth swerved aside and rushed on to shower fire and sparks from the stone wall well behind the mage. The dragon shrank with incredible rapidity to become a scaly little lap-dog that ran yapping about the chamber. The incinerated bat and spear were sputtering out into a little pile of black ash.

A bare instant later a covey of arrows seemed to erupt from Malisandis's chest to keen over Notable's head on their way to Arcala. The cat's big red head did not move; could not move. An uncomplicated, almost casual gesture from Arcala's left hand turned them from their course. They took up a new one—following the yapping lap-dog like a wake.

"The Rings of Senek, Malisandis," Arcala called, his right hand gesturing so that the ring caught the light in a firefly twinkle, "you treacherous swine!"

The screaming, long-tailed wyvern he sent racing at Malisandis like a missile was met by a circle of flame suspended in air. The wyvern passed through it and fell to the floor in a roaring fire, but the circle of fire, seeming to dance on tentacles in air, flowed toward Arcala.

"Keep them then, Arcala you smug bastard!"

And Shadowspawn thought, *Why* do *people insist on considering that word an insult?*

A sudden gush of water poured from the ceiling to dowse the fiery circle. The ashes of the bat and spear vanished without a trace, while the wyvern continued to scream and lash its arrowhead tail as it burned in a leaping pyre of yellow and white while the covey of arrows chased the yapping dog around and around the sprawling chamber while Notable trembled as Arcala's fire-quenching water spattered him and a seven-foot-tall man with a woman's breasts and a lion's tail rushed at Malisandis and launched

its spear just before the sorcerer sent a streaking covey of
darts like angrily humming bees to transpierce it—and
continued on its path, rushing at Arcala.

He was already creating another attack, and another, and
was forced to drop into a deep squat to let the spear whiz
over his head. Meanwhile two lovely white doves were
flapping toward Malisandis, who snarled a sneering "Ha!
Weakening, little mage?" and Arcala rose and opened one
hand in a tossing gesture that launched a boulder the size of
a coiled man.

"Arcala!" the Eye shouted. "Behind you! FALL!"

Arcala heeded. Swift reflexes dropped him to the stone
floor. The spear, which had turned in air like a well-trained
warhorse in combat, hurtled over his prostrate body for the
second time, this time from behind.

The spear headed home. The doves achieved a height of
about ten feet, each a few feet to either side of Malisandis.
The boulder hurtled at him, rolling through the air ponder-
ously and yet preposterously fast. Going home, home to the
mage with the ripped blue tunic. Sweat sheened the sorcerer's
face now, and suddenly Shadowspawn's fingers twitched.
Notable's tail came alive to lash and his yowl filled the air
as he regained control of the muscles of his jaws.

Suddenly dripping sweat, Malisandis turned the spear and
hurled himself aside from the boulder and a lurching green
gargoyle-bear-thing with fangs a foot long but additionally
armed with shield and spear, left him to head for
Arcala . . .

And the two doves spat simultaneous streams of liquid
flame at the man centered between them.

Malisandis's clothing blazed up and he screamed. The
gargoyle/bear seemed to flicker. Notable's tail lashed and
with a long yowl he headed for the yapping dog. Frozen in
mid-step, Shadowspawn felt movement return to his legs,
which had been in motion. He could not gain control of
them in time, and fell asprawl. Water showered from the

ceiling over Malisandis, turning flames into harmless smoke—and his own spear, having turned and begun its third rush, slammed into his back with a thoroughly sickening sound.

The bear/gargoyle vanished. Malisandis's eyes went wide and his mouth spurted scarlet. Amid a far more impressive shower of blood the spearhead appeared, ripping its way through his chest from behind—and disappeared before its full length had torn through him because the spell that had created it no longer existed.

Delighted to find a known target he could deal with, Notable pounced on the yapping dog—and it was not there. The pursuing arrows clattered to the floor—and were not there. Malisandis collapsed face-down onto the stone floor, wrecking his nose. And he was there. He lay still except for the reflexive twitching of a few gloved fingers. A shining track of crimson crawled rapidly from under him to form a rivulet on the dustless floor.

Shadowspawn dragged himself up from the floor, knife in one hand and sword in the other—and discovered that he had no target. No . . . living target. He was disappointed.

27

THERE WAS NO smoke, no ash, no creatures or sorcerous remnants. Odors did remain, none pleasant. They freed Mignue. The sweat of fear and terror gave her no better odor. Shadowspawn was fearful as to whose arms she would rush into, his or Arcala's. As it turned out, her being bound so long, seated with her ankles crossed, saved both men any embarrassment or disappointment or the elation of being Chosen: released, she collapsed. Her legs were not functioning and would not be doing so for a while.

Hanse squatted to slip his arms under her back and knees.

"She's unconscious, but all right," Arcala said. "Why don't I transport her out of here?"

Shadowspawn stared up at him with hooded eyes. "You mean magically?"

"Yes," Arcala nodded. "That will save—"

"I've had enough magicking tonight, thanks. I think we all have," Shadowspawn said, and picked her up.

Arcala sighed. Arcala nodded. He said nothing.

Then he did: "Hanse . . . are you perhaps in possession of a bit of *sand,* from Corstic's trove?"

Hanse turned slowly, trailing one of Mignureal's arms and her colorful skirt. He gazed into the other man's eyes for a long moment before he decided how to answer:

"Yes."

"We need it, Hanse."

"Now? Here?"

The mage only nodded.

Shadowspawn continued to gaze into the other man's eyes. At last he nodded. He passed Mignureal to Arcala, found the little bag of sand, and tucked its rawhide drawstring between his teeth. He held out his arms. He was ready for an argument and determined to make it brief, but Arcala handed him the colorful limpness that was Mignureal. And took the bag of sand.

"I wondered if that mightn't be something valuable in disguise," Hanse said wistfully, watching the mage walk to the lake of red where Malisandis lay.

"Oh, it's valuable all right," Arcala said. "Once." He emptied the sand into his palm and, like a framer sowing grain, tossed it onto the corpse.

Once again the hair on Shadowspawn's nape seemed to come alive as he watched Malisandis and his blood boil and bubble as if dropped into a vat of acid. Notable hissed and arched his back.

Arcala looked directly at him. "Be calm, cat," he said, and Notable's demeanor changed, because he was calm.

And Malisandis and his blood were gone. Not quite without a trace:

"Ils's beard, what a smell," Shadowspawn said, and turned to walk away.

It was over. Again.

As before, the Eye went ahead, leading the way back to Corstic's cellar. Arcala walked close, holding his inexplicable light. Paced by Notable, Hanse followed. He carried the unconscious Mignureal out of the tunnels. She wasn't heavy; she was Mignue.

No one spoke until they were outside the house and bathed in moonlight that did not seem cold at all. It was over. Arcala addressed the Wandering Eye:

"You were Garislas, weren't you? Before Corstic ensorceled you, years agone?"

"Yes," the Eye said.

"Do you want to be freed?"

"Freed? After I've lived a lifetime of rainy days? True wisdom is the inability to be deceived, sorcerer. You can't make me a man again."

"No. You know what I mean by freed."

"No, then. Maybe someday, Arcala, but not yet. Even as only an Eye, I am alive."

Arcala offered to put him out of his misery, Hanse thought, and his voice was quiet: "Stay with me, then, Eye old friend."

"I'll do that, Shadowspawn old friend."

"Hanse? I . . . I think I can walk . . ."

"Mignue!"

"Ouch! Hanse! Not so tight!"

She didn't say it, Shadowspawn thought. *She didn't say "Not so tight, darling."*

Arcala said, "Sleep, Mignureal," and she went limp again.

"Why in six hells did you do that, sorcerer?"

"My name is still Arcala, Hanse, and we're still friends and allies. She needs sleep. So do we all, but in a way she has been through more than we have."

Hanse sighed, nodded reluctantly. "It's just going to be a little more trouble getting her back down to town," he said.

That pulled the chain that tripped the spring that broke the tension they had never relieved. Arcala began to laugh. The Eye began to bob in air. Notable pounced on a moth.

It was over.

"We'll go back to my house," Arcala said at last, wiping his eyes. "We can watch over Mignureal there."

"No we won't," Shadowspawn said, and he was not smiling.

It was over. Arcala had the two rings, and Hanse felt that if they were safe in the hands of anyone anywhere, it was in Arcala's. Of course the master mage did not know that his friend from the south had judiciously retained the Ring of Illusion—which Arcala obviously did not need!

I think I'll just hang onto it for a while, Shadowspawn thought, and they rode down the hill.

In the apartment on Cochineal Street Notable had his snoot in a bowl of beer and was lapping with embarrassing noisiness. Mignureal lay where Hanse had laid her, conscientiously pulling down her skirts. Nothing was the same between them, and she knew it too, and so did Arcala.

The terrible thing, the loner Shadowspawn thought as he eased out the second-floor window, *is that she needs someone who isn't a loner—a man who needs her. Damn.* He swung up onto the roof. *Arcala needs her. I don't. Damn.*

He muttered the same word when he opened the oilskin packet and took out the tablet and one gold hearther. He shook the packet. It was empty. One of the two remaining coins had vanished.

"Damn. But Malisandis wasn't old enough!"

No, but the coin was gone, and the tablet coated with bees'-wax still bore the one name: Elturas.

The mystery remained and perhaps he would never solve it. Yet he still had that illogical feeling that he owed it to a dead calico cat who had been a woman, and to a live red cat who had been a man, to try. And the answer, perhaps in the form of someone named Elturas who might or might not still be wearing that name, lay down south; home, in Sanctuary.

He returned coin and tablet to its weatherproof pack and this time he took it with him as he swung back down and re-entered the apartment. Mignureal was not on the divan and something smelled good.

"Hanse? I thought some soup would be nice."

"Good idea!" *All as if nothing happened tonight,* he thought. "I'll get the fire going."

"I, ah, have it going already," she called back, but he had already taken the few steps into the kitchen.

He said, "oh." And then, "How? How, so fast?"

She looked away. With a dolorous feeling of resignation he thought, *She doesn't want to look at me because I'm in my blacks, and she knows they're my working clothes, and she hates that.* Maybe, but he saw that there was more. Mignureal looked guilty!

That was a change; looking guilty around here had been Hanse's job almost ever since they had moved in together.

Giving elaborate attention to the soup-pot, she stumbled over her reply: "I . . . uh . . . it's something Arcala taught me . . ."

"You . . . started a fire . . . by . . ." That pause between his low-voiced, staggering words stretched longer than the others. ". . . by magic?"

"Um-hm." She was striving to keep her face and voice serene; she knew how he felt about sorcery, and heard it in his voice now. "Oh Hanse, it's so easy, such a simple little thing, and harmless . . . and such a convenience!"

He didn't say anything. He went back into the other room to change out of his blacks. Notable made a tentative request for a bit more beer, was ignored, and almost instantly dropped off to sleep. Hanse changed clothes, thinking. She had a place in Firaqa, work in the tradition of her S'danzo people as a Seer, with a clientele. A man was very interested in her, and he happened to be the most powerful man in the city. And she liked his children. And now . . . and now she was accepting abilities from him, powers beyond the inherent S'danzo one. Gods! Mignureal a sorcerer!

Enveloped by the same dolor, feeling resignation and not liking it, Shadowspawn folded his working clothes. For travel. He had to go back down to Sanctuary. Had to. And he knew he would be going alone.

Quietly Hanse and Mignureal ate hot soup, and it was good.

Only when they were finished did he say it: "What do you remember, Mignue?"

Her mouth came open; her eyes went almost blank; she looked down. He saw her heave a sigh and wished he didn't like her breasts so much.

"All of it, I guess. It's just . . . it's sort of like a dream I had long ago. I didn't want to be there, and I think I sort of . . . went away. In a way." She jerked her head up. "Oh, Hanse! You saved me—saved my life."

Hanse did not smile. He shook his head as if ruefully. "No. No, Arcala did."

Epilogue

FOUR LEFT FIRAQA very late at night: a big gray horse, the impossibility of a floating bodiless eye, a large red cat—snoozing on the horse before his rider—and Hanse, not in black.

Many would have been surprised, and wondering and surely suspicious, if they had noted that he left by the southward gate and rode all the way around the city up the hill of tree-shaded estates. One last time, Hanse rode up to Corstic's manse, and went in. After twenty or so minutes he emerged in haste to remount and ride at good pace down the long hill.

By the time he reached the walls of Firaqa and started around them on his way south, the flames of Corstic's keep were licking the stars.

It was over.